AUTUMN DAFFODILS

JOANNA'S STORY

Peter Turnham

A CIP catalogue record of this book is available from the British Library.

Cover design and interior formatting by JD Smith Design

Copyright ©2019 Peter Turnham

All rights reserved

ISBN No. 978-1-9160979-3-3 (paperback)
978-1-9160979-2-6 (eBook)

Publisher: P&C Turnham

www.peterturnhamauthor.com
peterturnham.author@gmail.com

Also by Peter Turnham

Autumn Daffodils – Charlie's Story

When an enigmatic newcomer arrives, a group of people find themselves reluctantly sharing their past memories.

(The first book in the Charlie & Joanna series)

None Stood Taller

From the ashes of the Blitz to the D-Day landings. One woman's remarkable story.

Table of Contents

Acknowledgments

To my wife Carol,
my spell- and grammar-check,
my editor and IT consultant,
my indispensable other half.

A word from the author

This book comes with a spoiler alert.

This book can certainly be enjoyed in isolation. However, the reader should be aware that Joanna's Story is a continuation of my previous book "Autumn Daffodils - Charlie's Story". Together the two books are far greater than the sum of their parts.

October 2020

A Reminder of the Story So Far

Charlotte is looking for Charlie. She finds him sitting quietly reading.

"There you are Charlie. I've been looking for you. There's a woman in reception asking for you. She says she would like to talk to you."

I was obviously intrigued. "It's been a while since a woman came looking for me; did she say what it was about?"

"No, she says it's a personal matter."

Even more intriguing! I asked what sort of woman we were talking about.

She's a young woman, early thirties, extremely pretty girl, an American, I think. Said her name is Molly Wright."

I was even more intrigued. An American, Molly Wright. I had no idea! I said I couldn't wait to see this mysterious woman, and Charlotte said she would bring her through to me.

I sat waiting for my mystery woman to appear and, when she did, my heart jumped into my throat! It was Joanna! Except of course, it wasn't Joanna. This was a young woman. I immediately pulled myself together, telling myself I was an idiot for imagining things, but the resemblance was remarkable. Then I realised that my memory was playing tricks with me. This young lady was about the age Joanna was the last time I saw her thirty years ago.

She introduced herself and sat opposite me. She was obviously ill at ease, and it all felt a little awkward. However, after initial pleasantries, she paused and looked at me with a serious expression.

"You are Charlie Bartlett?"

"Yes, my dear, what can I do for you?"

"Can I just ask you three questions?" I was really hooked.

"Ask me anything, my dear."

She sat back in her chair and brushed a waft of blonde hair away from her forehead with the single stroke of a finger. I could see that whatever these three questions were, they were extremely important to her, such that she was struggling to utter the words.

I tried to help her get started.

"Whatever it is, my dear, I won't bite."

Molly drew a long deep breath.

"Is the Poppies Hotel near Clifton a significant place for you?"

Once again, my heart leaped into my throat.

"Yes," I answered.

Molly drew another very deep and slightly shaky breath.

"Does the name Joanna mean anything to you?"

Not only was my heart racing. I felt my hands shaking as well.

"Yes, I loved her."

Molly's eyes welled up with emotion, and I noticed her hands were also trembling. Then she said that Joanna was her mother.

"Do you remember the date 18th June 1982?"

"Yes," was all I could say.

"What I'm about to tell you, Charlie, is going to be a shock but I promise you it's true.

She paused for a long moment, but then finally said what she had come to tell me.

"I am your daughter."

There can be few times in life when just a few words have the power to hit you like a bolt of lightning, but this was one such time. Molly sat silently waiting for my response. For my part, my mental circuitry had tripped a fuse. I looked at her and raised my hand a little as if to say hang on a second, give me a moment to regroup.

I managed to compose myself sufficiently to reply.

"I don't doubt it for a second."

I'm not sure what reaction Molly had expected, but mine was obviously at the top end of her scale. She leaped out of her chair and hugged me, her tears running down my neck.

"We have an awful lot of catching up to do," I eventually managed to say.

Molly smiled that same broad smile of her mother's.

"I've got one more thing that I've been told to say, and you must think about it before you answer."

In truth, I wasn't sure I could cope with any more surprises, but I answered.

"Go ahead."

Molly took another deep breath.

"The message is 'I need a nice man to talk to. Are you still that nice man, Charlie'?"

Molly could see my reaction.

She glanced over her shoulder towards the car park.

"She's in the car, Charlie."

The Story Continues...................

Chapter One
THE DOOR OPENS

My decision to wait in the car had been an easy one to make. This was Molly and Charlie's moment. However difficult, this was something they both had to confront. I was quite another matter. Charlie didn't have to confront me again; it would have to be his choice. I had always known this moment would come. Having Molly reminded me of it every day. I acquired Charlie along the way, but she was born attached to him. It was inevitable that the thread joining us would eventually draw us together.

After what felt like an eternity, the door suddenly opened and Molly stepped through it. For a brief second, I thought she was alone; perhaps Charlie really had refused to see me. Then I saw that he was following close behind her, his hand clasped in hers. They took a few steps into the light. Charlie stopped in his tracks the second he saw me. Molly stepped back, putting her arm around him. I was both dreading and longing for this moment in equal measure. I stepped out of the car and stood in that moment. We just looked at each other; neither of us moved nor said a word.

At first Charlie appeared older. His hair was a bit thinner and just starting to go grey; maybe the smile lines around his eyes were deeper, more permanent. Charlie had changed.

This man was incredibly smart and elegant. I knew Charlie the builder had gone long ago, but I wasn't prepared for his replacement. We continued to gaze at each other until finally he left Molly's side and started walking towards me. It was probably no more than thirty paces. With every step, another year simply melted away. He may have been older and altogether more sophisticated than my builder, but he was definitely *my* Charlie!

I didn't know how to greet him. After all the intervening years, was I just a distant memory for Charlie? Should we just shake hands, and say hello? I was incapable of rational thought. Not knowing what to do, I simply reached out my hands. I sensed that he was as overwhelmed by the situation as I was; he reached out and delicately held my left hand. I felt he was cautiously probing for a response. I tried to smile reassuringly but felt almost paralysed with fear. Somehow, I managed to tighten my hold on his hand.

He took my other hand in his, and for a moment we just stood hand in hand. I had no idea what Charlie's reaction would be, I had no reason to expect him to be anything other than hostile towards me. I feared the worst but hoped for the best. Then something extraordinary happened, I could tell from the look on his face, he didn't hate me. He seemed almost pleased to see me. I had thirty years to worry about that day, and it had never occurred to me that Charlie would be pleased to see me. It was an outcome I had not even allowed myself to consider. Perhaps he saw my relief because he smiled. That was when I saw the Charlie that I had left behind all those years ago, a person I had never expected to see again.

I tried to say something, but simply couldn't speak. It was all too much for me, and I could see Charlie was equally overcome with emotion. Molly stepped forward and put her arms around us, I'm not sure what kind of reaction Molly was expecting, I had told her a lot about her father, and certainly about how much I loved him. It was important to me that she knew she was a love child and not the result of some passing fling. It was such an overwhelmingly emotional experience; I simply couldn't speak, and it seemed that we were both content to let our silence speak for us.

Molly finally broke our silence. "We can't go inside looking like this. Why don't you walk us around the gardens, Charlie?"

"Oh yes, of course, sorry! I'm a bit overwhelmed. No, I mean, I am *completely* overwhelmed. I can't believe it, Joanna, I didn't think for a moment that I would ever see you again. And Molly! All this time, I didn't know. I just don't know what to say."

I tried to reassure Charlie that we all felt the same, but I struggled to form the words.

"I know," I said, with tears in my eyes, "it's quite a day." It was a silly thing to say but it was all I could manage.

"I'm not sure 'quite a day' does it really," he said, trying to smile. "That's a good idea, Molly, let me walk you through the gardens. I still can't believe this, but it's wonderful to see you, *both* of you."

We set off around the garden, managing to gain some composure with every step. The initial fears I had about Charlie and Molly were instantly dismissed. He acted as if he had received the perfect Christmas present. My worry, that they wouldn't find an immediate connection, could not have been further from the truth. As we walked, I could feel the tension easing, so after a while we decided to go inside where we could sit down and start to answer some of those inevitable questions. Charlie headed straight to what was obviously his favourite group of chairs. As we sat down, I had so many things I wanted to ask him, and I knew he felt the same. The whole situation was so emotionally charged, I thought the sooner we started to ask those questions, the quicker we might start to relax a little more.

Charlie and I immediately spoke at the same time. "You first, Molly," he said.

"No, I don't know the questions to ask. You and Mom just talk, and I can get to know you both."

"Okay," I said, "Charlie, what are you doing *here?*"

He smiled and gave me the community sales promotion, explaining that they all referred to the community as the 'Village'.

"Whatever you call it, Charlie, you're far too young to be *here!*"

"You're probably right," he said. "I think I've recently come to realise that."

"So why did you come here in the first place?" I asked.

"People come to live here for many reasons. For some it might be as simple as the golf, or the attraction of the carefree lifestyle."

"That's not why you came here, is it, Charlie?"

"No, some people come here for other reasons. Maybe life has given up on them, or perhaps they have given up on life. I'm afraid I was the latter."

He explained how the years of looking after Annie had taken their toll on him, making him want to leave the worries of the world behind. He explained how his group of friends had come here for similar reasons, each hoping to forget the past.

It was Charlie's turn. "Why did I not know about Molly years ago?"

I had years to rehearse that answer, but still I didn't have a good explanation.

"When is the right time to tell your husband that his child is not his own, or to tell your daughter that her real father is someone she has never met?"

I admitted that these decisions had torn me apart. I had only recently told Molly, and I knew she hadn't forgiven me.

"So why now?" he asked.

"While Annie was alive, I couldn't risk what all this might do to her."

Charlie looked puzzled. "How did you know she's gone?"

"Sylvia, of course, who else?"

"You keep in touch with Sylvia?"

"Ever since that dreadful day in your office, Sylvia has been my eyes and ears. Do you think I wouldn't need to know about our daughter's father?"

Charlie was obviously taken aback. I knew he didn't know about Sylvia and me; we had agreed to keep it that way. He asked Molly if she was happy with my explanation, and she admitted her life had been turned upside down. She didn't say so, but I knew she felt that what Charlie and I had done was unforgivable. As for keeping Charlie a secret and not telling Alan, Molly agreed she didn't want her dad hurt; she thought that perhaps it was best he didn't find out. She hadn't said this to me before, so I was surprised and relieved.

Molly was far from content. "I feel like I'm part of a conspiracy, a truth that must not be spoken. What do you think, Charlie?"

To be fair, Charlie hadn't had time to consider any of this, which is why he astounded us both with his answer.

"Honour and integrity are the cornerstones of my life, which means being true to yourself and to others. I really struggled with my conscience during my relationship with your mother. I found it incredibly difficult to live with my situation. Finally, I realised there *can* be an even greater good, if another person's well-being can be protected by the simple omission of a truth. You have to decide where the greater good lies."

Molly said nothing and neither did I. Charlie had said it all. He changed the subject, asking what her plans were, and when was she going back to the States. She and I had discussed this at great length, so Molly explained.

"I've got a business venture here which I think is going to work out. I want to live here, at least for a while. Of course, I was also hoping that perhaps we might spend some time together, Charlie?"

He looked delighted. "Oh, thank heavens for that! I couldn't bear to lose you as soon as I've found you."

Molly smiled. I'm sure she already knew what his answer would be, but she was pleased, nonetheless. Charlie was quiet for a moment and I knew what he was going to say, so I pre-empted his question before he could ask.

"I'm not staying, Charlie. I've arranged for three weeks to see you, and to find a place for Moll to live. I have Alan and two sons at home, not to mention my first grandchild. That's my life now."

He suddenly looked aghast. "I can't believe it! You've also got two sons and a grandchild?"

"Well, *you've* got two daughters and three young grandchildren," I replied.

"No, I haven't, I've got *three* daughters and three little grandchildren."

We all smiled. I felt that, if there had been any ice, then we had well and truly broken it

Chapter Two
STANLEY'S LEGACY

As we were talking a very elegant lady walked into the lounge, heading straight for Charlie. She was beautifully dressed in a cream jacket and skirt, wearing a pearl necklace, and her brunette hair was gathered back into a French twist. Her presence was positively regal, and Charlie stood up to greet her as if she were indeed royalty! They hugged one another quite purposefully. My immediate impression was that they were more than just friends. She stepped back, obviously waiting for Charlie to introduce us. He was hesitant. In fact, he looked a little awkward.

"I would like to introduce you to my very dear friend, Audrey. And Audrey, this is Joanna and Molly."

Audrey spoke with a very refined English accent. I could see Molly loved it. "Hello Joanna, hello Molly, how nice to meet you both. Are you friends of Charlie's?"

I answered her saying I was a friend of Charlie's from a long time ago; we hadn't seen one another for thirty years. Audrey stopped abruptly in her tracks and looked at Charlie, who said nothing. It was the strangest thing, as if they were having a conversation without words. Audrey's eyes widened, and a smile radiated across her face.

"Oh my goodness! You're Joanna!"

She quickly sat down, in fact she almost fell into the chair, appearing to be completely taken aback. I had no idea how to respond to that reaction.

All I could think to say was, "This is my daughter, Molly."

Audrey said Molly and I looked so much alike that we could only be mother and daughter. Charlie's response then silenced the room.

"Molly's also *my* daughter."

Audrey appeared shocked and looked again at Charlie. They had another unspoken conversation, then she fell back into her chair.

"Oh my goodness!" she said again.

I had no idea what was going on, but one thing was clear. Audrey and Charlie were close, awfully close, and she knew all about me. I noticed she was wearing a wedding ring.

I started to say, "Are you and Charlie …?"

Audrey immediately interrupted me. "Oh no, we're just friends, although actually I *do* love him, but there's someone else I love even more than Charlie."

The pair smiled at each other, with another of their unspoken conversations.

"Why didn't you tell me about Molly?" Audrey asked him, after an embarrassing silence.

Charlie told her Molly had literally only just walked into his life, and once again Audrey fell back into her chair.

"You mean today, just now. Oh, my word! Thank heavens I came back in time!"

I thought: back in time for what? I was just plucking up the courage to ask for an explanation, when a man entered the room. He was tall and terribly smart, making quite an impression as he came striding towards us. He was the kind of man I would have to look twice at.

He slapped his arms around Charlie. "Who are your friends?"

Audrey intervened saying, "This is Harry, my husband, and this is Joanna and her daughter, Molly."

Harry shook my hand and almost crushed it, then did the same to Molly.

"Sit down, Harry," Audrey said with great authority. "This is Charlie's Joanna, and this is their daughter."

Harry stood motionless for a moment as if he hadn't heard. His eyes turned from Audrey towards Charlie, and I could see yet another unspoken conversation going on. Then as if he had suddenly lost the use of his legs, he slumped into a chair.

"Bloody hell!" He looked at each of us in turn and said again, "Bloody hell!"

No one spoke for a moment. I certainly didn't know what to say, and then Harry looked at me with the most wonderful smile.

"I think I might have guessed. You're everything Charlie said you were, but he never mentioned anything about a daughter."

"He didn't know," Audrey said. "We're *all* meeting Molly for the first time."

The whole situation was quite surreal. Molly was embarrassed, and I most certainly hadn't come all this way in order to meet these people. We needed to be alone with Charlie. I started to explain that we hadn't seen one another for thirty years, and there was so much that we needed to say.

"I quite agree," Audrey said, smiling sweetly. "I have so many questions. Isn't it wonderful that we can finally all be together!"

I looked at Charlie who, like me, was obviously exasperated. "I don't think now is the time, Audrey."

Just as he was about to continue, a jolly looking large gentleman came walking towards us. He looked a bit of a shambles. His clothes were probably awfully expensive, but he looked as if he had slept in them, quite unlike the others.

"Bill, I would like you to meet Charlie's Joanna," Harry said, "and this is their daughter, Molly."

Bill was obviously surprised. He also stood in silence for what felt like an age, before saying anything.

"Good Lord, Joanna! It's wonderful to meet you."

He didn't seem quite so taken aback by my presence, but then he said, "Did you say *their* daughter? Do you mean *Charlie's* daughter?"

Harry smiled from ear to ear, "Yep, this beautiful young lady is Charlie's daughter."

Bill appeared delighted. He kissed Molly's hand. "You're a lucky sod, Charlie," he said.

We all sat together like old friends, except that Molly and I had never met these people before. I despaired of getting rid of them. The thing I did notice was how pleased they all were to see us; they were obviously delighted. Perhaps Audrey realised that I was a little taken aback by the warmth of their welcome. She leaned forwards, taking my hand.

"We don't mean to overwhelm you, Joanna, but you're a part of our lives. You've affected us all, one way or another. You're the last piece of the jigsaw puzzle."

I looked at her in astonishment. "How can I be a part of your lives? I've never met you before."

"Charlie has told us so much about you," Harry said. "What you two shared together has inspired us all."

"Is this true, Charlie? Have you told them about us?" I asked.

"Well, yes. We share everything together."

"But Charlie, what we shared together was so personal. How much of our relationship have you told them about?"

"They know everything about you, but it's not what you're thinking. You see, I know everything about them; we have a kind of bond together."

"What do you mean a bond? What *are* you talking about, Charlie?"

"It's not easy to explain without telling you everything," Bill said, "and this is probably not the time."

"No, I'm sorry, Bill," I said, "I need to know what's going on."

Charlie looked a little awkward. "We four have a lot in common, but we didn't realise what it was, until we each shared the same experience."

"Charlie, what on earth are you talking about?" I said.

"You remember I told you I had given up on life, and I just wanted to get away from my past? My friends here were the same; we each had a past we wanted to forget. Then something happened to change our lives. Can you explain, Bill?"

"We met someone here, a dear friend," Bill said. "He knew we each had a dark secret, a burden which chained us to the past, and he took it upon himself to liberate us."

"What possible dark secrets do nice people like you have?" I asked.

They all smiled and looked at each other knowingly.

"Take me, for example," Bill said. "I was married to my wonderful wife Sarah for thirty-five years, and I had a distinguished scientific career. I also spent six years in prison for manslaughter and drugs offences. Keeping that a secret for all those years can destroy you as a person."

I didn't know what to say. I certainly didn't expect *that!*

I turned to Charlie. "What was in your past, Charlie, that you didn't want to divulge?"

He smiled his wonderful smile and said his story was not as dramatic as the others. In fact, he was the last of them to tell his story. Audrey stopped him at that point by placing a hand on his arm, as she looked directly at me.

"We have all seen tragedy in our lives, one way or another, including Charlie," she said. "He told us a wonderful story about the builder who met and fell in love with a beautiful woman. Charlie's tragedy was that their destiny was to not be together, and he was never able to repair his broken heart."

In a quite involuntary reaction, I said aloud, "Oh Charlie!" and tears welled up in my eyes.

They could all see how emotionally charged the situation between Charlie and me had suddenly become. It was Bill who now saw the need to save us from ourselves.

"Don't blame Charlie for sharing his life with us," he said, "it was something he didn't even know he needed to do."

He went on to say that I played a large part in Charlie's life. Through the telling of his story, I had also become a large part of their lives, and I shouldn't be surprised that they were all so pleased to see me. I still didn't really understand, but I could see how genuine they all were, and how important this 'liberation' was that they described. Eventually, and to my profound disbelief, I found myself asking questions. Who was this amazing person who had this apparent hold over them all? Bill explained that he was nothing less than a force of nature, whose name was Stanley.

Apparently, if he had walk into the room that day, everyone would notice and fall silent, and he would head directly towards me. Having been introduced, and with the kindest of smiles, he would have kissed my hand.

He would likely have said, "My dear, I am dazzled. Just the sight of you has quickened an old man's heart. You must tell me about that mid-Atlantic accent."

Bill might have been asking this question under the pretence of explaining about Stanley's modus operandi, but he was also clearly expecting an answer. I had to admit that a question posed in that way was deserving of an answer.

"I was born in the UK," I said, "but I have lived the last thirty years, half of my life, in America, and I now have dual citizenship."

Bill settled himself back into his chair and loosened a couple of his waistcoat buttons, and all the while his lips were pursed in an exaggerated fashion.

"Now tell me, my dear," he said, "what did we do so wrong that caused us to lose such a beautiful woman to our American cousins?"

"That's a very long story," I replied.

"Oh, my dear," Bill said, "now that you have opened the cover to this intriguing story, we must obviously start at the beginning. Do tell me about your early childhood."

At this point, Audrey said, "Do you see how, with the correct questions, you can be drawn in? This is what Stanley did to each of us in turn."

I could see that I was indeed being drawn into this conversation. "Not all of us has a past we want to share with others," I said.

They all reacted together, looking at each other, smiling. I felt awkward, not sure how to respond. I knew I had broken Charlie's heart all those years ago, I've spent the rest my life regretting it. Now a group of total strangers was reminding me of it in no uncertain terms! This was a situation quite unlike anything I had ever experienced. Just how much did these people know about Charlie and me?

I turned to Charlie. "When they say you shared your life with them, does that really include everything about me?"

Charlie appeared quite unabashed. "They know you nearly as well as I do, Joanna."

For me, our relationship was an intensely private affair, but now it appeared that it was not private at all! Audrey was quick to notice my discomfort, reaching across to take my hand.

"You have nothing to feel awkward about, Joanna. Your relationship with Charlie was a fairy-tale that most people can only dream of. You were both so terribly fortunate to have experienced it. We feel blessed that Charlie shared your story with us, because you've enriched our lives more than you can imagine. I can't tell you how pleased we all are to finally meet you."

I looked at Molly and invited a comment. "This is not what I had in mind at all, but I can't help liking Charlie's friends," she whispered.

My mind was racing in all directions. I immediately liked these people as well, but we were here to see Charlie. Then again, after all those years, these people did provide a useful foil between us. Charlie and I shared a passion the likes of which I had not experienced before, and which I never found again. This was all a heady mix; it's impossible to share such passion and now to somehow deny it. Perhaps I needed these people to stand between us.

Chapter Three
THE FIRST AFTERNOON

Charlie interrupted my thoughts to remind us that it was lunch time. Bill agreed gleefully, rushing off to organise lunch for Molly and me. I had to admit I was still reeling from the knowledge that they all knew the intimate details about me and Charlie. I also had to admit that this drew me awfully close to them. Their conversation was endless, and it was good for Molly to see her father engaging with his friends. Inevitably, the conversation kept returning to us. All of them especially Charlie, of course, wanted to know about Molly's life. Bill returned, announcing that lunch was organised, and would we like to go through to the restaurant.

We sat in what I had to admit was a very passable restaurant, and in no time, Molly was engaged in answering questions. She described her school and college days and went on tell them that she then acquired a Masters' degree from Harvard Business School. Her first job was in New York with Omnicom Group, America's second largest advertising, PR, and marketing agency. From there she transferred her skills to Cisco Systems. Three years ago, she joined a hi-tech company called Intuitive, where she's a senior executive.

Charlie was concerned for Molly's career if she planned to stay in the UK for a while. She explained that her business was involved in artificial intelligence, and where were some of the best brains in that field located? Not just in the UK, but right there in the Cambridge area. Her company had been in talks with several groups in the UK. Now it was Molly's job to establish a firm relationship with one of those businesses, in order to set up and manage a joint venture.

Charlie appeared delighted. "You must be so proud of our daughter."

I said I couldn't be more so, and it was obvious where she inherited her business acumen from. It was wonderful to see Charlie so obviously beaming with pride. I sat pondering the situation while Molly was talking, thinking how well everything had gone. Being part of a group like that was the last thing I had expected, but all things considered, in many respects I was relieved. There was also the possibility that Charlie might have rejected one or both of us. After thirty years, he didn't have to welcome either of us with open arms. Molly had quite naturally been terrified of meeting him. The prospect of telling a total stranger he had a hitherto unknown daughter was obviously daunting.

I had reassured her that Charlie was a lovely man, and that the meeting would go well, but nevertheless, I had to admit at that moment I was relieved. Molly remained the centre of attention, while Charlie was besotted with his new-found treasure. Bill and Harry were falling over themselves around her, while Alan the barman was attentive to the point of embarrassment. Molly was at the height of her powers; she has inherited my good looks, but for her that was just a bonus. Thirty years ago, I would have thrived upon the attention, but Molly doesn't need to, she is so much more. Nevertheless, having a beautiful daughter is my constant reminder of what age is gradually denying me. I caught Charlie's eye and he smiled at me. It may have been thirty years ago but the memory of his smile was fresh in my mind. I didn't mean to be so reactive, but I couldn't help smiling back. I may sit in the shadow of my daughter these days, but Charlie made me feel thirty years younger.

We went back to the lounge to sit in the same chairs, quickly followed by the over-attentive Alan asking us if we wanted drinks. I wasn't used to drinking in the afternoon, but it seemed to be routine for these people. As it was late afternoon, I was told this would therefore qualify as an aperitif before dinner!

"Stanley's buying. I'll have a single malt," Charlie said.

The others followed with drink orders, so Molly and I succumbed to a small gin and tonic each, the same as Audrey. When Alan returned, he placed an empty glass next to an empty chair and I had to ask why. Charlie explained about Stanley's bequest to them all, how he had left £1000 behind the bar for them; the empty chair and the glass were their way of remembering him. I had to admit I was touched; this man Stanley really had left his mark. I remembered that Charlie liked a glass of whisky, but I didn't recall his attention to detail. He swirled the glass and nosed the aroma, spending an inordinate amount of time smiling as he looked at it, almost as if he were having a conversation with it. Harry was drinking the same whisky.

"Ok then, Charlie, tell us what it is."

Charlie's smile broadened even more. "Oh, that's the easy bit. It's the Bowmore 12-year-old, but do you remember Stanley saying he could smell the surf gently lapping against the shores of Islay? I've finally got it!"

I had no idea what he was talking about, but the look of joy on their faces was contagious. Molly was as intrigued as I was, telling Charlie that he couldn't possibly leave it at that. What had he just said that was so important to everyone? Charlie started to explain about what Stanley's gift was. He produced a screwed-up envelope from his pocket and attempted to read the note within it. He only managed a few words when he had to stop. He passed it to Harry, who with a slightly shaky voice, tried to read it for me, but he didn't get very far either. Audrey took it from him and handed it to me. The underlying message contained in this little note was wonderful. It concluded with the words: '*Think of me when I buy the next round and listen to what the whisky tells you. Let that be my gift to you*'. I could see why they were all so upset. I found I had a lump in my throat, and I didn't even *know* the man! I said how lucky they were to have shared these memories together.

"The saddest thing is that Stanley's not here today to meet you both. He would have been so pleased," Bill said.

We chatted for another couple of hours. I think they knew it was not the time to talk about my relationship with Charlie. Instead, I found out a little more about Audrey and Harry, as well as Bill, and I have never felt so at ease with a group of strangers in my life. These really were lovely people. It was fast approaching evening, and while in some ways I had valued the separation that they provided between me and Charlie, I knew that we had things to discuss. Things that we could only say to each other.

Molly and I were staying at a hotel not that far from the Village, and I quietly suggested to Charlie that perhaps he would like to join us there for dinner? Charlie told the rest of them what was happening, and to my surprise they didn't insist upon coming with us. When they realised that we would be back the next day, they seemed content. Charlie excused himself, saying he would walk over to his apartment, have a quick change of clothes and be back as soon as possible. As soon as he was gone, Audrey came over and took me to one side.

"I need to ask you something, Joanna. We understand about Molly needing to meet her father, but are you here for Charlie as well?"

I knew exactly what she meant but I was amazed at her forthrightness.

"I'm here for Molly's sake."

Audrey made it abundantly clear that Charlie was special to all of them, but then qualified that by saying, that he was really very special to her. She went on to say that if I was here to pick up with Charlie where we had left off, then that would be wonderful, they would all be absolutely delighted for us both. She paused for a moment before continuing.

"Please don't break his heart again, Joanna."

I think I had every right to take offence at such an outspoken comment, but it was so obvious that Audrey was well intentioned, I found myself reassuring her! I assured her that I hadn't intended to hurt Charlie all those years ago. I admitted that I felt very responsible, and the last thing I wanted to do was to repeat the mistake. I told her she need not be concerned; I was going back to my husband and family. Audrey spent the next five minutes apologising for her outspoken comments. I then found myself consoling her, when I think really it should have been around the other way. Charlie returned, looking incredibly smart in a dark grey suit with a red tie and matching handkerchief in his pocket.

"You still clean up well, Charlie," I said, "do people dress for dinner here in the UK?"

Charlie smiled. "Not any longer, I'll probably be the only man in the hotel restaurant wearing a tie, let alone a suit. That's the whole point though, everyone else will be saying who's that terribly smart guy in the suit, with those two beautiful women?"

We got up to leave and Audrey came forward, kissing me on both cheeks, giving me an excessively long hug.

"Hurry back to us tomorrow."

Harry hugged me so tightly he almost squeezed the breath out of me, and Bill did much the same. Molly received the same attention. As I was leaving with Charlie, Bill put his arms around both of our shoulders.

"Do you remember, Charlie?" he said. "You told us about the very first time you met Joanna. You said she was the loveliest woman you had ever seen up close, and how you couldn't stop looking into her eyes. You said you were in danger of making a complete fool of yourself. Well, I know precisely what you meant now, Charlie. I hope *we* haven't made fools of ourselves, Joanna!"

I wasn't sure if this was a genuine concern of Bill's, or simply the nicest compliment I have ever received. Whatever it was, I left there perfectly convinced I was thirty years old again! Charlie said to leave our hire car where it was. He was our personal chauffeur from now on. His car was waiting by the reception entrance, and he opened the doors for us. It was only twenty minutes to the hotel, and we used the time to talk about his friends. He said there was so much more to tell about them, and I said I would like to know.

We soon arrived back at the hotel. Molly and I needed to go up and change. For a fleeting moment, I very nearly invited Charlie to my room so that we could finally talk alone, but the memories of our first night at the Poppies Hotel came flooding back. I had intentionally swept Charlie off his feet that night, and when we entered the room, I asked him to unfasten my dress. When I turned back to face him my enduring memory of Charlie was the look on his face, and how much I wanted him. I was surprised just how fresh those memories were in my mind. I wasn't sure that I could trust myself to be alone in a hotel room with him ever again.

Molly and I needed time to talk as well but having left Charlie alone in the bar we felt we must change and return as soon as possible. I put on my best outfit. He was overdressed for that place, so why shouldn't I be? And it wasn't by chance that it was a red dress not dissimilar to the one I wore for our first night together at 'Poppies'. Molly obviously felt the same as I did; when we met in the hallway, she looked absolutely stunning in a beautiful lilac silk, long flared halter neck dress. She so reminded me of me!

"Wow, Mom! You've still got it, you know."

I just smiled as we made our way back down to the bar. As we approached the doors, my heart was racing. I always enjoyed making an entrance but none more so than that first night at 'Poppies'. I felt every head turn that evening, but the moment Charlie caught my eye, no one else existed. Charlie would catch my eye tonight, but I knew that was where the similarity would end. This was going to be another significant evening, but for entirely different reasons.

The look on Charlie's face as we entered the room said it all, and I guess we did make quite an entrance. I was content that at least some of the faces were not only looking at Molly. As we sat together, I recalled the words Charlie had said earlier and suddenly it all made perfect sense. He was right, I was sure everyone in the restaurant was asking the same question. 'Who is that guy in the suit with those two beautiful women?'

We had only been with Charlie for a few hours and there I was thinking and behaving like an adolescent again. I couldn't remember the last time that Molly and I were dressed like that together. In fact, I tried hard to think of the last time I saw Moll in a dress. She's happiest in jeans and a t-shirt; at best, in a jacket. I often wonder if she rebelled against me and my lifestyle. Tonight though things were different, she had turned every head in that place. We each sat looking at the menu, and every time he glanced up towards Molly, Charlie could barely suppress a smile. The wonderful look in his eyes positively filled my maternal heart with joy. Molly, however, was looking thoughtful.

"Ok, we know one another well enough now to be open about this situation, so let's be clear, Charlie. What you and Mom did was inexcusable. How *could* you do it, Mom? How could you risk your marriage, possibly Dad's career; everything?"

I hadn't appreciated until that moment how upset she was. Obviously, when I finally found the courage to tell her about her real father, it was a terrible shock, but I had thought she was dealing with it. Poor Molly, she must have been suppressing all that emotion.

She rounded on me again, saying, "You told me you and Charlie were in love. Is that true, Charlie?"

Charlie had said nothing until then, but he obviously wanted to answer Moll's question.

"Let me answer that. I'm not sure how much you know about your mother and me, and specifically the 18th of June 1982, but I think you need to know."

He went on to tell Molly the exact circumstances of his arrival at our house in London. It cast me in the most terrible light. I had no excuses; this was the guilt I had carried with me ever since. Molly was mortified that I should have calculated the whole liaison. She was already so disappointed in me, this latest revelation looked set to widen the rift between us still further. I hoped Charlie would say something to offer some mitigating excuse for my behaviour. Instead, he said he could offer no excuses for what either of us had done.

"I'll do my best to explain," he said, "but it's going to sound superficial. That's because you need to understand not *what* we did, but *why* it happened. You have to understand our relationship."

Charlie asked Molly to listen and not to make assumptions, and she seemed to hang on to his every word.

"Superficially, what happened is that your mother and I simply couldn't help ourselves."

I could see Molly's eyes flash in anger. This was not a good enough reason, but she said nothing, as Charlie had asked. He continued, but I could see the emotion getting on top of him.

"I promise that you will get to know absolutely everything about your mother and me. We owe you that. Only then will you understand, so please be patient with us. Let me try to explain again."

Charlie reached for his glass of wine. I didn't know what to do or say. He hastily drank a large mouthful and put his glass down, before finally starting a long explanation.

"The fact is, Molly, for whatever reason, a kind of chemistry instantly existed between us. It happened for me the very first moment I looked into your mother's eyes, and it just grew from there. We didn't just love each other; it felt as if we occupied the same space. We truly were as one together. I felt incomplete every second we were apart. When we kissed, that was the moment when we crossed some great divide; we each inhabited the other, our two souls became one. That is what happened that day. It wasn't planned; it wasn't either of our intentions. Our mistake was that we kissed each other; that's all. It was just intended to be a kiss, nothing else. From the moment our lips met, there was no way back. There could only be one outcome."

Molly was silent; I was silent. I think if Charlie had said another word, he would have burst into tears, as would I.

"I can see it in your eyes now," Molly said, "you really did love each other, didn't you?"

I drew a deep breath. "We're different people now with different lives, but yes, I've never loved anyone like I loved Charlie."

Charlie held Molly's hand. "I can't justify what we did, and of course you were an unintended consequence. That applies to most conceptions; you know that. What we shared was so special, I never dreamed we could share it with another person. Well, it turns out that's exactly what we did. The love which united us then, lives on now, in you."

Charlie reached again for his glass and drained it, taking a moment to compose himself before he continued. He looked into Molly's eyes.

"I know you feel you have every right to despise us as parents, but I think you would be wrong. You were born of such a special love; you're a part of that wonderful gift we shared. It's a part of *you* now. This is our gift to you and it's yours to cherish until you want to share it, and trust me, when that time comes, you'll finally know exactly what I mean."

I wasn't sure who was the more deeply moved by Charlie's wonderful words. I desperately wanted to put my arms around them both, but I had to have Molly's approval first, so did nothing. It was the longest silence, but I could see the expression on Molly's face gradually change.

"Come here, you two," she said, as she opened her arms to us.

Molly said she wouldn't be here but for us, so there was little point in wishing it otherwise, and she admitted that Charlie's words had changed her outlook.

"I despise you both for denying me normal parents, but I realise what I have instead are two wonderful parents. I want to understand what it was that you shared together; I want to be a part of it."

Charlie and I looked at each other. I was apprehensive, but he was obviously serious when he said that Molly should know everything about us. I had always known this day would arrive, but I now had the feeling that something unstoppable had begun. I always used to say that Charlie could charm the birds from the trees, but his greatest gift was that he had no idea he was doing it!

I watched Molly gradually lower her defences as the evening progressed. They asked each other question after question, and they drew closer with each answer. Charlie was irresistible. I so wanted that to happen. There was much that could have gone wrong, but I needn't have worried. I could suddenly see afresh how Charlie had swept me off my feet all those years ago. The evening had gone by so quickly; we suddenly noticed the restaurant was empty and knew that day one was rapidly drawing to a close.

As we walked from the restaurant, Molly whispered into my ear, "Do you want me to leave you two alone?"

"No don't be silly, of course not."

We all smiled, and Charlie gave Molly a long lingering hug before turning towards me. I gave him a quick hug and thanked him for receiving us both so graciously.

"You didn't give me much option did you."

"No, but you could have refused to see me Charlie, I'm glad you didn't."

"I'm glad I didn't," he said. "Goodnight ladies, ring me in the morning at your convenience. Your chauffeur awaits your call."

With that he reached out and held a hand from both of us, leaning forward to kiss the backs of our hands simultaneously.

"Thank you for coming into my life, Molly, and thank you, Joanna, for making it happen."

He went through the hotel's revolving door and walked out into the night. We stood together in silence as Charlie headed towards his car, and as soon as he had disappeared, Molly held my hand.

"It's actually been a wonderful day hasn't it," she said. "I didn't dream for one moment that it would go as well as it has."

"I know, I was terrified, when I first saw Charlie I could hardly breath. I don't know what I would have done if he had rejected us."

"He was never going to do that was he, I realise that now. He's just like you said he was, I think he's lovely."

"Oh Moll do you mean that?"

"It's not every day you meet your father for the first time, not at my age. Perhaps it's the anti-climax of being so frightened to meet him and then finding that actually it wasn't so terrible after all."

"I know what you mean, I think we had better go to bed and start again."

Chapter Four
AUDREY TAKES CHARGE

The following morning, Molly and I met for breakfast as arranged, and for at least two minutes Charlie wasn't mentioned! During a brief silence, I looked at her and asked the only question in my mind.

"Well, tell me what you think about your father."

Molly smiled, which was reassuring, then reached out for my hand, which was doubly reassuring.

"I know now why you fell in love with him," she said. "Not that I'm excusing what you did, but I must admit he's rather gorgeous isn't he."

We hugged each other for an age, no doubt making something of a spectacle of ourselves, but what the hell, this was one of my life's most important moments. Eventually, I commented that I was interested about her using the word 'gorgeous' to describe Charlie. It was how I had often described him, to his great embarrassment. Molly said it just seemed like an appropriate word; she thought he was utterly charming.

"He can really charm the birds out of the trees," she said. "The thing is he does it with such innocence. I doubt he could sell a lousy second-hand car even if he tried!"

I was really taken aback. These were *my* words. No doubt she had heard me using that expression before, but it was as if

Molly was seeing Charlie through my eyes; it was the strangest feeling. The man who could have so easily become a permanent wedge between us, was in fact drawing us closer together. I could hardly dare to believe it!

"What's the plan for today?" Molly asked.

I told her there were several avenues I wanted to explore but I was not sure about the order of things.

"Such as?"

I said I had a lot of explaining to do, both to her and to Charlie. I needed to choose the right circumstances, but Charlie's friends had changed everything.

"I know what you mean," Molly said, "it's almost as if Charlie comes as a package with them."

At least we had no need to worry about finding her a place to live. I explained all of that was in the most capable hands of Sylvia, who we needed to see as soon as possible.

"This is Charlie's secretary?" Molly asked.

"Oh, never make the mistake of thinking Sylvia is just his secretary! She used to run Bartlett Homes, and now she runs Charlie!"

We laughed as we agreed our plan was to formulate a plan. I said I would give Charlie a ring now, which would give us time to wash and brush up before he arrived. The number only rang once before Charlie answered it.

"This is your personal concierge service, madam; how may I help you?"

"Good morning Charlie, that's so kind of you."

"Tell Molly she looks wonderful this morning."

I passed on his message without thinking. Then he asked if we always dressed the same as each other for breakfast. I suddenly looked around the restaurant to see Charlie sitting in the far corner. He came over to us and apologised for the subterfuge, saying he simply couldn't resist it. Molly was as pleased to see him as I was. We stood with our arms around each other for an age, obviously making the accustomed spectacle of ourselves.

We agreed to get ready as quickly as possible, and Charlie said he would be waiting in the car right in front of the hotel. As we made our way up to our rooms, I asked Molly what she thought I should wear. When she said I looked great just as I was in jeans and a t-shirt, I asked if perhaps it was a bit casual. She replied that on her it was casual, but on me it was a statement.

"Are you just saying that?"

"Mom, it's your confidence you're losing, not your looks."

In next to no time, we were sitting in the car with Charlie and there was obviously no question about where we were going. I asked again about Audrey, and Charlie told us some more about her extraordinary life. I was surprised to find myself looking forward to seeing his friends, especially Audrey. I did find the community, or the Village as they called it, a dreary place, though 'dreary' was the last word that could be used to describe that group of people. We could tell how pleased they were to see us when they met us at the door. Audrey took my arm, while Harry just about beat Bill to Molly's arm.

We were escorted to what I assumed were their usual chairs, and we sat down. Molly was once again the centre of attention, but it was obvious who the mystery woman was here, as they also wanted to know about me. I wasn't remotely relaxed about it. Audrey could see I was uncomfortable.

"Why don't Joanna and I go for a little stroll together, so we can discuss things that only we ladies will understand. You gentlemen can devote all your attention to Molly."

Audrey did have an air of authority about her, she left them all with no room for discussion. I felt much the same and simply fell in line behind her as we got up to leave the room together. We strolled arm in arm into the gardens. I had a slight feeling of trepidation; what did Audrey want to say? I didn't have to wait long. Audrey really isn't backward in coming forward.

First, she said that the important thing we shared together

was Charlie, and she knew I wanted to understand. She went on to describe their relationship, or more accurately the absence of a real relationship. Despite that, it was clear they shared something very significant between them. I asked what had been holding them back and she was so candid with me, it quite took my breath away.

"It's complicated Joanna, we both have a lot of baggage from the past. I was never really sure what was holding us back, I used to think it was just my old-fashioned British reserve, but Stanley made me see everything afresh."

"I really wish I could have met Stanley; he must have been quite a character."

"Oh he was, I simply didn't realise how heavy my burden of guilt was until I put it down. Then when Charlie finally told us his story everything became clear. He has had such a troubled life, and then you came along Joanna. You changed his life, his love for you was something he felt he could never repeat. As soon as I realised that I knew why he was not able to make a commitment to me. You see the truth is, you stood between us. You were this beautiful woman of Charlie's dreams, I couldn't compete."

"Oh, Audrey, you make me feel awful, I didn't mean to hurt Charlie like that, much less you. I am so sorry for what I have done, I really am."

"You didn't know, but I admit I despised you at the time. I wanted Charlie and you stood between us; I think what I despised the most was the fact that I knew I couldn't be like you. You see you are the kind of woman, Joanna, that the rest of us sometimes dream of being. You're beautiful, and above all, you're so attractive to men. Frankly, you have whatever it is that makes a woman sexy; even at your age now you still have it."

I was embarrassed, but not so Audrey, as she continued.

"I was envious of you then, and now that I've met you, I'm still envious of you. I can't be like you, Joanna, but I can be envious and yet still admire you."

I had no idea what to say but had the distinct feeling that Audrey did. She continued, saying that she knew she couldn't emulate me, and perhaps more importantly, she realised Charlie knew that as well. This, she felt, was the real issue for them as a couple. I stood between them in both of their minds.

I was mortified. Knowing I had broken Charlie's heart was bad enough; the prospect that I had broken Audrey's heart as well was too much to bear. She could see my reaction and immediately put her arm around me.

"None of this is your fault, Joanna. You simply remind people that we live within boundaries of our own making."

She went on to say that, above all, Charlie was a decent, honest man. She described the evening when he told her that much as he loved her, he would not stand in the way of someone who loved her even more than he did.

"Charlie said that?"

Audrey smiled. "I know, I couldn't believe it either. It was the most selfless thing I had ever heard. The thing is, I knew he really meant it, and the wonderful thing was that he was right. Harry and I couldn't be happier."

"Do you have any regrets?"

"Certainly not," replied Audrey, "but there's been a lot of pain getting to this stage of my life. May I ask you a personal question?"

"Of course."

Once again, Audrey just came right out with it.

"Why on earth did you go on looking for someone else when you had Charlie?"

I was no longer shocked by Audrey's frankness, and besides, I suddenly felt she had every right to know.

"I've asked myself that question a thousand times. I think the fact was, when I had Charlie, I didn't realise what I had. I was living in a totally different world to him and I did everything I could to convince myself it was a better world. It was only when I finally lost him that I realised what I had let go."

Audrey seemed to intuitively understand.

"I guessed as much when Charlie told us about the day you telephoned him asking if he had reconsidered leaving his wife."

I was really taken aback. "Did Charlie really tell you about that?"

Audrey just smiled.

"Not only did he tell us, but he also admitted that if he had his time again, he would have said 'yes'."

There was no longer any need to be reserved with Audrey. I simply admitted that if I had my time again, I would never have let him go.

"Hindsight is a wonderful thing isn't it, I think you made a terrible mistake, but none of us can have our time again. What about now, Charlie's by himself and if I'm any judge he still adores you."

Audrey had cut right to the chase. I could feel my heart was racing.

"I came here thinking Charlie might hate me. So much of what we have is the memory of what we left behind. We're different people now; I have a husband and sons at home, a different life."

Audrey was concerned for me, but as upset as I had become, I was determined to continue.

"There's more to this than you know Audrey, more about me, and more about Charlie. I can promise you one thing Audrey, I didn't come here to break his heart again. I intend to see Charlie happy."

"I can't imagine how you're going to do that if you won't be a part of his life, but I know I can trust you."

I was flattered by what she had said, and so I elaborated a little.

"I can't tell you just yet, but I came here with a plan, and when the time's right, I know you will help me."

Audrey obviously didn't want to embarrass me by asking about it, so she changed the subject.

"That day when Molly was conceived, why did you ask to see him?"

"Wow, you really do set your own boundaries, but I guess I deserve it."

Audrey apologised, saying that it really was none of her business, but I corrected her. We share so much of Charlie, I felt she should know.

"I was leaving the country permanently; I was in a dreadful turmoil. There was something that I had never told Charlie, it was something that was so important to me, I had to tell him. I knew it was my last opportunity."

"Charlie told us," Audrey said, "but why didn't you tell him you loved him before?"

I couldn't believe Audrey was asking me this.

"I can't tell you why, not now; maybe another time."

Audrey accepted that without another word. Then she asked, "Do you have any regrets about that day now?"

"How can I? Charlie and I produced Molly! I can never have Charlie again, but in a way, I can never lose him. How could I regret that day now that we share our Molly?"

Audrey didn't need to say anything else; she understood. We talked endlessly. I asked about her previous marriage, about Freddy, and why such an intelligent woman was deceived by someone like him. She was just as forthright talking about her own life as she was about mine, admitting that she was blinded by what she thought was love. I asked her what she meant by 'thought' was love, and the seemingly prim and proper Audrey amazed me yet again.

"I had no experience of men at all, but in that regard, at least, Freddy and I really hit it off, if you know what I mean!"

"I know what you mean, Audrey."

"I suppose the truth was that during those first couple of years, we were pretty much obsessed with one another. Well, I know I was. I wonder now how much of it was real for Freddy, or was he just using me. There were many times when I was concerned about the business and all Freddy had to do was to whisper something in my ear and my concerns simply melted away. When he was near me, it was all I could think about. Silly girl! I thought it was *love.* "

It was my turn to smile an understanding smile. Audrey's candour had left me momentarily speechless. This was not the Audrey that Charlie had described to me at all; she was such a strong and confident woman. I felt myself warming towards her with every minute we spent together. To my complete amazement, I glanced at my watch to see that it was nearly 2-o-clock, and nobody had come to enquire about our whereabouts. We walked arm in arm into the lounge to find they were gone. Audrey said we should go to the restaurant; they would have a table waiting for us, and she was right.

Suddenly, as I sat down between Audrey and Charlie, I had an indescribable feeling of union with these people. I had never spoken to anyone in the way I had just spoken to Audrey, and her to me; it was liberating. None of them asked what we had been talking about. We had a wonderful lunch together which simply spilled over into the afternoon. I found out much more about Bill and Harry. Whenever a detail was missed, Charlie would intervene saying 'you missed so and so', or 'don't forget that'. I was transfixed by these people; by the end of the afternoon I felt as if I was being absorbed into their lives. Listening to some of Molly's questions, I could see she was as well.

Bill had been so lucky; his life with Sarah sounded sublime, and I couldn't help but wonder if that might have been me and Charlie. As for Bill's prison term, Charlie was of course right. Had I been there at the time, I would have condemned both Bill and Sadie. How terribly wrong I would have been! When Audrey explained how this had all come to light without them realising Sadie was indeed Bill's wife, I could immediately see why they reacted as they did. It was a wonderful story.

As for Harry, I can only say I was deeply moved. I have

never met such a man, truly a towering figure. I have been lucky enough to meet all manner of impressive people. I have been introduced to the Queen of England, and I have danced with the President of the United States, but nobody has left me feeling humble before! When I looked at him and Audrey, I could see how they complemented each other perfectly.

Charlie glanced at his watch and made an announcement as if something serious had happened. "Good heavens! Do you realise it's more than an hour past the yardarm?"

The others gasped in horror, as Charlie immediately waved to Alan, the barman, shouting out, "Stanley's buying."

The usual round of drinks appeared, and I learned that Alan would decide on the single malts so that nobody knew what they were drinking. Once again, the empty glass was placed by the empty chair and the toast was to Stanley.

"What are you planning to do this evening, Joanna?" Audrey asked.

I must admit we had lost track of the day completely; I couldn't believe it was already evening.

"Will you have dinner here with us?" Harry asked.

It would certainly have been an easy option, but I pointed out that we were hardly dressed for dinner and would appreciate a chance to freshen up. Charlie immediately offered to drive us to the hotel, but this had been such a monumental occasion for Molly, I felt we needed time alone. She said she would leave her gin and tonic so she could drive, pointing out that Charlie was probably well over the limit. Everyone seemed saddened at the prospect of us leaving, not least Charlie. However, it had been an emotionally tiring day, and I wanted to relax with Moll. We said our goodbyes before they could talk us out of it, agreeing we would be back in the morning. Audrey gave me a warm hug, as they all did.

"Thank you for this morning, Audrey."

"No, I think it's I who should thank you."

Charlie escorted us to our hire car, and he looked quite

forlorn not to be joining us for the rest of the evening. Molly was right, though, he really shouldn't be driving. She hugged him and sat in the car, leaving us standing there, looking at each other. I had quite forgotten my young builder; this man standing before me was simply Charlie, the same as he always had been. We just stood for a moment looking at each other, not knowing quite what to do or say.

"Come on, Mom, I can't sit here all night."

A bit embarrassed, we said goodnight, and I stepped into the car. As we drove out of the Village, Molly asked if she had done the right thing and I assured her she had. We talked about our day until we reached the hotel, where we arranged to meet for dinner in forty-five minutes. I had a shower and used the time to count my blessings. Everything was going better than I could possibly have dreamt. I was terribly tired, no doubt the consequence of all the stress mixed with jet lag. As we went down to the restaurant, I knew we had made the right decision to dine alone; I felt so weary. Finally, we were sitting together in the restaurant.

"I love you, Moll; you're the one thing which makes sense to me, right now."

We hugged each other, and I was past caring if we were making a spectacle of ourselves. Molly said she had lots of questions and didn't know where to begin.

"Start with the hardest one," I said.

"Is your relationship with Charlie over?

"Of course it is, but if you're asking if I still feel something for him, then yes, I do, I always

have. I don't think I could ever forget a relationship like we had. Even if we hadn't had you, I guess Charlie would always have been a part of me."

"I thought it would all be really awkward, I thought per-haps the two of you would find it really difficult to reconcile your differences. That's not the case though is it, I can see there's something between you."

"I'm surprised as well. I didn't know what to expect; I honestly thought he would loathe and despise me; he had a good reason to – I treated him so badly."

"Why did you Mom, it seems so out of character. I can't imagine you being cruel to anyone."

"I hate myself for it, it's the blackest part of my life."

"What do you mean, what did you do."

"I can't bring myself to talk about it, not now. I know I have to, and trust me, I will tell you, but I'm just not ready yet."

"I need to know Mom; I need to know everything."

"I know I have to tell you, and I promise I will, but the time isn't right. I desperately hoped I would get on all right with Charlie, because there's something I would like to do for him. I wasn't sure how to go about it, but I think perhaps now I do."

Molly gave me a quizzical look. "What else are you up to?"

"I'm shocked to find Charlie in a retirement community. I can't believe any of them are ready for that, they're too young. Have you noticed how they've become habituated to a kind of institutional life?

"What do you mean, Mom?"

"They always eat in the same place, they sit in the same chairs, they drink the same drinks, and every evening at 5-o-clock they are going to say, 'The next round's on Stanley.' They are all wonderful people, but I feel they've allowed themselves to give up."

"I agree, Mom. I thought it was just me because I'm younger, but I could never see *you* living like that. But are you just blaming yourself for Charlie giving up?"

"Well, maybe I am, but that's all the more reason to show them that they're far too young to have given up on life. Let's take them out of themselves and put the life back in."

Molly had no idea what I meant but nonetheless looked enthusiastic.

"What are you up to, Mom?"

"What do we all do when your Dad comes back exhausted from one of those international meetings?"

Molly smiled, knowing exactly what I meant.

"We drop everything and fly off somewhere exotic for a day or two."

"Exactly, so why not Charlie and his friends, we could do that for them. And what do you think about the way they dress, and I'm thinking especially of Audrey?"

"They all wear really expensive clothes, but it's all so dated."

"Perhaps I could change all that, perhaps I could show them another life, really take them out of themselves."

Molly worried that I would be interfering, and of course I would be, but I was sure they would all thank me. Besides, I would be good at it! My life was so totally different to theirs, if anyone could save them from life in the village it was me. Molly was not convinced, but she agreed to play along with me. We talked well into the evening, and inevitably our conversation kept returning to Charlie. I told her as much as I was comfortable with, but I knew my day of reckoning was approaching.

Chapter Five
THE PLAN COMES TOGETHER

The next morning it was apparent that Molly had been thinking about my little plan. No sooner were we sitting down than she said, "South of France, somewhere like Nice, Cannes or Monaco."

I knew all these places well; it would be perfect. I was more concerned about my makeover idea; how could I get them to change their fashion ideas without causing great offence? This was indeed a conundrum. We exchanged a few ideas, but nothing stayed afloat.

"Why don't we approach it another way?" I said. "Why not take Audrey to a fashion house under some other pretence and just see what happens."

Molly liked the idea except for the 'other pretence' part, and I had to admit it sounded shaky, but I did have an idea. I had always relied on Sylvia for help and advice for anything to do with Charlie, so she was the obvious person to turn to. I had already phoned her to arrange a meeting.

"We need to finish our breakfast," I said. "Sylvia will be here in less than an hour."

I knew Sylvia would be on time, and I was sure I would recognise her. I hadn't seen her since that dreadful day in Charlie's office, although it didn't feel like that. I kept in constant telephone and latterly email contact with her ever since then. We have shared numerous photographs. I have come to know her well, and I would say we're good friends. So when the time came for us to meet in the foyer, I was really looking forward to seeing her. We both arrived at the same time, quickly followed by Molly a few moments later.

I recognised her immediately, and she said she knew instantly that it was me. Sylvia is about my age, but I wouldn't have thought so to look at her. She was an attractive girl the last time I saw her, and although still quite slim, oh dear, she had let herself go! Her hair was lank and more a grey than brunette, and she wore no makeup at all. Her clothes looked like her mother's, and I swear those shoes really must have belonged to her mother! Despite her drab appearance, Sylvia is just about the sharpest lady I know; no wonder Charlie allows her to run everything. She was so pleased to meet Molly, but I didn't want to delay the difficult news for fear of making it all the worse. I just came straight out with it.

"Charlie is Molly's father."

There was a very awkward moment. Sylvia seemed to take the news badly, it was a difficult situation. We discussed it with all its implications, and she seemed accepting at least, if not pleased. I suspect she already had an inkling about it. I moved the subject on to Molly's accommodation, anticipating she would have everything in hand. Sylvia opened her briefcase, produced a dozen files, and looked over her reading glasses.

"I've narrowed the list down according to your criteria and I've been to see the ones I feel are most promising. There's one I suggest you should see first."

Molly was taken aback, but knowing Sylvia, this attention to detail did not surprise me. She handed Molly the file detailing a nice little estate house, obviously newly built.

Sylvia said quite casually, "It's such a shame that Bartlett Homes doesn't have a development in this area. However, we have had dealings with this developer before, so I've managed to negotiate a very good price for you. I think this is a better option than renting just now."

It was perfect, exactly what we had in mind. Molly had no idea all this was being done for her; she was speechless. When she finally managed to regain her composure, she could not stop thanking Sylvia. They went over the details of the house together and it did indeed fit the bill perfectly.

"Ok, you and your Mum go and see it when you can," Sylvia said, "and as soon as you confirm the purchase, you can leave everything else to me."

I sat quietly thinking, what an extraordinary woman Sylvia was. She was so immensely capable, who could possibly be a better accomplice in my plans for Charlie and his friends? I decided to tell her about my idea for Audrey's fashion makeover. Sylvia laughed at the prospect, but did have some sympathy with the basic idea, although I could see the words 'fashion makeover' had really fallen on stony ground. 'Sylvia' and 'fashion' reminded me of what Charlie and friends had told me about their friend Lizzy. Sylvia was to fashion what Lizzy was to be skiing! However, I was not about to give up.

"Would you do me an enormous favour, Sylvia?" I asked. "I wouldn't ask if I didn't know that you will thoroughly enjoy it anyway."

Sylvia and Molly were both intrigued, so I continued.

"We have to persuade Audrey to have a fashion makeover, because only then will the rest of them follow, and we know she wouldn't volunteer. But I am sure she would come along to see *you* have a makeover, Sylvia."

Sylvia appeared mystified. "But I'm not having a makeover, that's not the kind of thing I would do."

I felt we were making progress.

"That's the point, Sylvia, you're the same as Audrey in that regard, but if you *did* have a makeover, don't you think it would encourage Audrey to do the same?"

I continued to unfold my proposal, saying I would pay

for everything and even if it didn't work with Audrey, Sylvia would really enjoy it.

"After everything you've done for me," Molly said, "don't think of this as doing Mom a favour; think of it as a thank you from me. You *will* love it!"

This was all well outside Sylvia's comfort zone. I felt it could have gone either way, but reluctantly she agreed, though only as a favour to me; I was delighted. I had worried for weeks trying to imagine how I might create the right situation. We left it that we would see the house the next day, and by then I would have a better idea of how to organise the makeover.

Sylvia left, looking a little bewildered, but I did detect a slight spring in her step. Molly thought it was a hairbrained idea that might just work, but what about the details? I said I had no idea where to go or who to see in this country, but fortunately I knew someone who would know. Molly's face lit up at the same moment mine did, as we said in unison, "Emma-Jane!"

We both knew Emma-Jane well, a dear friend of mine back home, but for some years now she and her husband had been posted to the UK. She was the American Ambassador's wife, and her life was a continual makeover. I immediately grabbed my phone. Luckily, Emma-Jane was free and had time to talk to me. I explained our predicament and it was obvious that I could not be speaking to a better person. She said it would give her the greatest pleasure to be of assistance; to just let her know when. My idea was starting to take shape, but as it was becoming a reality, my concerns about the repercussions grew. Molly shared my concern, my intentions were good, but there was so much that could go wrong. We continued to discuss it in the car heading towards the Village.

"I can't wait to see how you intend to talk Audrey into this!"

I didn't answer but was thinking the same thing. No sooner had we arrived than we were sitting in the usual chairs with cups of tea and biscuits. There was the usual excited chatter between us, and I waited for an opportunity to unveil my plan. Molly helped, telling them about how Sylvia had found a house for her, and how capable she was.

Charlie seemed a little bit put out. "I could have found you a house, Molly."

Audrey was as forthright as ever. "I know you, Charlie Bartlett. When you say you would find Molly a house, what you really mean is you would ask Sylvia to find one!"

We all laughed because she was quite right, but here was my chance.

"Talking of Sylvia," I said, "can you believe she asked me if I knew where she might go to have a fashion makeover?"

They all knew Sylvia, she was often about the place with papers for Charlie, and the prospect of her having a fashion makeover did seem slightly ludicrous.

"I know," I said, "but she was adamant."

I was delighted to see that Audrey was intrigued. "Have you arranged something?" she asked.

I explained that I had no contacts here, but my friend the American Ambassador's wife was helping us. I could see I had really caught Audrey's attention.

"Did you say the American Ambassador's wife?"

It was difficult trying to conceal a smile. I was sure Audrey had taken the bait, and Molly stepped in on cue.

"Do you think I could come along? It sounds like fun."

Audrey then said she would love to come as well, not to take part, just for the day out.

"I hadn't thought of making it a girls' day out. What a wonderful idea, Audrey."

Now was also the time for the other part of my plan. So, I jumped in with my idea about a fun trip away. I said it would be a lovely way for us to get to know each other, in a different environment. It would be a little adventure we could share together. Bill said it sounded like a great idea, what did I have in mind? Something like Southwold would be nice, he thought. Charlie said Southwold was a lovely place, and we could even find a B&B for the night. I looked at Molly who raised her eyes toward the ceiling. I explained that I was used to something a little more exciting than a B&B in Southwold. Harry missed the point entirely, saying we could always stay at a hotel in Southwold.

Molly helped me out. "What did you have in mind, Mom?"

I tried to make it sound like a spur of the moment idea.

"Well, only somewhere that we can get to in a few hours, perhaps the South of France, for example. We could stay in Nice and then take the helicopter taxi into Monte Carlo for the day, or we could stay in Monte Carlo. I know the most perfect restaurant there."

My suggestion was greeted with silence until eventually Audrey spoke.

"Sounds lovely, Joanna, but surely we've all had enough of queuing in airports?"

"Obviously, I don't mean queuing at airports. I meant a private jet."

The silence was deafening, but once again Molly sprang to my assistance.

"That's a great idea, Mom, just like we do at home."

Audrey looked a little bewildered. "Do you mean you have a private jet?"

I explained that my husband Alan was the President of the World Bank, and occasionally we can use one of the bank's jets, but if nothing was available, we just charter one. They looked at me incredulously.

Harry then said, "Actually we used to charter private jets all the time in the business. Difficult putting soldiers with guns onto domestic flights!"

Here was an opportunity not to be missed. "Who did you use Harry, anyone you can recommend?"

He thought about it and said they had contracts with two

operators, one for heavy transport, and another for smaller personnel flights. He offered to telephone his old business to see if anything had changed.

"Do you suppose we can book a flight through one of your company contracts? That would save us some red tape." I asked.

Thinking about it, Harry replied, "I can't see why it would be a problem."

"Where's the nearest airport?" Charlie asked.

Molly was ahead of him. "Cambridge has an airport," she said, looking at her phone.

"Where would we stay?" asked Audrey.

I did know the South of France well. "It all depends on what you like. If it's Nice, then for me it's got to be Le Negresco. I just love the architecture and the décor; it is like stepping into another world. If it's Monte Carlo, I know the most perfect place."

Bill was concerned about the food. I assured him he would love it, but said the real treat was to be had in Monte Carlo. I told them there was the most wonderful Michelin two-star restaurant tucked away just a couple of hundred yards from the waterfront. They were usually booked for weeks if not months in advance, but I knew some tables were always reserved for the superyachts, just in case one of them visited. I was in no doubt they would be delighted to reserve one of those tables for me.

The enjoyment of good food and wine was one of the common denominators among us all, and I knew my description of this wonderful restaurant would be my carrot before the donkey. They were no longer thinking why they should not go. They were now thinking why they *should* go! I sat quietly, very contented that the pieces were coming together, though it was like juggling a dozen things at a time. I knew I should only interfere with these people's lives if they would thank me for it afterwards. It seemed that I had won them over; I was delighted when they all agreed that we should do it.

The conversation then moved back to Molly's house, and Charlie especially was extremely interested, so their conversation gave me time to think. I looked at them all, and that dreary place, and was convinced I was doing the right thing. I remembered Charlie's description of giving up on life, and I knew from their stories that each of them arrived here with the same attitude. These were all such high achievers, very exceptional people. I was sure if only I could just show them that they were still those same people, they would be liberated. Charlie was my biggest concern. For such a successful man to feel he wanted to turn his back on life was tragic, and my own part in that still haunted me.

I had to admit there was a certain comfort in the dependable nature of their daily routine. Suddenly it was lunchtime, and we all acted as if it was a surprise. We made our way to our usual table, ordered our usual food, and enjoyed a glass of our usual wine. It was so easy to enjoy. I loved them all, and my special relationship with Audrey, but it always came back to Charlie.

The others were reminiscing about a disastrous picnic they once had. Stanley had saved the day with his knowledge of an old tractor, and Audrey had fallen in the mud. It all sounded hilarious and we laughed until our sides ached. Just as we were laughing again at a description of Lizzy, Audrey suddenly changed the subject.

"You're really one of us now, Joanna, and you're the only one of us with a secret. Do tell us about yourself, and Charlie."

They looked at me in anticipation. We had promised Molly that she would know all there was to know about her father and me. I was perfectly happy with that, but it was the other side of my life that troubled me. I knew Charlie wanted an explanation for the way I had treated him; could I really bring myself to tell him? What about Molly and how would she react? I could only worry that it might go badly. I had no regrets for anything that I had done, and if there was one thing I had learned while being there, it was that truth is a great liberator. Was there ever going to be a right time for this? I thought probably not, so I decided now was as good a time as any. I drew a deep breath.

Chapter Six
JOANNA'S STORY

I told them I had a happy childhood. I was born in High Wycombe where my Dad worked in a furniture factory. My Mum was the driving force in our household and came from a good family. Grandfather was an accountant, and Mum had a good education, going on to study accountancy, albeit without obtaining a qualification. I always felt she was destined for something so much better than the rented house where we lived in Wycombe. My Dad wasn't an ambitious man, working first as an apprentice, then as a turner. He worked in the same factory all his working life. He would have worked there until he was 65 but the factory closed 5 years before his retirement. Mum never complained about her lot, but she could have been so much more. Maybe she just wanted me to achieve everything that she didn't, or perhaps she just chose to live through me. Either way, she sacrificed everything for me. I was an only child and the centre of her life.

"It sounds like you felt under pressure to do well," Audrey said.

That was exactly how I felt, and the pressure was increased because, goodness knows how, she managed to pay for me to have a private education. Mum worked part-time during the day as a bookkeeper and on three nights a week in the evening, she worked for local firms, doing their payrolls.

"Your mother obviously sacrificed a lot for you," Harry said. "I'm guessing this really had a lasting effect on you."

I nodded in agreement; my relationship with my Mum has shaped everything about me. The fact was that Mum worked herself to death for my education, and then I let her down. Despite my privileged education, I simply didn't take advantage of it. I should have gone on to university and could have been exactly what my mother expected of me. Instead, I left school when I was eighteen and got a job as a sales assistant.

"What did your mother say about that?" asked Bill.

"She loved me too much for us to fall out over it, but I know it broke her heart. I have no doubt it contributed to her early death."

"Why did you do it, Joanna? Was it just an act of rebellion?" Audrey asked.

That was not an easy question to answer, because looking back, I wasn't sure. Perhaps it was teenage rebellion, but that was not the whole story. By the time I was eighteen years old, I was very aware of myself. I was always the prettiest girl wherever I was, and doors always opened for me. It seemed to me that despite all my education, my looks were my real asset, so I decided that I would be a fashion model. The job as a sales assistant was just a means to an end, but my Mum could not understand any of it.

Bill was extremely sweet. "I don't need to ask if you were a success, but *how* successful were you?"

I told them that I wanted to follow in the footsteps of girls like Maudie James, and like Jean Shrimpton who was born in High Wycombe the same as me. I suppose it was unfortunate for me that Twiggy made such an impact upon the fashion world just a few years before me. The body shape that Lesley made so fashionable just was not me. Perhaps I should have gone more into the glamour side of the business, but that held no appeal at all.

As well as fashion, I told them I was just as likely to be

promoting things like cars or yachts, or holiday destinations. My career was quite successful, but I never achieved the national recognition I would have liked. I became friends with Sally Cummings, a young unrecognised fashion designer. It was Sally who gave me my big break, when I modelled one of her new creations. Almost overnight she became a fashion sensation. The photographs appeared in Vogue magazine, and I modelled the dress on the front cover. Poor Sally was killed in a car accident only three years later. In a perverse way, that has contributed an almost mythical status to her famous Red Dress. The dress was always the centre of attention. I did not get much recognition. As I was telling them, Charlie was smiling; we both had a connection to that dress.

I was waiting for him to say something, but he didn't. Audrey obviously knew about the dress as well; I could tell by the expression on her face. They all sat strangely quiet and attentive, so I just continued, telling them about when I met my first husband Martin. I was probably at the height of my modelling career, soon after the famous dress. However, the fact was that Martin and his family were terribly upper class and well connected. He was an old Etonian, as was his father. It was just at the time when they would have seen the big promotional photographs of me in the lingerie departments of Marks & Spencer. It was a significant career success for me, but it was all very unacceptable for Martin's family.

It amounted to an ultimatum. If I was to become a member of Martin's family, then I could not appear on the walls of Marks & Spencer. Martin loved the idea of boasting to his mates that his future wife was a fashion model, but his family fortune was significantly more important. I admitted to them that I was also seduced by the social position, connections, and family fortune to such a degree that eventually I agreed to end my modelling career.

"It sounds as if your marriage started off on the wrong foot," Harry said.

He was right, of course. With hindsight, it was obviously destined to fail. When I look back now, I don't think I ever loved him. He was the perfect husband insofar as he was rich and handsome. I was the perfect wife insofar as I was the trophy he wanted to show off to his friends. Other than that, I now realise we were a disaster together. Suddenly we realised that we had hardly eaten anything of our lunch, everything had gone cold. I apologised for distracting everyone. Bill looked positively affronted.

"Apologise, my dear! Don't be ridiculous! What's a cold lunch compared to the privilege of being allowed to share part of your life?"

I looked around at them all. I was not being judged in any way; these people really valued me. Charlie said we should leave the cold lunch behind and retire to our comfy chairs, and everybody agreed. As soon as we sat down, it was apparent that I was positioned in the middle, in the 'hot seat,' as Charlie called it. Perhaps it was the astonishingly frank conversation I had with Audrey which I found so liberating, but whatever it was, being a part of the group made it easier. I felt more comfortable with these people than without them.

Charlie asked me when I first became aware of Martin's gambling, and I said I always knew about it, but of course had no idea as to the scale of it. Martin worked in the family insurance business and seemed unable to appreciate either his wealth or position. He wasted money on cars and clothes, and obviously on gambling. We had no real need for an extension to our house in Bath. It was already a large house, but Martin just decided upon a whim that it should be even larger. The first I knew of it was when he told me a builder was calling to look at his idea. This, of course, was that fateful day when I met Charlie.

Everyone's eyes lit up. They knew the story of our meeting from Charlie, but wanted to hear my side of the story, as did Molly. So, I began to recall my life with Charlie which started inauspiciously. I did not even realise he had arrived; I was doing something in the garden. When I came back into the house, I found Martin talking to someone.

He introduced me. "Joanna, this is Charlie Bartlett, he's a builder, come to look at the extension."

I found it extremely difficult to describe to them just how significant my first meeting with Charlie was, probably because I didn't understand it myself. I glanced across the living room to see Charlie staring at me. I was perfectly used to men staring at me, normally I would enjoy the attention and then simply look away, but for some reason I didn't do that. I walked towards him removing my sunglasses and the second he could see my eyes, his expression changed. His eyes did not leave mine for a second, and I was equally transfixed.

I stepped forward, offering to shake his hand, and all the while our mutual gaze was unbroken. It was several seconds before I realised that I was just standing there, holding his hand, looking into his eyes. Suddenly I felt embarrassed and simply said, "Hello Charlie," removing my hand from his. Charlie averted his gaze and changed his whole posture, as if he had snapped out of a trance. I could see Charlie looked decidedly uncomfortable, which in turn made me feel awkward. He hurriedly talked about the extension and was not making much sense. I found his schoolboy reaction rather endearing. Martin suggested I make a cup of tea, which I seized upon as an opportunity to lighten the situation. I went to the kitchen and tried to reason what had just happened. Obviously, this guy was hitting on me in the most overt way, but why had I reciprocated?

I carefully glanced round the kitchen door in order to look at him again. He was not exactly scruffy, but there was nothing exceptional about his clothing, just jeans and a quite smart shirt. I noticed he had a pencil tucked behind his ear. He was tall with fair, slightly wavy hair. As he turned, I saw his wonderful smile again. He was gorgeous, with arresting eyes, but nevertheless I could not explain the reaction between us.

Molly sat smiling at my description, as did the others.

Charlie looked a little embarrassed as I was telling the story.

"You *are* gorgeous, Charlie! You made such an impression on me that day." I said.

My comment only made him even more embarrassed. They all sat in silence, no one asking me anything; seeming to be spellbound. Eventually Charlie smiled, obviously reliving the moment with me. I suddenly realised I was on the threshold of sharing my most intimate secrets with my daughter, not to mention a group of people I had only recently met. I could feel the butterflies in my stomach; this was going to be an incredibly significant moment.

"Please, carry on, Joanna," Audrey said.

Molly was equally absorbed with my story. "Yes, come on, Mom. What happened next?"

There was no turning back now, so I continued, telling them that I went back into the room carrying a tray of tea and placed it on the table. As I looked up at Charlie, he seemed to react toward me all over again, as if he had just seen me for the first time. Our eyes met again, in an awkward but intense moment. It was obvious Charlie felt he had overstepped the mark. He quickly drank his tea and left, somewhat with his tail between his legs, leaving me wondering what had just happened. Initially I dismissed the whole episode as just another lecherous man hitting on me, but somehow it did not exactly feel like that. When Martin later said he had given the extension contract to Charlie, I was immediately pleased.

I explained how it was about this time when I sensed Martin's gambling was becoming a problem. His finances were running into trouble. Perhaps the additional cost of the extension was a factor, but I sensed all was not well. Martin's response was to go on holiday and to spend even more money while the extension work was being carried out. That holiday was a disaster. I described the tension that grew between us with each day. Finally, interspersed with a stream of expletives, he admitted that an enormous rift had opened between him and his family. His father had given up on him; there was going to be no more money. I asked him what that meant.

"It means exactly that," he said, in a drunken rage, "there's no more money; in fact, there's even *less* than no money. My father refuses to cover my debts."

By the time we came home from that holiday, Martin was intolerable. I described how we had final demands falling onto the doormat every day. Within a week of our return home, I decided that I simply could not tolerate another night in the same building with him. I telephoned my Mum and told her the full story.

She said what I knew she would say, "You must come home right away," which of course is exactly what I did. My solicitor advised me to start divorce proceedings immediately, and although Martin didn't contest any aspect of the divorce, it all dragged on for ages because he seemed to be incapable of dealing with it. He was eventually declared bankrupt, and I came out of the marriage with no career and not a penny to my name.

About three months after I walked out, I found the various letters and invoices from Charlie's building firm. I phoned his office and spoke to a lady who I now know was Sylvia. She said Charlie wanted to come and see us about the outstanding invoice, and so I had no option but to arrange a time. I was dreading it; all I was going to be able say was that he would not be paid, and I felt sick with worry.

I told them that I had no idea where Martin was. I obviously had to deal with this by myself, it was a dreadful position to be in. Charlie arrived at the house exactly on time and I opened the door. I had no idea what to expect, but to my surprise and relief, Charlie's face lit up the second he saw me. He could see I was terribly upset. There was no way to avoid the inevitable, so I just came out with it as best I could.

"What did Charlie say when you told him?" Molly asked.

I answered, telling them that Charlie seemed to take the news in his stride. He was so kind and understanding; it was more than I deserved. I felt so utterly drained and just wanted to unwind and calm down. He asked me what I intended to do but of course I hardly knew myself. I said the first thing that came into my mind.

"I just need a nice man that I can talk to. You look like a nice man, Charlie. Take me out to lunch."

The second I said it, I realised it was a mistake. This was not a social meeting; what on earth was I thinking! I expected Charlie to be furious, having lost thousands of pounds, but instead he was dreadfully concerned for me. He said he thought a nice lunch was exactly what I needed, and where should we go? I mentioned one or two places and finally we drove a short distance to the local Italian restaurant. As soon as we arrived, we immediately started talking and hardly paused for breath. I thought perhaps I was nervously talking too much, but Charlie seemed to hang on to my every word, which helped me relax. Eventually, when I had calmed down, I asked him questions about his life. Gradually our situation began to feel a little more normal.

I described how Charlie could not take his eyes off me, and that when our eyes met, neither of us made any attempt to look away. He was blatantly flirting with me and I was not discouraging him. Finally, and with some reluctance, he told me that he was married, which is what I had assumed all along. In a strange way it was a relief. I would have felt vulnerable at that time, flirting with an eligible man. The time went by quickly; suddenly we realised the restaurant was empty.

Charlie drove me back to the house and we sat there in the car looking at each other. I could sense he felt awkward. He had a certain schoolboy vulnerability about him. I knew from the way Charlie looked at me that he wanted to kiss me, but I could tell he was far too reserved. The strange thing was that, despite hardly knowing this man, I really wanted to kiss him, so I did! I drew him towards me, and we kissed. You know the second you kiss someone if that kiss is intimate if it's a searching kiss. In my experience it rarely is, which is why I will never forget that first kiss with Charlie.

All I could say was, "Wow, Charlie Bartlett! Where did that come from!"

As I was telling the story, I was suddenly aware that Charlie and friends were smiling, and Molly was smiling along with them.

"Has Charlie told you all this before?" I asked.

Bill agreed that he had, but added, "Charlie told us *his* story but now you're a part of our lives as well."

Molly said we should not forget that she wanted to be part our story as well, so I should continue. They all agreed I should. It seemed I had no say in the matter, so I continued, telling them that none of the day had gone as I had expected. It never occurred to me that Charlie would be so sanguine about his financial loss. Not only had he taken it in his stride; he was far more concerned about me and what I was going to do.

I left that house behind, together with my marriage. I tried to explain to them how frightening it was to be starting again absolutely from scratch. One moment I was on the front cover of Vogue magazine wearing the famous Red Dress; the next moment I was out of work and penniless. Perhaps I might have got back into the modelling industry, but I felt my time had gone.

Above all, I knew I had let my mother down. She hadn't sacrificed everything for me to end up with nothing, not at my age. I made a vow to myself that I would never be poor again, that I would make a success of my life regardless of what I had to do. Somehow, I would repay my mother for all the sacrifices she made for me. I knew I had no special talent other than my looks, and although I didn't like myself for thinking it, I knew to achieve my goal I would have to marry again. This time I needed to be sure of my wealth and position, but in the pre-internet age, finding the right husband was not going to be an easy task. In the meantime, I had to earn a living.

This was the point in my story which I feared the most. How would Molly react? How would Charlie react for that matter? I suspect they could all sense my apprehension.

"So, what *did* you do, Mom?"

Chapter Seven
JOANNA'S DARKEST SECRET

Somehow, I was going to have to explain to Charlie and to Molly why I had treated him so badly. I hated myself for it then, and I still hated myself. Could I really share such a dark secret with my daughter and the others, knowing it was inevitable they would think badly of me? I drew a deep breath and just come out with it.

"I got a job in London's leading escort agency," I said, trying to make it sound like just any other job.

There was an instant look of shock and disapproval on Molly's face. This was the moment I had been dreading for all those years.

"Isn't that like being a prostitute?" she asked, with a pained expression.

My heart was in my mouth, I desperately did not want to be a disappointment to Molly, but now it was unavoidable.

"No, it's not the same thing at all," I said, feeling a desperate need to ameliorate her disapproval.

Molly was unconvinced. "I'm not going to pre-judge you, Mom, but this is not what I expected, I need to adjust to this."

Audrey did not appear to be shocked in the slightest, she even helped me along at that point.

"Well done, Joanna, you did what you had to do. So, tell us about being an escort."

I was taken aback by her response, I had not anticipated support from any of them, certainly not from Audrey. It was going to be a horribly difficult question for me to answer; that was the moment when I realised the full extent of the hole that I was digging for myself. If I were somehow hoping that I could tell them I had worked as an escort and leave it at that, I was sadly mistaken. I could sense that

Molly had found herself in a difficult position too. She wanted to know what being an escort actually meant, but at the same time she did not want to know what it meant for her mother.

It was an excruciatingly difficult position to be in, but it was a situation of my own making; somehow, I just had to deal with it. I was not ashamed about working as an escort; in fact, I mostly enjoyed it. My shame was admitting it to Molly. I had to explain to Charlie why I treated him as I did, and therefore, despite my discomfort, they needed to know. I had no option; I took another deep breath and did my best to describe the life of an escort.

I told them I worked for a very professional and highly regarded business. We were extremely expensive and dealt with a very select clientele. I explained that the contract with the client was quite explicit; the escort did not have sex with the client. I would usually accompany the client to a restaurant, or to a social gathering. It was essentially the same as going on a date, above all I had to be enjoyable, interesting company. Occasionally our job might be to escort a client or an associate of *our* client to a business meeting. In those circumstances, the escort's job was to impress the client's friends or associates, and to enhance his stature in any way possible. I explained that on some occasions I had personally helped deals and treaties to be signed where this would not otherwise have been achieved. In this way, for some clients I provided a valuable business service. Molly then took me completely by surprise.

"Did you have sex with any of them?"

I should have expected that question, but I certainly had not expected Molly to be the one to ask it. The answer was 'yes', but I knew Molly needed a more comprehensive reply, so I just continued explaining the role of the escort. First and foremost the escort must be enjoyable stimulating company. There was always a sexual connotation; my job was also to be flirtatious and desirable. There was nearly always food and alcohol, often dancing; in other words it was usually very enjoyable.

With the agency I worked for, it was always made explicitly clear that the girls were unattainable. Paradoxically, I think that was what made the agency so successful. A closer relationship would only happen if the escort found the client attractive and wanted it to happen. This immediately established our relationship with the client. We were not treated as prostitutes, and we would never behave like one. In fact this was the key to the agency's success, the client invariably worked hard to seduce us. It could be exceedingly difficult at times appearing to be sexually provocative, while not actually being attracted to the client. I admitted that I did find some of them attractive, and yes, I did go to bed with some of them. It was also true that I was often given 'gifts' afterwards. I could not deny that I found it to be an extremely exciting, often enjoyable job which paid well, but it was always just a job. On a personal level, it introduced me to a social world that I would otherwise never have known.

"Above all," I said, "I did what I had to do. I have never done anything that I feel the need to apologise for."

Audrey was wonderful, immediately saying, "Why the hell should you apologise, it sounds like your job was far more exciting than mine."

Bill and Harry were completely non-judgmental, and even Molly threw me the olive branch of a half-smile. It was Charlie who did not react. Bill said he thought I must have quite a few stories I could tell. I had to agree; the life of an escort was nothing if not interesting. I had always held the view that I would never allow myself to be judged by other people's morality, I wasn't about to start then. The exception of course was Molly. Charlie was quiet, his expression was not exactly approving, but I hoped it indicated his acceptance.

"I guessed it was something like that," he said.

I nodded in acknowledgement. "I knew that you realised, Charlie, would it have helped if we had talked about it?"

"No, I think we both knew it was best left unsaid."

"Why did you put up with me, Charlie?"

"I couldn't help myself; I was hopelessly in love with you."

"Oh, Charlie!"

I was already close to tears; it was the tension of the situation. When Charlie said that, I completely lost whatever dignity I had left. I apologised to everyone and rushed outside. Molly suddenly realised there was much more to our relationship than she had previously assumed. She followed me, grabbing my hand.

"You and Charlie, it was nothing like a normal relationship was it, Mom? Do you intend to explain all this to me?"

"As long as you're there for me, Moll, we'll never have a secret between us again, I promise."

Molly was a great comfort. She might not have despised me any the less, but a mother in distress overrides all other considerations. When I had finally composed myself, we went back to re-join the others. I apologised for my absence, and they pretended they hadn't noticed.

Charlie was the first to say something.

"I've never been judgmental about your mother; I don't think you need to be Molly."

"Thank you, Charlie," I said.

Molly didn't answer him, but her expression spoke volumes. It was apparent that Molly respected everything Charlie said. The afternoon was still relatively young, and it was clear they all wanted me to continue. I was left wondering just how much of my life I would end up sharing with them. After thinking about it for a moment I decided to confine myself to my time with Charlie. The less I said about the job the better.

"Let me skip forwards in time about a year," I said.

This was when I met George. I explained that I met him at a function where he was one of several executives I was asked to impress for the client. George was one of three directors of a large multinational company with which my client was hoping to do business. The client misunderstood my role completely, allowing two of the other directors to think I was their plaything for the night. They were extremely offensive. This is a situation an escort was less used to dealing with. If it's the client who pushed the boundaries too far, I could just walk away. In this case, I had to rely on the client to support me, and that was not happening.

George was the one who intervened and put the two 'boys' in their place. He was a thorough gentleman in all respects, and when he asked if he could take me out to dinner one evening, I said yes. He was in the process of divorcing his wife and was rather fragile. He didn't ask anything of me; I think he just needed a welcome distraction from his troubled life. George was quite a bit older than me and I freely admitted that I found his wealth and position extremely attractive. He was the first real marriageable prospect I had found, and when he realised that I was living in a small, rented flat, he offered to buy me a house.

"There are no strings, Joanna, just tell me where you want to live," he said.

Looking back, I was obviously seduced by his wealth and charm, not to mention the offer of a house. This was beyond my wildest dreams; it was everything I had hoped for. I accepted his offer. After my divorce, my only real friends were a couple who lived near Bath, not far from where we used to live. I wanted to be nearer to them if possible. George seemed to have interests in all manner of things, and quickly came up with an idea for a house not far from the M4, quite near Bath, yet still convenient for London. As soon as I knew George was talking about a new build house, I immediately offered a suggestion.

"My ex-husband and I used a really good builder in that area; we should ask him to look at this," I suggested.

I could see my friends looking at me with those knowing looks, including Charlie. Molly however was the one to ask the question.

"What was your first thought Mom; Charlie or the house?"

She was right of course; Charlie was never far from my mind. Despite the brief nature of our encounter I could not forget him. George was happy to accept my recommendation. He arranged to meet Charlie at the site and asked if I would like to come as well. I had to try hard not to appear over enthusiastic.

"You should have seen your face Charlie, when I stepped out of the car that day."

Charlie smiled his wonderful smile as he recalled the moment, agreeing he was struck dumb.

"Did you have any idea how fast my heart was racing, Charlie, when I saw you that day?"

"I wasn't aware of much else at all, it was such a shock to see you."

Everyone smiled. Following that brief encounter, I described how I invented a reason to be at the site on a day when I suspected Charlie would be there. I had gone to a lot of trouble to look my best, it was totally inappropriate for the situation, but I just could not help myself. Charlie couldn't help himself that day either, every time our eyes met, he just couldn't look away.

We went through the pretence of looking at the plans until I found myself saying "Take me out to lunch, Charlie, I still need a nice man to talk to."

It was difficult to explain to myself, let alone to the others, what the attraction was between Charlie and me. We sat in that pub making love to each other with our eyes and yet I hardly knew the man.

"I know you felt the same that day, Charlie, but neither of us admitted it, did we?"

Charlie has a wonderful sense of humour. "I tried not to be too obvious, unless you count my words on the pub chalkboard saying, 'I want to make love to you'."

Everyone laughed. "Charlie, you might just as well have written those words, and I could have written 'me too.'"

I continued my story. After our lunch together we left the pub and stood in the car park. I admitted that all I wanted to do was kiss him, but he just kept talking. I think he was nervous. Charlie never seemed to know what to do at times like that, so I pressed a finger against his lips as he was talking.

"Kiss me, Charlie," I said, whereupon Charlie threw his arms around me with such enthusiasm I almost fell over. We kissed so passionately; for that brief moment, it was sublime. As I drove away Charlie was standing by his car, looking forlorn. My mind was racing; I so much wanted him, but knew I couldn't have him. He was married, and he was a builder, he was not what I was searching for. Nevertheless, I was unable to stop thinking about him.

The following weeks and months were filled with all kinds of excitement. The house building progressed rapidly, I continued my job as an escort which was as eventful as ever, and my relationship with George continued.

Audrey interrupted me at that point. "We know from Charlie that you didn't marry George; it sounds as if you always knew that would be the outcome?"

She was right of course; Audrey was very perceptive. I tried to explain that while George was a dear, I simply did not love him. I tried to convince myself that my future wealth and position was more important, but I remained unconvinced.

It may even have been the case that if I had not met Charlie, I might have accepted a comfortable life with George. As unattainable as Charlie was, I could not stop longing for him He was my constant reminder of what would have been missing with George. It was perhaps inevitable that we would go our separate ways; George and I parted company very amicably. He was such a sweet man, saying he could sell the house for a profit, while trying his best to pretend he was taking it all in his stride. I knew I had broken his heart, I hated myself for what I had done to him. It was a depressing time for me.

I moved the story forwards. It had been nine or ten months since I had seen Charlie, but it felt like yesterday. I had not contacted him because there was no future for us, and I really thought the way I was tormenting us both should stop. It was at a time when there had been two consecutive escort jobs where I had to try really hard to be attractive, and flirtatious. When it didn't work it was exhausting. I was earning a lot of money, but I felt my life was not progressing. It was one of those days when I was very depressed. Inevitably at such times my thoughts turned to Charlie. We had no relationship, we had met a few times, we had kissed a few times, but I could not stop longing to see him again. I lifted the telephone to call him without really thinking beyond that point. Charlie was obviously pleased to hear from me, the usually shy reserved Charlie surprised me.

"It sounds like you need a nice man to take you out to lunch," he said.

Not only did I need taking out, but I also wanted to see him right then, and he agreed immediately. Everyone was smiling; I realised they all knew about this from Charlie, but they urged me to continue, and I needed to do this for Molly.

We agreed to meet at a pub, and despite my long drive I was there first. I sat in a corner waiting, feeling almost desperate to see him, looking constantly toward the door. When Charlie appeared, I was momentarily taken aback, he was wearing a suit. I had never seen him in a suit; somehow, I didn't associate Charlie the builder with looking that smart. He looked wonderful as he walked towards me; perhaps it was just that I had not seen him for months, or perhaps it was the suit. Whatever it was my determination not to be gushing failed immediately. The first thing I said to him was that he looked gorgeous.

Typical of Charlie, he was embarrassed, so I just wanted to hug him. We talked endlessly as we always did, but it was clear from our conversation that he sensed I was feeling a bit low. He asked more probing questions of me than before, and I was evasive, unable to bring myself to tell him about my real life. None of that made me feel good about myself, and I could feel he was questioning this strange relationship we had. When I told him about George, he tried hard to disguise his relief. His reaction told me that he really wanted me. Knowing Charlie and I could never be, I suddenly realised how wrong all of this was. We were both tormenting the other for no good reason; I became determined to end it.

"I think we need to go, Charlie."

I could not bring myself to say what I meant to say, but I hoped he would hear the meaning in my voice. We walked out to the car park together and stood by my car. I desperately wanted to kiss him, but I intended to just step into my car, which is what I started to do. I dropped my bag onto the passenger seat of my little sports car, and started to put my foot in, but I simply couldn't do it. I turned back, and we fell into each other's arms.

That kiss lasted for an age and nothing else existed. I had never felt so at one with another person before. When we broke apart neither of us said anything. Something so unexpected had just happened, I could not begin to explain it. We had just kissed in the most intimate way, as if in every respect we were lovers, except of course we weren't. Eventually we said goodbye; all I could say was that I would give him a ring. Once again, I drove out of a car park, leaving Charlie standing alone, looking dejected. My common sense said this must be the end.

Looking around at my new friends, they all appeared to be spellbound. Charlie had told them his version of the story, but they obviously still wanted to hear my side of it, as did Molly. I was becoming more comfortable sharing those memories with her. I continued, telling them that several months went by - it might even have been the best part of a year since our last meeting. My life continued as before. I was meeting some exciting people, but I hadn't met the right person. Perhaps if I had done, things might have been different, but the fact was there was probably not a single day when I did not think about Charlie. There must have been a hundred moments when I nearly telephoned him. We obviously couldn't see each other on the same basis as before, that was cruel, but how could I take it further? It was clear to me that Charlie could never be a one-night stand. I wanted him so much, but also knew we could never have a normal relationship in the conventional sense. I was expecting Audrey to ask me one of her probing questions, but it was Molly who asked the difficult one.

"We know you got back together, Mom, but were you *sure* Charlie wouldn't leave his wife, and if you were sure, why did you start it all again?"

Molly had gone right to the heart of it! I'd had years to think about that very question, and still didn't have a satisfactory answer. I knew one thing for sure; I had to be honest now with myself, and above all with Molly and Charlie. Everybody looked at me in anticipation; I knew I would not come out of this well. It was always clear to me that Charlie would never leave his wife. He was so honourable, and duty bound, despite the horrendous problems he had. Reluctantly, I also had to admit that I was determined to achieve my ambition of finding the perfect wealthy husband. I did not allow myself to see the real Charlie. For me, however gorgeous, he was always Charlie the builder. He was not the wealthy man I wanted to marry, even if he had been eligible.

"I'm sorry, Charlie," I said.

Charlie smiled. "In my mind, I *am* still just a bricklayer, I've never thought of myself as anything else, so why should you?"

They all knew how my relationship with Charlie progressed from that point. There was no way round it, I would have to admit to everyone that, despite knowing there was no future for us, I simply took advantage of Charlie and indulged my selfish pleasure.

"I can't make any excuses," I said, "I just didn't have the strength to overcome my desire for him."

Audrey, never judgmental, said, "I think we can all understand that feeling, Joanna We know from Charlie what happened at the Poppies Hotel. It was such a fairy-tale story, I was in tears, but it was tears of joy for you both. Do please tell us your side of the story."

I was not expecting that. Any mention of Poppies Hotel makes me take a deep breath; Audrey had brought tears to my eyes again. Molly put her arms around me.

"When you sent me in to see Charlie that first time, with that message about 'Poppies,' I knew it was important. You *have* to tell me about it, Mom."

"Okay," I said, and with some reluctance I continued the story.

Poppies was a wonderful little hotel, I had been there on two occasions before, just for meals. It was superb in every detail, I decided if I was going to make love with Charlie, then this was a wonderful place for us to do it.

Molly interrupted me. "You *knew* that would be the outcome, but you hadn't seen Charlie for months."

It was difficult to explain, but I said, if Charlie agreed to meet me, then us making love was inevitable. We had this strange relationship where we had made love with our eyes and our kisses over such a long time. It was so obviously what we both wanted; I simply made up my mind that it *would* happen. I was just concerned that once the cork was removed from the champagne bottle, there would be no putting it back.

I told them I telephoned his office and when I made my suggestion of dinner together, his reply confirmed everything that I already knew about him. I did not have the courage to suggest he take an overnight bag, although I knew he would need one, because I had already booked a suite for the night. On the day I was like a teenager on my first date which completely surprised me. Making an entrance and sweeping men off their feet was what I did for a living. I did it very well, but it was always just a charade. Suddenly I was doing it for real.

I described my preparations for the evening. I had outfits for all occasions, but I had one dress that stood out from all the rest. It was full length, red silk satin, it was Sally Cummings' famous Red Dress. After I had modelled it for Sally on the front cover of Vogue, she gave it to me in lieu of a modelling fee. All her work is now held in private collections. Her red dress is known in the fashion world simply as 'The Red Dress'. I still have it; it is my most treasured, and my most valuable possession.

The style is fitted at the waist with a plunging neckline. There is exquisite detailing, with hand embroidery and sequins, and the bias-cut sections reflect the light in the most extraordinary way, making it both fitting and flowing at the same time. It is the most beautiful dress I have ever worn. I had never worn it in a personal capacity and refused to wear it as an escort. That night with Charlie had become so important to me, it suddenly became imperative that I wear the dress for him. I returned from my hairdresser that afternoon, wearing my hair up to accentuate my height.

The moment I got home I removed the dress from my wardrobe and lifted off the cover, and just stood staring at it for a moment. It was not like stepping into a dress, it was like stepping into another world. I felt obliged to treat the process with reverence. I wore my diamond necklace and earrings.

They may not have been entirely real, but they were absolutely beautiful. My red shoes were by Givenchy, with high heels and ankle straps. As a fashion model I had been dressed by some of the world's greatest designers, but as I left for Poppies, I knew I had never looked as radiant as I did that evening.

Having booked the room, I should obviously have checked in and changed there. It was difficult to explain to Molly, and to my friends, why I didn't do that. The truth was, I didn't want Charlie to know I had planned it. What a surreal experience it was, driving there dressed as I was! Poppies Hotel was a grand establishment, but they did not offer a car parking valet service. This, however, was about to change. I pulled up in my car outside the entrance. The doorman opened my door, I could tell he obviously did not expect to see what stepped out of the car! I slipped off my incongruous trainers and put on my high heels; he was quite unable to suppress his delightful expression.

"Good evening, madam," he said, "leave your keys with me madam, I will see your car is parked for you."

I walked into the foyer where the receptionist was dealing with a guest. The moment he saw me, he left his guest to greet me.

At the same time, the concierge said, "Good evening madam, will you be dining with us this evening?"

I said I would, and he beckoned the maître d who almost fell over himself in his haste to cross the room. I explained that I was meeting someone for dinner.

The maître d's face lit up. "I believe the gentleman in question is waiting for you in the lounge bar madam, may I have the honour of escorting you."

I offered the maître d my arm, and the room stood still as he led me to the door.

"This will be far enough," I said, as I thanked him with a smile. He reached forward to open the door for me.

"Not just yet, give me a moment will you," I said.

"I understand. In your own time, madam."

I drew a deep breath; my heart was pounding in my chest. I looked at him and nodded. He opened the door with a wonderful smile.

"May I wish you both a wonderful evening, madam."

I stepped into the room and stood for a moment looking for Charlie. I was so nervous, it was like stepping out onto the catwalk at a fashion show, but much more intense. The moment Charlie saw me he devoured me with his eyes, I enjoyed every second. Everyone there was beautifully dressed for dinner, but I knew no one would be dressed remotely like me. I was aware that, one by one, I quickly gained the attention of the entire room. As I walked towards Charlie, it felt as though I had entered a stage set with a single spotlight trained on me; nothing else existed. Perhaps it was my nerves or just the intensity of the situation, but when we met, I simply fell into his arms, and we kissed passionately. I was oblivious to anything else, it felt like an age before we broke apart. Every single person there was looking at us. Charlie was deeply embarrassed; I love that about Charlie but I didn't give a damn what those people thought.

We talked more intimately that night than ever before. I remember I told him that I intended never to be poor again. I would use what few attributes I had in order to achieve my ambitions. I did not have the courage to say I was working as an escort, but apart from that I really tried to be honest with Charlie. I said that we had separate lives, and perhaps that meant that we had no future together. I admitted that I couldn't think about the future, I just needed him now. Charlie looked at me with an expression which melted my heart. He said something quite wonderful.

"Needing means so much more than wanting," he said.

That part of our conversation didn't last long, I didn't want to spoil our reunion.

John the maître d escorted us into the restaurant. I told them

I was unsure if it was Charlie or the Red Dress, but it felt as if I was floating over the floor as every head in the restaurant turned towards us. It was the most magical moment. Even Charlie had to comment upon the dress. He said he had never seen anything like it, except of course he now remembered seeing me modelling it on the cover of Vogue. The photograph was hanging on the wall of my house in Bath where we first met. Of course, Charlie hadn't heard of Sally Cummings! We spent the evening talking endlessly, but above all we did not stop making love to each other with our eyes and body language. It was a slightly surreal situation, here we were again, we had never been intimate, but we acted in all respects as if we had. Charlie was drinking rather too much, as always, he was slightly nervous. I knew I could have that effect on some men. They might want me, but I could also intimidate them. I did not want Charlie to feel like that, and I knew alcohol didn't help.

I said something without thinking. "Let's not drink too much if you're going to make love to me tonight."

It was too late to take it back. I said it, and Charlie looked as if he had been run over by a bus! The prospect of what I had just said made my heart race even faster; I could think of nothing else but making love with him. We had finished our meal and might have enjoyed coffee together, but now that I had popped the champagne cork there was no putting it back in the bottle. I now found myself in an extremely strange situation, describing those events to my daughter. But Molly wanted to know, she was hanging on to my every word.

"How did you know Charlie would be able to stay the night, that he had made no plans?" she asked.

"I knew how much Charlie wanted me; I knew he would find a way."

I continued the story telling them how we went to reception, where I said I would book a room, while he telephoned and made some excuse to his wife. In fact it was just a case of picking up the keys, I had already booked the room.

Molly interrupted me. "You orchestrated the whole thing, didn't you? You seduced Charlie from start to finish. Do you not feel that was wrong, Mom?"

"Oh Molly, it might have been many things, but it was never wrong. If I had left it to Charlie it would never have happened, and we would not have experienced the most wonderful night of our lives. How *can* it be wrong?"

I explained how events happened so quickly that night. Charlie described it to me later as being like a whirlwind, and that was exactly how it felt. I hardly remember the sequence of events that led us up to the room. I know I instigated the whole situation, but I was quite sure Charlie hadn't told the others that I dragged him kicking and screaming up those stairs. We both wanted each other more than anything else in the world. I can hardly remember entering the room, I just remember asking Charlie to unfasten my dress. I felt almost faint with passion and excitement as I turned back to face him. It was at that point that I paused for a moment with my story; I looked at Charlie.

"Oh Charlie, the look on your face that night."

Everyone was smiling. I thought this would be uncomfortable for Molly, but she was smiling too. I tried to convey to them all just how significant that night was in my life.

"I've had an exciting life, but if I could relive just one single moment again it would be that night at Poppies. I know Charlie feels the same."

"I was so happy for Charlie when he told us that story," Audrey said, "now I'm happy for you as well Joanna. You're both so fortunate to have shared such a wonderful experience."

Molly then surprised everyone. "Audrey's right, Mom. You might have caused each other more than your share of heartache, but who wouldn't want what you and Charlie shared that night."

I was so relieved to hear Molly say that. I have so much guilt attached to my relationship with Charlie, and it's all of my own making. It has clouded my memory of our relationship for thirty years, but beneath it all something beautiful always shone through. I needed Molly to know that. I needed Charlie to know that!

I continued the story into the next morning when I woke up in Charlie's arms. The morning after is always the moment when a night of passion is viewed in the cold light of day; for me it had so often been a bad experience. That morning it could not have been more different. In my half sleep I was aware of Charlie's chest beneath my cheek, my lips pressed against his skin. I could feel his heart beating; my senses were full of the smell and the taste of him. It was wonderful, I did not want to fully wake up. Charlie smiled as I told my story, I could see from his expression he was reliving the moment just as I was.

"You lifted my head from your chest, and ever so gently you moved me over to the pillow, and then you kissed me. Do you remember, Charlie?"

"Like it was yesterday," he replied with a smile on his face.

"Oh Charlie, I don't think I've had a happier moment in my entire life."

Audrey really surprised me. "Charlie told us what you later said about that moment Joanna, about wanting to tell him you loved him. Would it have changed everything if you had?"

"We both knew we loved each other, Audrey. I just could not admit it. If I had been honest with you Charlie, if I had been honest with myself, I would never have let you go."

The implications of what I had just said were obvious. I made my choice to pursue a life without Charlie - I had just admitted to everyone that I had made an awful mistake. Perhaps that was also the moment when I finally admitted it to myself. Nobody said anything, and I am not sure I could have said anything even if I had tried. I think we all needed to digest the full meaning of my admission. How different our lives might have been if I had just mentioned those three words. Charlie's resigned expression said it all.

"I'm sorry Charlie," I said, "I can't continue with this today."

By then the day had slipped effortlessly into the evening and I was feeling totally drained. Reliving those moments with everyone was difficult, and some of the questions they asked of me were exhausting. I really could not face anymore so I suggested Molly should drive us back to our hotel, where I was looking forward to an early night. Everyone expressed disappointment. Audrey did her best to persuade us to stay for dinner, but I could tell from her tone of voice that she understood how I was feeling. Charlie probably had other ideas, but he also understood that I genuinely needed a quiet evening. We made our excuses, saying we would see them all the next morning.

As the father of my child, I could never forget Charlie, but I had tried so hard to put those feelings behind me. It had not occurred to me that our reunion would awaken such vivid and painful emotions. One of my enduring memories of him was his face on the numerous occasions when I drove away, leaving him standing somewhere. Once again, he stood by the car on that evening and waved goodbye. As we drove away, those emotions came flooding back like a spring tide, I still felt the same.

Another reason for leaving was that I felt I needed an evening alone with Molly. This was not just about me and Charlie; this was very much about me and Molly. It had been a momentous day, I felt so tired, and it was quite late. I suggested we simply went straight into dinner dressed just as we were. Molly was happy to do that, so we sat down in the hotel restaurant, and I prepared myself for some more searching questions.

My daughter had not ceased to amaze me throughout this whole affair. Considering what I had done and its consequences, she had met me more than halfway. She had no idea about my brief life as an escort, and of course, however I dressed it up, some of it was paid sex. This had been my darkest secret. I always dreaded telling her; now I dreaded hearing her opinion of me. We ordered our meal and I waited to hear what she had to say.

"Don't look so worried, Mom," she said, "it's just a case of getting to know you all over again."

"I realise that, but I'm so frightened you won't like what you find."

Molly took my hand and what she said took my breath away.

"As soon as I was old enough to realise, I could see you were different to the other Moms; you always stood out from the crowd. The way you look, the way you dress, the way you talk to people; you are that amazing woman in the room that everyone gravitates towards. I have always been so proud of you, and nothing you said today changes that. I wish I were like you, Mom."

It had been such an emotional day, I just could not help it, I burst into tears.

"I always assumed you rebelled at the way I looked and dressed."

"I don't think I was ever a rebel, not consciously anyway. I just always thought that I couldn't compete with you, so why try?"

"But look at you Moll, you are an amazing, beautiful woman. You have the world in the palm of your hand."

"I suppose in some ways I do, but it's *my* world in the palm of *my* hand. I can never be like you, Mom! I just do not have the confidence; look at what you did at the Poppies Hotel. You wore that fabulous dress, worth thousands of dollars, and you walked into that place on your own as if you owned it. You swept Charlie off his feet and into bed without a second thought. How many women would have the confidence to do that? I certainly haven't!"

My daughter never ceased to surprise me, but what she described of herself was not the Molly I knew. I told her that for many years now, what she was describing as me was actually the perfect description of herself.

"I've been to some of your conferences and business gatherings Moll. There is only ever one person in the room, everyone gravitates towards you. I am the lone woman beaming with pride that nobody notices. All I want is for someone to ask who I am so that I can say, that's my daughter."

Molly looked at me, and I really think she had not realised how other people see her. We suddenly saw each other in a new light.

"I've learnt a lot about you today, Mom, and about Charlie. The pieces are starting to fit together. I simply couldn't understand how you and Charlie could have done it, but after what I've seen and heard it begins to make sense to me."

"I so hoped it would, Moll. I have hated hiding secrets from you, especially about me working as an escort. I wish now that I hadn't done it, but I am not ashamed of anything I have done, I did what I felt I had to do at the time. I just hope *you're* not."

"It *was* a bit of a shock to find out that your Mom has worked as a hooker, but I can see it was just a job. I suppose, in a way, I even admire you for doing what you felt you had to do. Does Dad know about it?"

"Yes, that's how we met. It was at a function, your Dad wasn't a client, but he knew exactly why I was there."

"If it's okay with Dad, and with Charlie, then I guess it should be okay with me."

"Do you mean that, can you really forgive me, Moll?"

"I don't think I'll go around telling people that my Mom was a hooker, but it was all a long time ago, what's to forgive?"

I thought about Molly's comment, as well as the use of that

dreadful word 'hooker' which I hate. I wanted to take her to task over it, but of course, however you describe it, I guess she was right. That was a good time to call it a day.

Chapter Eight
REGRET LEAVES THE BUILDING

When we met for breakfast, the world seemed like a happier place to me. Molly seemed to share my sentiment.

"We have a lot to do today, Mom. We need to see the house Sylvia found for me, you need to tell me the rest of your story with Charlie, and we need to put your plan into operation."

"You're right, but there's something you've overlooked," I said, "when are you going to tell me about Giles?"

Molly looked surprised. Giles was the owner of the IT business Molly had come here to collaborate with. I met him a couple of times when he was in Washington DC negotiating with Molly, and I was aware of the hours they spent together in video conference.

"You know what's going on with Giles; it's business," she said.

"This is *me* you're talking to Moll. I've seen that look on your face. After all the things I have been confessing to you, come on, tell me."

"I should have known you would realise. Okay, he's adorable and I can't stop thinking about him. There you are, I've told you."

"But you told me it was only business."

"I know I did, Mom. The thing is, I feel a bit guilty about it."

"I knew you were hiding something from me. That's not like you, Moll. What have you done to feel guilty about?"

"This deal with Giles is the biggest thing I've ever done. It could be ground-breaking, but I am no longer being objective, because I can't stop thinking about him! Not only is that a ridiculous mistake at the corporate level, but he's also married, which means it's a ridiculous mistake on a personal level as well."

I was more than a little taken aback. I could tell from her voice that she was very emotionally involved in this situation. I knew how much was at stake, and suddenly realised why she hadn't been herself recently. I realised what disastrous timing the revelations about her father had proven to be.

"I'm sorry sweetheart," I said, "if only I had known, perhaps we could have delayed meeting Charlie until you have this situation sorted out."

"It's too late now, Mom. I just have to deal with it."

"If you knew he was married, why did you allow yourself to get involved with him, especially in these circumstances? You know it can only end in tears."

"That's great advice coming from you, Mom! Look at you and Charlie. He was married, and yet you fell in love with him."

"You're right of course but look how it all ended."

"You said your relationship with Charlie was the most wonderful experience of your life, it might not have ended well, but surely you don't wish it never happened, do you?"

Molly was right, I was trying to give her the advice that I certainly hadn't taken, so perhaps she had a point.

"You're really serious about him, aren't you, does he feel the same about you?"

Molly seemed to be in little doubt. "I'm sure he does, but

we haven't talked about it; we're kind of pretending it's not happening."

I knew that situation only too well. I so remember my early meetings with Charlie, when we would sit and make love to each other with our eyes, neither of us admitting it.

"I won't give you advice, Moll, but if you ever want any, Charlie and I wrote the book."

Molly smiled in agreement. "Giles has been completely honest with me, his marriage is a disaster, but he has a little boy to think of."

"How involved are you? Have you been to bed with him?"

"*Mom*, you're not supposed to ask me that! No I haven't! I'm sure Giles wants to, but that would mean betraying his wife, and I don't think he can take that step."

"If that's true, then he's the first man who couldn't."

"That's being cynical, Mom. He *is* that kind of man, he's very principled, that's what makes him so wonderful. Neither of us wanted or encouraged this thing to happen."

"Are you sure about that. You might say that Charlie didn't initially encourage me, or me him, but I'm not sure it would be entirely true."

We agreed, Molly should tread very carefully. I so much wanted her business venture to be a success, but I didn't want my baby's heart broken in the process. It had been an eventful start to the morning, I had already spoken to Emma-Jane and to Sylvia on the phone, as well as to Harry. My plan was progressing well, but now I also had Molly's revelation to think about.

As we set off in the car to see Charlie and the others, we were both preoccupied, and little wonder! We had stepped into the unknown with this reunion; so much could have gone wrong, but rather than weakening our relationship, I began to feel that Molly and I were being drawn ever closer together. I couldn't wait to see Charlie again that morning and was really looking forward to seeing the others as well. We both felt amazingly comfortable with them; when we arrived, they welcomed us with open arms.

"What's the plan today?" asked Audrey, with an excited smile on her face.

"Well," I said, "this afternoon we're going to see the house Sylvia has found for Molly. Tomorrow morning, we ladies are all going to Sylvia's fashion makeover. This evening I want you all to have dinner with us at our hotel, where we can plan our little trip, because in just two days' time we will all be in the South of France!"

Harry had obviously told them what he had told me that morning, about a charter flight being available for us in just a couple of days' times. I expected Audrey to be in a panic about getting ready, but instead there was an air of excitement. Harry quickly spotted the voids in our diary.

"Let's have lunch *here* today, that'll be quicker, and then we can all come with you to see Molly's house."

Bill offered the next suggestion. "You said this house was just outside Cambridge, not far from Girton College. Well it just happens that I know the most wonderful restaurant near there, so shall I try to get a table there for this evening?"

"That's wonderful," Audrey said, "and that leaves this morning free for Joanna to continue her story."

"What about me," Charlie asked, "can't I make a suggestion?"

"No, be quiet, Charlie! It's Joanna's turn now," Audrey said, giving Charlie one of her condescending looks.

"Yes come on, Mom, I want to know the rest of it."

I was already prepared for that, so just cleared my thoughts in preparation.

"Where did I get to last time?"

"Oh, it was that wonderful night you and Charlie shared at the Poppies Hotel," Audrey replied.

I looked at Charlie, knowing he had already told them our story, but for some reason I needed his approval to continue. He smiled his irresistible smile, and I drew a breath.

"Poppies," I said, "marked the beginning of our real relationship. We were lovers from that moment on. Every second we spent together was intense. I never dreamed for a second that anything could surpass the experience of our first night together, but every night at Poppies was equally wonderful, though in a different way. This was how it continued; it was sublime wasn't it, Charlie?"

"Happiest days of my life," Charlie replied with a broad smile.

They all sat in silence listening to my every word. I just knew the question that they wanted to ask me. If I loved him so much, why didn't I abandon my desire to find a wealthy husband? I knew it could not be avoided, especially for Charlie, so I tried to explain the unexplainable.

"I know the way I treated you was unforgivable, Charlie. I am so sorry, if only I had my time again!"

Nobody asked me anything, so I just continued. I had been working as an escort for eighteen months or so by that stage and was used to fitting my social life around my work. My torment began as soon as Charlie and I became lovers. Our relationship was so special, but he was married, and this gave me the reason I needed for pursuing my goal. I knew his marriage was a disaster, but I never once tried to convince him to leave Annie.

I think I needed him to remain unavailable, because somehow that justified what I was doing. I hated myself but continued to get on with the job. I would come back from an escort job feeling guilty, unable to force myself to tell Charlie what I was doing. We loved each other so much; in my heart of hearts I knew my quest was really a denial of our love. My way of dealing with that was to never say those words, and never allow Charlie to say those words; I could not admit to what was so obvious.

One of my worst moments came when for the first time during our relationship I met a wonderful marriage prospect.

That lovely man was crazy about me; I had been seeing him for a couple of weeks. We were sitting together in a London restaurant one evening, when he spoke to me about his plans for the future. He was hinting that perhaps I might fit into those plans. I became drawn into the conversation, then suddenly it hit me that a future with that man would mean saying goodbye to Charlie. It was a quite involuntary reaction, I simply burst into tears, right there in the middle of the restaurant.

"Do you remember, Charlie, that night when I met you at your yard, and I ran from my car into your arms, and wouldn't let you go?"

Charlie obviously did remember. "You never did tell me why you were so upset. That was probably the moment when I realised that I really was going to lose you one day."

We looked at each other, both reliving the tragic mistakes we made.

"Even after that awful experience," I said, "I still forced myself to continue my quest to find a wealthy husband; I was so determined. Charlie, I can't believe it now, but somehow I convinced myself that wealth and position was more important to me than our love."

Charlie managed a forced smile and nodded his head in resigned agreement. I moved the story on to describe that terrible day when Annie found out about us.

"You know the details from Charlie," I said, glad that I didn't need to relive it all again. I went on to briefly explain to Molly how we entered Charlie's office, and our world of subterfuge came crashing down around us when we found Annie and Sylvia standing there.

"Oh, my God!" exclaimed Molly, "what did you do?"

I explained there was little I could do; this was something that Charlie and Annie had to deal with. It was a turning point in our relationship in more ways than one. I thought if Charlie was ever going to leave Annie, then this would be the time. It was only later when I realised why he didn't. I explained to Molly about Annie's alcoholism, and how there was the risk that his girls might have been taken into care. I also knew I should have been there for Charlie that dreadful night, but for me it would have been the commitment I had convinced myself I couldn't make. Our love affair continued for several months after that dreadful day, in fact in some ways it was even more intense between us. Then I met Alan, my husband, an international banker.

I realised that this was the part of my life which would be the most painful for Charlie to hear, I also knew I had to continue. Alan was handsome and charming, and I knew he represented everything I was searching for. Except for the one thing - he wasn't Charlie. This was to be the start of the most painful experience of my life.

As my relationship with Alan progressed, I knew there could only be one outcome for me and Charlie. I tried to tell him but I just could not do it. When Charlie suggested we go away for a weekend together, somehow, I knew he understood. We both acted as if nothing was untoward that weekend. When we made love, I felt a desperation to be a part of him, I knew this was the last time. Somehow, I needed to experience everything, forget nothing. I could not begin to explain my anguish; neither of us could bring ourselves to mention it. The pain was so raw, I could scarcely bring myself to think about it, much less mention it, I could tell Charlie felt the same.

As we drove back on the Sunday afternoon we hardly spoke. Every minute that elapsed was a minute less remaining of our relationship. I mourned the loss of every second. Finally, that awful moment arrived. There was so much that should have been said between us, but I simply couldn't speak. We kissed for the last time; it was a kiss like no other I have ever experienced. I felt we were both searching for something, a part of each other that we hadn't found before, a part we could keep for ever. I was in such conflict, a part of me desperately wanted to tell Charlie I loved him, that I couldn't live without him. The other part was my driving ambition, telling me my future was with Alan. Somehow, I forced myself out of the car and I walked away. Every step was a torment; my legs were weak and I feared I might fall over. The moment I sat in my car, the enormity of what I had done swept through my body. I was crying hysterically; my hands were shaking so badly I struggled to put the key in the ignition. When I tried to pull away, I stalled the engine and had to start again. Even when I finally managed to drive away, I found myself going in the wrong direction.

"Oh Charlie, I just couldn't stop crying! I'll never forget how I felt that day, just thinking about it brings it all back again." I could see Charlie was reliving that moment just as I was, we were both going through it all over again. "I know you felt the same, Charlie. I bet you drove off just like me, not knowing where you were going."

I looked at Charlie across the room; he had sadness in his eyes.

"You *do* know me too well, Joanna; that's exactly what I did."

Everyone sat glum-faced. What I had described was so tragic because it need not have happened. I destroyed a large part of both of us for an ideal which I had convinced myself was more important. It may seem absurdly foolish now, but at the time my vision of the future was resolute. I had made a pledge to myself, and to my mother, that I would never be poor again.

I moved the story forward a couple of months to when Alan and I were making all the arrangements for our wedding. I was unable to stop thinking about Charlie, wondering whether I was making a terrible mistake. I would relive a moment from our wonderful time together, and then in an instant the memory would collapse into that agonising goodbye, and I would be distraught. One afternoon, I found myself in floods of tears again. Here I was, about to be married, and I was crying about my lost love! Alan was everything I was looking for. I had achieved my goal in life. Charlie was not an international banker; he was a builder, and he was married. I would have to deny everything that my life stood for if I were to reject Alan.

It was perhaps the only time in my relationship with Charlie that I was being completely honest with myself. I simply could not bear the pain of being without Charlie, so despite everything, I resolved to telephone him. I told him about my pending marriage, and stupidly all that I asked him was whether he had reconsidered leaving Annie. Really, of course, what I was saying was, 'I'm getting married but it's still not too late for us to be together.' Charlie said he hadn't reconsidered leaving Annie. I should have said more, much more, but I didn't.

"That was the moment, Charlie, when we finally lost each other, wasn't it?'

He looked at me with his sad eyes, took a deep breath as if to say something, but instead he just nodded in agreement. Charlie had already told Molly about the events of the 18th of June 1982, and I knew the others had no need to hear it again. It was certainly not my finest hour, and something I was really reluctant to re-live. But I did feel I needed to tell Molly and Charlie what I had told Audrey, so I summoned up the courage to continue.

I knew what I had done that day was horribly selfish, a cruel thing to do, and I could not justify any of it. I just could not go to America and leave Charlie forever without seeing him, and finally telling him I loved him. I simply cannot explain why the expression of those three words became so important for me. When I search deep into my soul, perhaps the one guilty regret which exceeds all others was my denial of our love. Nothing can excuse what I did. I just had to say those three words to Charlie, I was blinded to everything else.

"Had it not been for Molly," I said, "I would have spent the rest of my life regretting what I did that day. But how can I regret that day now? We could have done things so much better, Charlie, you and I, except for that last day. It was the one thing we finally got right. Look at what we did, Charlie!"

I looked at our beautiful daughter and then at Charlie.

"Please try to forgive me, Charlie. I am *so* sorry for the way I treated you, but I can never regret our last day. We have Molly, and now I can never lose you."

Charlie could see how distressed I was, he walked over and put his arms around me. Molly immediately followed, as did the rest of them. I have lived with so many regrets about my relationship with Charlie; I had even been unable to tell him about the one good thing we *had* achieved, Molly! Now I felt as if a great burden of guilt was being shed with every tear.

"I think it's time that all this guilt and regret left the building," Charlie said.

There were still so many questions unanswered, but I felt the time had come to leave the past behind and look towards the future. Lunch provide a welcome break, an opportunity for Molly to take back the centre stage. Everyone wanted to know about the house, and Bill was also particularly interested to hear about the artificial intelligence which Molly's company was developing. I was so happy not to be the centre of attention any more, feeling that perhaps Charlie was also pleased that our past could now return to its rightful place. He had said little, but I knew there was a whole world of regret just beneath the surface, which made me even more prepared to take any risk to see him happy.

My mind was elsewhere, I couldn't concentrate on the conversation, and lunch seemed to come and go without me noticing. We sat in the lounge with our cups of coffee and arrangements were being made all around me. The next thing I knew Charlie was agreeing that he would drive Molly and me to view her house, while the others followed on in Harry's car.

"If that's fine with you and Molly, I suggest we get going?" he said.

"Oh well, yes I suppose so, yes thank you Charlie," I replied.

They arranged to meet later in the car park, and Audrey asked if Molly and I would like to use her apartment before leaving, we accepted her offer. It had been such a difficult morning for me, I am not sure I would have got through it without their support. So I made a point of thanking Audrey.

"Thank you for helping me through this morning, that was a difficult moment for me."

"You amaze me Joanna, I so admire how you faced that ordeal."

"I don't think I had an option. I promised Molly, and I promised myself I would tell Charlie."

"I can't imagine the ordeal you must be going through, Molly; you're both dealing with it amazingly well."

"It has certainly been a lot to take in Audrey, but Mum's right; once we set out on this reunion there was no way back, was there?"

We talked some more for a while, and when we were ready, we walked back towards the car park, where the others were waiting for us. Audrey had helped to raise my spirits, and the prospect of viewing Molly's potential new house gave me a sense of purpose. Charlie opened his car door with a smile, and I felt we were moving away from the past, into a new future. We had not driven more than a couple of miles when Molly needed to ask more questions.

"You weren't honest with Charlie, were you, Mom? Do you *really* forgive her, Charlie?"

"I guessed she had a secret life that I was never a part of, so of course I knew. I also realised she was looking for something I could not offer; I suppose I just didn't want to know the details. We both had another life; neither of us was ready to commit to the other. There is nothing to forgive, Molly. Well, maybe one thing. You were in such a rush, Joanna, if only you'd given us both just a little more time."

"When you first told me, Mom, I was so shocked, and angry! To be told your father is not your father, that your entire life has been a lie! I hated you for it. I hated you Charlie, even though I didn't know you. I was convinced I was some sort of tragic mistake, the consequence of something sordid."

"Please tell me you don't still feel like that?" I said.

"I don't. After everything I've learned about you, I want you both to know, I'm really proud to be your daughter."

Charlie stopped the car on the side of the road. Molly clambered forward from the back of the car and we hugged each other. It was a moment I will always remember. When we arrived at the house, I think we all felt the past was somewhere behind us. We walked from the car, arm in arm; it felt like we were a loving family. I did nothing to break the spell.

The house was perfect in every detail. Just big enough for a guest bedroom, and an office for Molly. It was compact, cheap to run, low maintenance, ideal for Molly's busy life. The location was also perfect, just fifteen minutes from Giles' business. It was fully equipped with curtains, carpets, all the fixtures and fittings. The furniture was perfect in every detail, the beds, everything. Audrey could not believe it.

"Does all this come with the house?" she said, with a note of disbelief in her voice.

"It was the show house," Molly said. "Sylvia's arranged all this; everything comes with the house, at no extra cost."

For someone like Molly, who would walk through the front door holding only a suitcase, this was everything she could have dreamed of. Sylvia really was a genius! Bill was a genius as well; the nearby restaurant that he knew was perfect. We arrived early, but it gave us more time to sit and talk together. We talked again about Molly's house, and then the conversation turned to her business venture. She was so excited and enthusiastic. It was Giles this, and Giles that, and Giles and I will do this, and Giles and I will do that. She positively sparkled.

"Sounds like you're marrying Giles, rather than going into business with him!" Audrey said innocently.

Molly looked embarrassed and went rather quiet.

"Oh dear, have I said something." Audrey exclaimed.

I am afraid the cat was out of the bag for Moll; she'd given the game away. Of course, Audrey wanted to know all about Giles, and to my surprise Molly told them everything, including that he was unhappily married with a small son. Bill was concerned about the conflict of interest, Harry asked if she were sure she could trust him, Audrey just seemed pleased.

"Please be careful, Molly. I don't want my daughter hurt," said Charlie.

What Molly told us in the car earlier changed everything that day. She had gone beyond forgiving Charlie and me. Everything changed between us, and I could see that applied to Charlie as well. We had a lovely evening in the restaurant; it was Molly's moment to shine and she was radiant. I felt so much more relaxed, as did Charlie.

Finally the evening had to come to an end, and Charlie drove us back to our hotel. Molly smiled and chatted all the way; it had been such a good evening. I felt we had reached a turning point, nothing was going to change the past, but we had got beyond that first difficult step towards our new reality. I didn't know what the future held for us, but at least now I was sure that there would be a future. A part of that future would be seeing Charlie the following day, that was understood now. When he dropped us off at our hotel there was no awkward goodbye, he gave Molly a long hug, and I kissed his cheek, saying we would see him in the morning.

Molly and I walked up the stairs to our bedrooms, and to my surprise she walked into my room with me.

"I can't leave it, Mom. I have got to ask you how Dad fits into all this. Do you intend to just go back to Dad and pretend that nothing has happened?"

"That's exactly what I intend to do; what good could it do to tell him?"

"I don't want him hurt either, he will always be my Dad. Did you ever love him, Mom?"

"I did come to love him. It's not the way I loved Charlie, but what we have is real."

"Did Charlie come between you both, is that why it could never be the same?"

"I suppose it was, it took me years to realise just how heartbroken I was."

"Do you think you can really just carry on as before? What you and Charlie had; it's not really gone away, has it?"

"Of course it has, that was a long time ago."

"I'm not sure if you really believe that or not, but that's not how I see it."

"What do you mean?"

"There's a kind of spark between you, do you not realise how you look at each other?"

"We don't do we?"

"I can see it."

"Well I'm sorry, it's not intentional."

"No need to apologise Mom, I've come this far, and he is my father!"

"It's bad enough that I broke Charlie's heart all those years ago, I'm certainly not going to do that again. And the same applies to your Dad, I am not going to break his heart either. I know what I have to do."

"I'll support you, whatever you do, Mom. But now that I have found Charlie, I'm not letting him go. He's a permanent part of my life now."

"I know! He's been a part of my life for the past thirty years."

Chapter Nine
THE MAKEOVER

Next day, it felt as if a great burden had been lifted from my shoulders, like a new beginning. Molly had changed her plans and was rushing off to see Giles. When she emerged from her room after breakfast, she looked wonderful.

"Not bad for a business meeting!" I said.

"Do I look okay? I've not overdone it, have I?"

"You look gorgeous, Sweetheart, don't change a thing. Poor man, he's not going to know what's hit him."

I could see she was anxious to see Giles. No sooner had we finished getting ready than Molly was on her way.

"Good luck with the makeover today, I'm sure it will work out just fine."

"I do hope so, it's a bit of a gamble isn't it."

"Don't worry, it's one of your better ideas Mom."

When my baby left in a taxi, I was not sure if I was pleased for her, or envious. Moments later, my own taxi appeared, in the shape of Charlie. This was the first time I had been completely alone with him, but after everything that had been said, I felt no apprehension between us. Our conversation was centred upon Molly. I needed to be reassured that he at least understood why I held my secret for so long. He in turn was more concerned to assure me how much he adored Molly, how she had stepped into a void in his life. When I set out on this reunion, my two biggest fears were that Charlie would come between me and Molly, or that I would come between Molly and him. I hadn't dared to dream the complete opposite would be the case.

We stepped out of the car at the Village and walked towards the entrance. I was aware that we were at ease with each other, the tensions and difficult moments seemed to be behind us. Audrey was the first to greet us, giving me a hug. I could see immediately that she had dressed to make an impression. Her expression said, 'I don't *need* a makeover.' Sylvia was there sitting with the others, and oh my goodness, she really *did* need a makeover! I felt so sorry for her. She's an incredible woman, always a part of everything that Charlie does, but always on the outside. As soon as we had greeted them, all the gentlemen hastily excused themselves. I could see the prospect of a fashion makeover was a bit alarming to them.

"Are you ladies ready?" I asked.

"Where's Molly?" asked Sylvia.

"Giles!" I didn't need to say anything else.

"Where are we going, and how do we get there?" asked Audrey.

I checked my watch. Having already spoken on the phone that morning to Emma-Jane, I knew she had everything organised. What I was not prepared for was what arrived outside the door. Two enormous black cars appeared with blacked-out windows. A burly man wearing an earpiece got out from the front passenger seat and opened the back door for Emma-Jane. She stepped out, looking as she always does, like a Hollywood film star. She was accompanied by a strangely dressed androgynous figure. I had not seen Emma for several months; it was great to see how pleased she was to be a part of today's adventure. I introduced Audrey and Sylvia, and she introduced her androgynous companion.

"This is Antony, my personal style guru; he's wonderful, simply the best."

"Darling, you *know* I hate that term guru. Fashionista, *please!*"

Antony did not just appear before us, he seemed to explode into view. He kissed and hugged each of us in turn as if he were a long-lost friend; it was all a bit disquieting. I had never seen anyone dressed like it! His clothes were all brightly coloured, in thin flowing materials which exaggerated his every movement. His shirt was long tailed with billowing sleeves, while his harem pants flared out with an excess of material. This was complimented with his silk scarf and red beret, while a yellow silk handkerchief in his breast pocket added the final flourish.

"So, my darlings," he said, "a little bird tells me that a sprinkle of stardust is required. Let me look at you wonderful creatures; allow me to cast my spell."

To add to our discomfort, he then walked round each of us in turn, surveying us up and down. He walked around me, pushing, and prodding my clothes. Albeit discreetly, he pushed my boobs up, and ran his hand down my back. I felt uncomfortable but not remotely threatened. Antony certainly did not regard women as sexual objects; this much at least was quite clear! He stepped back, looking at me.

"This I can work with. You have *great* potential, darling."

Then he turned his attention towards Sylvia who was obviously terrified. She stepped back, but to no avail. Antony did possess a disarming charm, but as he walked around her, touching and prodding, Sylvia closed her eyes tight.

"Oh dear! We *have* let ourselves *go*, darling. *How* exciting. A blank canvas for me to explore."

He then turned towards Audrey, who immediately made excuses.

"Oh no, I don't need any advice."

"*Of course*, you don't, darling. What exquisite clothes. Was this jacket your mother's?"

Audrey was mortified but seemed determined not to make a scene.

"Just play along," I whispered to her.

"Come along, Antony, let's get going. Where to first?" Emma-Jane said.

"Well, I'm sorry, my darlings, but I *can't* work here in the wilderness. We'll have to go back to *civilisation*."

I suddenly realised that Emma must have set off incredibly early that morning from the Embassy, then travelled all this way, and now we had to return to London! There were two huge cars, two drivers, and who was the other man? I had somehow thought this would be sorted out locally and now I felt I had asked too much of Emma.

"I wouldn't miss this for the world!" Emma said. "Don't worry about John, he's my personal protection officer. He won't get in the way."

There was a sense of excitement in the air, I think even Sylvia managed a smile. We set off in the lead car, while John, Antony, and driver followed behind. I thought we were driving far too fast, with the car behind much too close. Emma just smiled throughout.

"Don't worry, we're in very good hands," she said.

This was out of my control now. I had no idea where Antony was taking us. Eventually we pulled up simultaneously outside a hairdresser in central London. We parked in a no-parking area, which apparently was not a problem for us. Antony introduced us to a team of incredibly enthusiastic hairstylists. He then went into raptures about his ideas for each of us, and the hairdressers ran their fingers through our hair like children opening Christmas presents.

"I'm sorry, you've made a mistake. I'm only here to watch," Audrey said.

"I thought I was here to watch as well," I said, "but why not? This could be great fun."

Audrey had little option but to take part which, of course,

was my intention. There was much debate among the hair-dressers, with Antony running around between us, waxing lyrical about our various bone structures, and where we needed enhancing. The whole process took me back to my time as a fashion model. It was all familiar to me, but I could see the others were bewildered. We went from looking absurd, to ridiculous, and then finally being transformed.

I offered no suggestions to my hairdresser, other than I did not want my hair shortened too much. I know from experience that they generally do know best. Antony was beside himself, saying my hair swept up like that was *perfect* for my bone structure. I am lucky with my hair, having virtually no grey at all, but they returned me to my youthful natural blonde colour. I had not even realised it was fading. The interesting thing was, without prompting them, they had styled me exact-ly as I was on that first night at Poppies.

Audrey was equally transformed. I thought her hair looked good anyway; it was her clothes I had been worried about. Antony, however, had seen an Audrey that I hadn't suspect-ed. She looked fully ten years younger. The real shock was Sylvia. Her hair had been so out of condition, I doubt she could remember the last time she had it properly styled. The transformation took all of us by surprise.

Antony was pleased, the hairdresser was delighted, and Sylvia was speechless. Her lank brown hair was replaced by a rich chestnut coloured bob. She didn't look like Sylvia at all; she looked years younger, a different person. For someone who had only come along to encourage Audrey, this was a wonder-ful outcome. Audrey desperately did not want to admit it, but she too was delighted, how could she not be! Sylvia seemed almost to be in shock. We left there on a tremendous high.

"Where to next, Antony?" I asked.

"One step at a time, my darlings, one step at a time. Next stop is Annabelle."

"Who's Annabelle?" asked Audrey.

The Makeover

"She is an *angel* descended from heaven to perform mira-
cles," said Antony. "The darling girl is the finest makeup artist
in the world."

Eventually we stopped in Shaftsbury Avenue at the Queens
Theatre.

"Are we seeing a show?" asked Emma.

Antony looked bemused. "If we want to be in the presence
of greatness, *we* have to go to *her*, and right now she's *here*."

We were quickly ushered in via the stage door. There were
people everywhere milling around. John was greatly concerned, talking up his sleeve to the drivers. We spotted several
well-known faces.

"Oh look, isn't that…?" Audrey tried to say.

"Of *course*, it is, darling! Come along now," said Antony.

We were directed into a dressing room, and in there was the
very ordinary-looking Annabelle. She had little time to spend
on us, but like all expert professionals, she could do in twenty
minutes what would have taken me two hours. Antony was
right, I have worked with more makeup artists than I care to
remember, but this young lady was in a class of her own. Her
skill was not so much applying the makeup; it was in seeing
how every feature of your face could be enhanced. Sylvia was
first in the chair, and although she was embarrassed by us all
watching, we could not tear ourselves away. Annabelle just
looked for several minutes, then swung into action.

"You have good features, Sylvia," she said. "I just need to
widen your eyes a little and accentuate those eyebrows. We
need an understated sophisticated look to go with that wonderful hair of yours. The only real statement you might like to
make for an occasion, say, would be a really bold red lipstick."

In little more than twenty minutes, the result was breath-taking. If I had not seen the transition first-hand, I would have
walked straight past Sylvia without recognising her. She looked
incredible! Next up was Audrey who by now was showing
some enthusiasm. It was not quite the dramatic transformation

we saw with Sylvia. Audrey already had good makeup skills, but the professional can always see things you don't. She told Audrey some of her colours could be improved, especially her eye colour, and skin tone. The changes were subtle, but again it was transformational; she looked wonderful.

We were running out of time. Annabelle beckoned me.

"You've had this done before, haven't you? Have you been in the fashion business?"

I nodded. "A long time ago."

She looked for an embarrassing amount of time, before finally making changes to my eyes, skin tone, lips, everything. When I looked in the mirror, I could hardly believe what I saw. Antony was right, she was a genius!

We could not thank her enough and left there with our feet hardly touching the ground. The next stop was a boutique, but not just any boutique. Occupying two shop fronts in Bond Street, this one was incredibly special. They were of course friends of Antony's and were ready and waiting for us. The staff flitted around us like so many butterflies.

"What's the occasion?" they asked.

I stepped in to say this was not any one specific occasion. Sylvia and Audrey needed smart causal, something for a warmer climate. We also needed something a little formal, suitable for a company secretary like Sylvia. We needed shoes, of course, and finally, we needed evening dresses to grace the finest restaurant in Monte Carlo. The prospect of such a lucrative sale sent the staff into a spin.

"I won't need an evening dress, not at these prices," Sylvia said. "I don't go anywhere to wear one."

"Never mind," I said, "have one anyway. It's nothing, after all that you've done for Molly."

Sylvia worrying about money was a little silly; this was all my treat. In any event, she could afford it far more than I could. Sylvia is one of the largest shareholders in Bartlett Homes. Clothes began to appear from all directions, and

Antony was beside himself once again. At first, I had been a little apprehensive about his strange androgynous appearance. I was not sure if he was simply a gay man, or any one of several other possibilities.

His clothes were his fashion statement. However outlandish, he certainly wanted to make an impression. This was when I noticed his shoes, very feminine, sequin covered sling-backs. I had really warmed towards him, despite his outrageous appearance. He was immensely talented at what he did, and he was a real joy to be with. His sexuality was none of my concern, something I didn't think about any more. This was probably just as well because he thought nothing of stepping in and out of the cubicles while we were changing. He went in after Sylvia; she was probably horrified.

We all heard him say, "Oh, good *Lord!* What on *earth* is *this?*"

The next thing we knew, he put his head around the curtain and shouted to the assistants.

"*Bras* please, for Sylvia."

I had no doubt Sylvia was mortified, but he was right, there were things that Sylvia just did not seem to notice. Audrey is tall and slim, made to hang clothes on. She tried on one item after another, looking good in everything the staff produced. There was one evening dress, however, that particularly caught my eye. I tried not to influence her too much and was delighted when she decided on the same dress. She looked sensational in it, and the overall look with the new hair and face was breath-taking.

"You look absolutely beautiful." I said.

Audrey was tearful, quite overcome with emotion.

Antony only made matters worse when he came out of Sylvia's changing room and saw Audrey standing in her evening dress.

"Oh, my *Lord!* Audrey my *darling,* you look *wonderful.*"

We were giving all our attention to Audrey and didn't

notice Sylvia emerge from her changing room. Emma said nothing, just tapped me on the shoulder. I looked round to see Sylvia standing in an evening dress. No one said anything, I looked at Antony, who was equally speechless. Audrey looked over and said nothing. All the staff in the shop stopped what they were doing, and just stared.

"I don't think I can wear a dress like this," Sylvia said, "it's too revealing."

The dress was not especially revealing, that wasn't what had taken our breath away. It was just the sight of Sylvia looking like a totally different and beautiful woman. We gathered round her, everyone smiling.

"Do you think I look all right?" she asked.

"*All right!*" Antony said, "My darling, you're *gorgeous!*"

We had to persuade Sylvia to have the dress. She genuinely seemed to have no idea what an attractive woman she is. Antony could not have been happier, seeming to be transported to an even more exuberant level.

"Sometimes a little of my stardust can end up on the floor of the changing room, but today my darlings, I have *excelled!* A talent such as mine can be so *tiring*. Will you forgive me, my angels, if I retire so that I can relive today's *triumph!*"

There was not very much we could say to that. Antony was a little unusual to say the least, but his was a special talent. We all kissed him goodbye, and he disappeared in a flourish.

This had been by any measure a wonderfully successful day. Audrey had finally been seduced by the whole thing; I had succeeded in my task. We left there feeling like three princesses, with Antony having sprinkled the way ahead with his stardust. The staff ran around carrying our vast number of bags and boxes. It was not desperately late, and so because we were not far from Grosvenor Square, Emma-Jane invited us to the Embassy for afternoon tea and cakes.

"As long as it doesn't take you too long to get past 'Check Point Charlie'," she laughed.

We had no real proof of identity with us, and so it did take a little while. Eventually we were sitting in a grand reception room, enjoying wonderful afternoon tea and cakes. The Ambassador eventually joined us, and Emma introduced him to us all.

"Joanna, wonderful to see you here," he said, "how's Alan and the family?"

"They're fine, Ted, thank you. Molly's here with me in the UK."

"Any chance we can meet up?"

"Oh, Molly would love that, but she's really tied up just now with her latest business venture. She's working on a tie-up with a British IT firm."

"She's one hell of a girl, that daughter of yours. If there is anything that I can do to grease a few wheels, you know where I am."

"You're a sweetheart, Ted."

"Nonsense, I'm just a sucker for a pretty face."

We had a wonderful time at the Embassy, the time seemed to go by so quickly. All too soon we had to say our goodbyes to Emma and the Ambassador. Emma said that one of the drivers would take us back to Cambridge. They were so excited and pleased with their day; I have to admit it was a triumph. We talked nonstop all the way back. I didn't like to mention it in front of Sylvia, so as soon as I could after we arrived at the Village, I spoke to Audrey.

"We've got most of the morning to get ready for the South of France tomorrow. We don't need to leave until the afternoon."

"Oh, my goodness, I'd almost forgotten that in all the excitement."

"I'm living out of a suitcase anyway, so it won't take me long to get ready," I said, "I'll be here late morning tomorrow. I have to get back to my hotel now. Will you all join us there for dinner?"

"Oh no, I couldn't possibly. I've got to start getting ready for tomorrow. Charlie will drive you back. I'll make sure Bill and Harry are packing the right things this evening."

Sylvia came back for another armful of bags and boxes to carry to her car. Once again, I could hardly recognise her. She said how much she had enjoyed the experience, and we laughed again about Antony and the bra incident.

"I've never been so embarrassed in my life," she said, laughing. "The entire shop knew about my ghastly old bra."

"Are you pleased now that you did it?" I asked.

"I thought I would hate it," she said, "but I didn't, I absolutely loved it. I can't thank you enough, Joanna. Look at me, I don't even recognise myself. As for my old bra, good riddance to it."

Sylvia gave me a lovely hug, which really made my day.

She drove off just as Charlie arrived.

"I've just seen Audrey, she looks amazing," he said. "Oh wow, look at you, you look…."

Charlie stopped mid-sentence, just looking at me.

"Nothing wrong, is there, Charlie?"

"No, nothing's wrong. You just remind me of someone I used to know, that's all."

I smiled; it was a lovely compliment. He offered to drive me back to my hotel, and I insisted he stay to dine with us. As we set off, I noticed the box full of CDs in the car and thumbed through them. Charlie had always loved music. I used to say he was a philistine because he only ever enjoyed popular music. There were always lyrics he remembered that fitted every occasion. We might be listening to his favourite Barbra Streisand, or Diana Ross, and he would kiss me, and whisper whatever the appropriate words were from the song. I loved that about Charlie. Sometimes when he sang me song lyrics, he became so emotional that he would choke up, and be unable to finish the words. Charlie doesn't walk through life, like most of us. Charlie feels his way.

There were recent recordings in amongst his CDs, but all our special songs were there from the past. I knew *'I will always love you,'* would be there, and I looked for *'Stairway to Heaven.'* Charlie played it a lot, but we seldom listened to it together. I knew Charlie thought the lyric applied to me. I attempted to play *'Silly Love Songs'* another of our favourites. There was already a disc in the player so I tried to play whatever it was, but Charlie stopped me.

"No, don't. I can't listen to that now."

I ejected the disc, it was John and Vangelis, *'So long ago, so clear.'* It's a beautiful evocative song, I thought it best not to comment upon it. We soon arrived at the hotel and I left Charlie in the bar while I went up to change. I knocked on Molly's door; she was there, ready and waiting for me, looking radiant. I guessed that she'd had a good day. We went to my room together so we could chat while I changed.

"How did the plan go?"

"Perfect in every detail," I replied. "How did it go with Giles?"

"Perfect in every detail."

She was clearly overjoyed with her meeting and I could not wait to hear the details. We were both aware that Charlie was waiting for us, so we resisted the temptation to talk at length. I changed as quickly as I could, and we went down to join him. We found him at the bar, and quickly made our way to the restaurant, as it was already late. The businessman in Charlie was really interested in Molly's venture, and I could see she wanted his opinion. He knew nothing about AI, but certainly knew his way around a merger deal. They talked in detail for some time; she was very attentive. When I could finally get a word in, I asked about her and Giles. She smiled a wonderful smile; obviously, it had gone really well.

"This is the first time we've spent a whole day together," she said. "Most of it was business, but we had lunch together. Every time he looked at me, I couldn't look away; he just kept smiling at me. Do you know what I mean?"

I smiled at Charlie, and he smiled back.

"Yes, we know what you mean," he said.

Charlie asked more questions about Giles. He was particularly interested in how Giles approached his business, and how much was dependent solely upon his personal input. The point he wanted to make was that if the business was dependent upon the intellectual ability of one man, then the value of the business was him alone. He asked what kind of a man he was. I sensed he was walking a line between Giles the very clever IT geek, and the Giles with amorous intentions towards his daughter. It was clear which way Molly's mind was working; she missed the business connection completely.

"I know, it's ridiculous. I just can't think clearly when I'm with him."

"How can you be sure he's not playing you along to get a good deal?" Charlie said.

"I just know," Molly replied. "I know you're right to consider that Charlie. I *need* you to consider that. I'm not sure about the venture, but I'm 100% sure about him."

"You can't negotiate something this big, feeling like that," Charlie said.

"I know, what can I do, Charlie?"

"You need an intermediary; someone you can trust implicitly, who can negotiate for you. It would also be helpful if that advisor didn't want a percentage of the deal."

"Who do you have in mind?" asked Molly, with a smile written across her face.

"I only know one person who works for nothing these days."

We all laughed; suddenly Molly's father was a part of her business. I was delighted, she had made a good decision.

"There's only one advantage to getting older," Charlie said. "Every year is another year's experience. If I haven't seen it before, then I know someone who has. Look at Audrey, she went into business with Freddy. I am not saying Giles is like Freddy. I hope not, Harry would kill him."

"My business head knows you're right, Charlie, I need you in my corner. When you and Mom get back from the South of France, you must meet Giles. You'll love him; I do."

Molly said she would now prefer not to go with us the next day, there was too much for her and Giles to do.

"But everything's booked, the hotel rooms, the restaurant," I said.

"I know, I feel terrible letting you down. Why don't you ask Sylvia instead? She can take my place."

"That's an idea; phone her, Charlie, and ask her."

"Ask Sylvia? Well, I don't know; not the sort of thing Sylvia does. She probably wouldn't want to go."

"Tell her you *want* her to go. She won't refuse *you*, Charlie."

He did as he was told and phoned Sylvia. I could hear that she didn't sound too enthusiastic, and I raised my voice across the table so she could hear me.

"Charlie wants you to come with us, Sylvia. Come on, it will be fun, like today."

Charlie ended the call saying he would see her tomorrow morning at the Village, so she had obviously agreed.

"That's great, I don't feel so bad now," said Molly.

We ended our evening in high spirits. A lot had been decided, and Charlie and Molly were moving ever closer together. We said our goodnights to Charlie; he hugged Molly for ages, I was so happy. Molly and I walked up to our bedrooms with our arms around each other.

"It's been a big day, Mom."

"It sure has, and it will be an even bigger day tomorrow."

"You're still sure you're doing the right thing, Mom? This is a huge gamble you're taking with Charlie."

"Oh God, I hope so."

"It's gone according to plan so far; I think you might just pull it off Mom."

With that, we called it a day and said goodnight.

Chapter Ten

MONTE CARLO

Molly left the hotel after an early breakfast.

"I've got to dash, Mom," she said. "Have a good trip. I hope you don't regret it."

"I've been working on what I'm going to say; I'm having second thoughts."

"I'll keep in touch on the phone, Mom. You'll do the right thing. I know you will."

Molly dashed off and I felt quite alone. I spent an hour or so working out what I wanted to say to Charlie. I had to stop every so often and pack a few things in my case, then I would go back to my notepad. Suddenly it was time for Charlie to pick me up, and I was still full of indecision.

We drove back to the Village and Charlie talked continually about Molly's venture, and about her and Giles. I am afraid I couldn't concentrate. I kept thinking about what I planned to say to Charlie, and all its repercussions. When we arrived, he asked if I was OK, saying I seemed distracted, but I made some excuse. I was greeted by Audrey who looked wonderful in one of her new outfits, and the boys were all in a swoon over her. She looked simply marvellous; at least that part of my plan had gone well. Eventually Sylvia appeared. We could see her talking to Charlotte at the reception. Charlie looked over and obviously didn't recognise her.

"Who's that with Charlotte?" he asked.

"Sylvia," I said.

"No, it's not, she's not here yet."

Sylvia then walked into the room towards us, and Charlie still didn't recognise her. When she said, "Morning, Charlie," his eyes nearly fell out of his head. I must admit I hardly recognised her myself. The transformation was simply amazing. Charlie was completely lost for words, as he stood in silence, surveying Sylvia up and down. I could see she was embarrassed.

"Doesn't she look wonderful, Charlie?"

"Wow, you look incredible, Sylvia. Where have you been all these years?"

Sylvia acted coy, but I could see she enjoyed Charlie's flattery. Audrey and Sylvia spent what was left of the morning talking about the day before; the boys didn't get a word in. We had a nice light lunch, and there was the buzz of excitement in the air. I asked Harry if he had final confirmation of the jet.

"Yep, all in hand, it's a little Cessna Citation. He'll be landing at 1.30."

"What time's the car coming, Bill?" I asked.

"Any minute now."

We made our way outside to find the 12-seater waiting there. It was all happening so quickly. My heart was racing, this was all my idea, if it went wrong, I would have created such a disaster. I sat in the car without saying a word.

"You're very quiet, Joanna, are you sure you're okay?" Charlie asked.

I brushed it off, but I was nervous. The formalities at the little airport were very tolerable; we seemed to be walking towards the jet before I had time to worry any further. It was small inside, but extremely plush. We had four seats facing one way, and two seats facing the other, so we could all see one another. Harry had already warned Bill about the toilet arrangements. I knew from experience of small jets that there is no flush loo, and the privacy's not great either. Audrey pretended to be mortified.

"What on earth are the arrangements then?" she asked.

"Chemical toilet," Harry said, "I've got a lot of funny stories about them."

"Oh, good heavens, surely not," Audrey replied.

"The funniest one," Harry continued, "was when we were stationed in the Falklands…"

Audrey stopped him immediately.

"Harry, don't even think about it; you're not in the army now."

Charlie said, "Tell me later, Harry."

This all caused great amusement; we laughed and laughed. We taxied into position on the runway and waited for clearance to take off. When that clearance came, it seemed to me that we catapulted along the runway, and then just went vertically up into the clouds.

"Oh, my God!" Audrey said, in a shrill voice.

Everybody was smiling as we levelled off and settled down for the short flight. I have spent a lot of time in private jets, and just wanted to arrive, but the others were really enjoying it. When we arrived at Nice, the first thing we noticed as we stepped off the plane was the warm air. The contrast with the UK was very welcome. We walked straight through to the VIP lounge; our luggage quickly followed us. Then it was straight through passport control, and on to the taxi rank. It's not terribly far to Monte Carlo from Nice, about 40 minutes by taxi.

Our timing was perfect. Part of my plan was to remind them that they can still be spontaneous. They can be in the Village for lunch, and in Monte Carlo for dinner, and here we were. We checked into our superb hotel, and all were open-mouthed from the moment we entered. There was just time for a drink or a cup of coffee before we needed to get ready, so we sat ourselves down in one of the reception rooms. I told them again about the restaurant we were going to that evening. It is the most sought-after restaurant in Monte Carlo; I knew it well. Admittedly I was building it up for them, I did so want them to experience it to the full. Bill was terribly excited, he had already heard of Roberto's, and said he couldn't wait to get there.

I later offered to help the ladies with their makeup, knowing Sylvia especially would have no idea how to recreate what the makeup artist had done the day before. To my surprise, they were both enthusiastic. I hoped Audrey would be, but it did not occur to me that Sylvia would be as well. We had fun getting ready, it was all adding to our sense of occasion. At the arranged time, we met in the foyer, and it was quite a meeting.

"Bloody hell! You girls look wonderful," Harry said.

Audrey told him off for using coarse language. Even though I say it myself, we ladies did look sensational; the boys didn't look bad either. We were overdressed for a restaurant where smart casual would be the norm, but if we were going to be the stand-out crowd, then it would be because that was exactly what we were. We left our hotel and walked among the smart and trendy people enjoying a drink in the warm evening air opposite the Casino.

"It's nice to see all these chaps bringing their granddaughters to a place like this," Bill said.

"They aren't granddaughters, Bill," I explained.

"What are they then?"

"Never mind, we're almost there."

Roberto's is deceptively unassuming; the terribly smart staff uniforms are perhaps the only clue. My heart jumped a little as we approached. I have a lot of history with the place. Roberto very sadly is long gone; his son Emmanuel is now the face of the restaurant. I have some history with him as well! No sooner had we set foot in the place than he spotted me, his face lighting up as he came towards me.

"Joanna, mon ange, quel plaisir de te revoir!"

"Emmanuel cheri, laisse-moi te regarder," I replied.

He put his arms around me and kissed my neck, as I tried not to look enthusiastic. I may not have succeeded, so as soon as it was polite, I returned us to the matter of a table. We were finally escorted to a table in a magnificent position. Our evening had begun. The others were full of questions about Emmanuel, and how was it that no one can get a table there for weeks, but I could get us the best table in the house with just two days' notice? Charlie, of course, had some song lyrics for the occasion, although I doubt the others knew what he meant. I knew only too well that they came from '*Stairway to Heaven*'. I was not about to tell them the full story. I just said that I came here several times when Roberto was alive; Emmanuel was a young man then.

Audrey whispered in my ear. "What are you not telling me?"

"I was working when I was here, you know what I mean?" I whispered very quietly.

"Yes, I'm not *that* naïve, Joanna! I know what you mean!"

"Emmanuel was a young man then, and well, let's just say you never forget your first time, do you, especially when it's with me!"

Audrey was more than a little taken aback.

"Oh, my goodness! Oh my! I told you your job was more interesting than mine."

We laughed aloud, and everyone asked what the joke was. Audrey said it was nothing. I made her promise not to mention a word. It was the most memorable evening, and this was before I had made my little speech. Emmanuel was very attentive. Audrey kept smiling at him and looking at me. The food was exquisite; Bill was beside himself, in raptures over every course. We had our desserts still to come and sat in anticipation of another culinary masterpiece. My heart was racing; I wanted to say what I had rehearsed but had not yet found the courage to discuss it with Audrey. I obviously needed to talk to her first. As I was worrying about these things, a voice whispered into my ear from behind me.

"Do you realise, Madame, you are sitting at my reserved table?" the voice said, in a Russian accent.

My heart sank; I thought it was all going too well. I turned around and standing there was Alexei, towering over me.

"When Emmanuel told me it was you, Joanna, I couldn't believe it! How long has it been?"

I stood up and hugged him.

"Oh, my darling Alexei, it must be five years! I remember, it was the World Economic Forum at Davos."

"How's Alan?" he asked.

"He's simply fine, and how is that lovely new wife of yours? I saw on the news that you got married again."

"She's here, let me bring her over."

She was a delightful young thing - I could have been her mother. I didn't want to admit it, but I could probably have been her grandmother.

"Alexei, these are my dear friends. Alexei and I go back a long way. We both remember this place when Roberto was here."

They sat with us, chatting, and we exchanged more memories as we enjoyed our desserts.

"I'm forgetting myself, Joanna, if I can't have my usual table, I must take my wife back to have supper on the yacht. Why don't you all join us?"

"Oh, we couldn't possibly impose, not at this time of the evening." said Audrey.

"What a wonderful idea, lead the way, Alexei," I said.

Before we had time to consider it, we were walking in the warm evening air toward the harbour. It's always full of boys' toys, and the bigger the toys, the more miserable the lesser toy owners become. I had a sneaky feeling Alexei's toy would be making *everyone* miserable. Imagine my surprise when we were directed towards a modest sized power boat. As we walked along the wooden pontoon, it moved slightly beneath our feet. I was not quite sure if it was the pontoon or the wine. As we neared the boat, I wondered what kind of adventure lay ahead.

The moment you enter the harbour at night, you feel as if

you have entered another world. The smell of food is always present in the warm breeze, and the gentle sound of rigging tapping against masts seems to echo into the distance. Above all it is the myriad of little lights all reflected and dancing upon the water; perhaps it serves to remind us of Christmas and fairy lights in colder climes. I slipped off my high heels before I stepped on board, remembering Alexei telling me off about that, all those years ago. We sat down on the plush leather seats as instructed, and suddenly we were gliding away from the quayside, into the world of sparkling lights.

"It will only take a moment," Alexei said, "the harbour's quite full tonight, we were too big to get in,"

Soon we were looking up at the most enormous yacht, or was it a boat? Perhaps it was a ship, I have no idea about these things. Whatever it was, it towered above us. Our 'little' boat moored alongside a cavernous hole in the side of the yacht. We stepped off and there we were, in another world. A crewman escorted us to the main deck where we were directed into an enormous space looking down the length of the yacht. It was a series of reception rooms, each leading into the other with partial glass walls between them. We walked through a sumptuous dining room, and into a reception room.

The wooden furniture items were all beautiful antique period pieces, in complete contrast to the rest of the décor. There were cream leather sofas and armchairs, which stood on the pale beige carpet running the length of the deck. The shiny ceiling had a recess around the edge with concealed lighting which reflected against the glass of the windows. In the ceiling were numerous tiny little lights; the effect was that when you looked up at the stars, they seemed to continue across the ceiling. We were invited to sit down, a bottle of champagne appeared and the steward filled our glasses. Charlie was beside himself, he asked to see the bottle. He sat gazing at it, seemingly mesmerised.

"This is Krug Clos Du Mesnil 1998!" he said to Alexei.

"Yes, it's rather special."

"Special, I should say so! I've never tasted it, but I've seen the enclosed vineyard, about two hectares."

Alexei was obviously delighted to be sharing his champagne with someone who really appreciated it. The pair of them drifted off into another world the moment they tasted the wine. I have to say it *was* wonderful.

"Have you seen the South of France at night, Charlie, from the sea?" Alexei asked.

He said he hadn't, and we all agreed that we hadn't, either.

"In that case, we will cruise along the coast to Cannes."

Before we had any say in the matter, the crew were ordered to set sail. Audrey looked bewildered, while Sylvia's expression was one of disbelief. Harry and Bill looked at each other in astonishment. One moment we were having lunch in the Village, the next moment we were having dinner in Roberto's. Now we were sailing towards Cannes in the dead of night. The look on everyone's face was memorable.

"This is a bit different to a B&B in Southwold, isn't it," I said.

The only one of us who seemed to be oblivious to it all was Charlie. For the moment at least, his world did not extend beyond his glass of Clos Du Mesnil.

We had a wonderful evening; in fact, it was 1 o'clock in the morning, before we had time to think about it.

"I can see a logistics problem here," Harry suddenly said, "we're heading towards Cannes, and our hotel is behind us."

"Forget your hotel, Harry," said Alexei. "I haven't seen this lovely lady for five years. I am not letting her go until the morning. You must all enjoy my hospitality tonight. Anything that you need, clothes, toiletries, makeup for the ladies, anything at all, just ask my steward."

Nobody argued; I don't think any of us wanted it to end. Audrey and I went off to the ladies' room, and I finally plucked up the courage to tell her what my plan was.

"You can't say that Joanna, it might be true, but you just *can't* say it. Can you imagine what the others would say, and what would Harry say?"

"Yes," I said, "but you know I'm right. I would risk anything if I could make Charlie happy."

We made our way back to the others and Audrey tried to talk me out of it. Maybe she was right. Alexei and the child bride excused themselves for the night. He said he needed his beauty sleep; I got the feeling that his beauty wouldn't be sleeping just yet.

As soon as they had gone, Bill asked about Alexei, and I explained that he was your archetypal oligarch. He was not just the oil tankers, he was the oil, as well as the gas. I met Alexei at Roberto's, thirty-odd years ago. The memories came flooding back as I remembered one occasion being there at Roberto's with Alexei. It was a wonderful evening, and yet all I could think about was being home the next day, because I was seeing Charlie.

"You look miles away, Joanna, are you sure you're okay?" Charlie said.

"Sorry, Charlie, I was just thinking about you."

Chapter Eleven
JOANNA'S MONOLOGUE

It was late, and perhaps Audrey was right; perhaps I shouldn't interfere. Molly thought I shouldn't do it, as well; these things weighed heavily on my mind. There was only thing I *was* sure about; I wanted to see Charlie happy, and felt convinced I was right. Despite the late hour, there was never going to be a better time, and there was certainly never going to be a better place.

"I've got something I need to tell you, Charlie; all of you," I started nervously.

Audrey stared at me, willing me not to say anything. The others realised I had something important to say and sat in silent anticipation. My heart was racing, my insides were churning, as I took a deep breath.

"When you walked into my life, Charlie, all those years ago, you were Charlie the builder with your measuring tape and your schoolboy charm. You stood there in my house, and the first moment our eyes met, I fell for you, Charlie Bartlett; you were the man of my dreams. I was a fool Charlie, we loved each other, didn't we, and I let you go. I know I broke your heart so badly that it has never mended. I hated myself then, and I will always hate myself for being so selfish and stupid. I am so sorry Charlie.

You were the man of my dreams when I let you go, and you are still the man of my dreams. But the thing is, Charlie, it *is* only a dream. I have another life, and you have another life. Ours is a dream from the past, it's time now that you mended that broken heart of yours. Do you remember what you said to Audrey? As much as you loved her, there was someone who loved her even more, and you did not want to stand in her way. I don't want your memory of me to stand in the way, Charlie. You may be the man of my dreams, but for someone else you're not a dream, you're real, and she's loved you from the first day she saw you.

"Why do you not see it, Charlie? Sylvia has been by your side in everything you have done, she's devoted her life to you. She has sacrificed everything for you, Charlie. She has long since been estranged from her husband, Jack, because of *you*, Charlie. When you moved away to Cambridge, she gave up everything to live near you. Sylvia's my dear friend. I know she loves you; she has always loved you. You and I shared something wonderful, Charlie, but that was another time. We will always have those memories but you can't allow them to come between the two of you. It's me that is standing between you, and I just can't bear it. Look at her, Charlie, open your eyes, you've got to let me go."

There was a deathly silence. Audrey sat with her mouth open. Bill and Harry sat wide-eyed. Charlie looked as if he had seen a ghost, half surprised, half in terror. Sylvia burst into tears, unable to cope with the situation. She looked at Charlie with an expression that confirmed everything I had said. She knocked over her glass of champagne as she jumped to her feet. Without a word, she hurriedly walked away and out of sight.

"What do I do?" said Charlie.

"Anything other than what you've *been* doing," I said. "Go after her, put your arms around her; just hold her."

Charlie rushed after her, as I slumped back into my chair.

The others were obviously still in shock; no one said anything. Then it suddenly hit me like an emotional tidal wave. I had lost Charlie all over again! I was shaking and reacting the same as Sylvia had, wanting to run away. As I rose to my feet, Audrey grabbed my arm to prevent me, and Bill rushed forwards, putting his arm around me.

"I can't believe it," Audrey said, "I know how much you loved him; I can't imagine the courage it took to finally let him go like that."

Bill still appeared to be in shock.

"I had no idea about Sylvia, why has no one told me?"

"That's because none of us knew," said Audrey, "I only found out today when Joanna told me. But now that we know, it was always obvious, wasn't it?"

"I suppose you're right," Bill said. "Sylvia's always been a part of Charlie; we seem to have taken her for granted."

"How did *you* know, Joanna?" Harry asked.

"I've been friends with Sylvia for thirty years, and more recently it's been easier to talk about these things via the email. I must have told her a dozen times to tell Charlie how she feels about him, but she's just been unable to do it."

"I suppose in their position, once you establish a code of conduct, it must be difficult to change. I can understand," Bill said.

"Now that we know," said Harry, "it does all make sense. I've seen how Sylvia looks at Charlie, and it's for sure he completely relies on her."

"So why on earth has Charlie not seen it as well?" asked Audrey.

"You know why," I said. "It's the other three women in Charlie's life that have prevented him from seeing what was always right there in front of him."

"Do you mean us?" said Audrey.

"Yes! You, me, and Annie, but especially me."

They were all so supportive, I could not have got through

it without them. Bill provided the common sense that we all so desperately needed. He suggested we leave Charlie and Sylvia to talk, and we should all retire for what was left of the night; now was not the time to relive it. I wanted anything that might distance me from the anguish I was feeling. I just wanted oblivion. They escorted me to my suite, and Audrey came in with me, sitting on my bed for a moment.

"I know I said not to do it, Joanna, but I think you were right; it was such a brave thing to do."

"I've practised those words so that I didn't really have to think about them. It was as if it wasn't real. I managed it until I had to say he must let me go, and then suddenly everything was horribly real. Oh Audrey! What have I done?"

"You've done the right thing. You have a husband and family in another country. You know you must let him go. What's more, Charlie must let *you* go, and I don't think he could do that by himself."

"I know you're right, Audrey, but it just hurts so much. I know it's because of Molly, but Charlie has always been a part of me, I'm not sure I can ever be complete without him."

"You will be. If anyone can, you will."

Audrey was such a comfort; I'm not sure I could have coped without her. She said I should try to get some sleep, though I felt there was little chance of that. I just lay there in bed, unable to sleep, unable to do anything, except watch the distant shore lights gently moving up and down. I knew my future was back in Washington with Alan and the boys, and that I had done the right thing. Then again, if I had done the right thing, why did I feel so distraught? I could not bear the prospect of standing between him and Sylvia, so why did I feel so unhappy. Would I ever be able to reconcile this madness?

The next morning, I was woken by a knock on my cabin door. It was Audrey; she came in and sat on my bed.

"How are you?" she asked.

"How do I look?"

"Honestly? You look terrible!"

"Oh God, are we meeting for breakfast or something? Are Charlie and Sylvia there?"

"No sign of them yet. Just come up on deck when you're ready, and don't worry, we're all here for you."

Audrey gave me a hug and left. There was another knock on the door. I had just got out of the shower, so I shouted out to come in, thinking it was Audrey again. When I stepped back into the room in my robe, I realised it was Sylvia. She had obviously had no sleep either, looking as dreadful as I did. I had no idea what to expect.

"Why didn't you tell me what you were going to do?" she asked.

"You wouldn't have come, would you?"

"Do you mean you planned it all!"

"I'm sorry, yes I did, you weren't filling in for Molly."

"What about the fashion makeover – was that all part of your plan?"

"Yes, that as well!"

"Why! Why did you go to all that trouble?"

"I'm sorry, I felt dreadful not being honest with you. I wanted you both to see each other in a totally different light. I wanted you to see *yourself* in a different light, you are a lovely, amazing woman, Sylvia. I just wanted Charlie for the first time in his life to recognise that. I thought in the South of France, and Roberto's - I thought I could bring the two of you together. I just wanted to see you both happy with each other."

"Well you have certainly brought us together."

I was suddenly made to feel like a ghastly interfering and manipulative woman, even though I only had the best of intentions.

"When I told you I loved Charlie, I never dreamed you would do something like this. I have tried to tell him so often, but I always end up as the company secretary, or the finance director. Nothing would have changed without you Joanna; I realise that I suppose I should be thanking you."

Just to know that Sylvia didn't despise me was such a huge relief.

"Can you forgive me, I only meant to bring you together."

We hugged each other.

"I know you meant well."

"Do you think it will work with Charlie?" I asked.

"I'm only alive when I'm with him. It is going to be so difficult to change our relationship, we just need to take it at our own pace, take it one step at a time. At least, thanks to you, we've taken that first step. I would never have taken that step without you."

"Oh Sylvia! I only wanted to do the right thing for both of you."

"I think maybe you have. Get dressed and we can go up for breakfast together."

I knew what Sylvia was suggesting. If we appeared together, it would diffuse whatever atmosphere there may be among the others and help to put Charlie at ease. We arrived together for breakfast on the open deck dining area, next to the palatial dining room. We ladies were each dressed in one of Alexei's wardrobe outfits supplied by his steward. Charlie was there, as well as the others, along with Alexei and the child bride. We all avoided the obvious topic of conversation. None of it would have been appropriate in front of Alexei. Molly telephoned me, asking how Charlie and Sylvia had reacted. It was difficult to speak, so I just said everything was fine, and I would phone her back later.

The yacht was anchored just off Cannes, with the Lerins Islands off to the right. From our distance, the hotels of Cannes looked like so many white Lego blocks, while the sunshades looked like tiny pebbles on the beach. The morning sun was warm and welcoming, as the gulls swooped around us in the hope of some discarded offerings. All the while there was the gentle sound of water lapping against the side of the yacht.

In any other circumstances, this would have been sublime.

Charlie said little, Sylvia said even less. I had to rely on the others to be sociable with Alexei. Between them, they were good company, but this was a strange situation. None of it was helped by the child bride. Charlie said later that he thought she must have undergone surgery to attach her hand to her cell phone.

After breakfast, we cruised further along the French Riviera, past Saint-Raphael, and around the bay at Saint-Tropez. The lunch prepared by Alexei's chef was quite breath-taking. Alexei's hospitality knew no bounds. I was just sorry I wasn't better company. Once or twice he put his arm around me and asked if I was okay.

"You're not your usual self, Joanna. You know I will help, whatever it is."

"I'm sorry, Alexei; perhaps I'm just jealous of that beautiful new wife of yours."

"You know I don't believe you, but I'm here for you whenever you need me."

"I know you are. I can't tell you what that means to me, Alexei."

The child bride approached us, and so we ended our conversation. The day would have to end at some point, we all knew it couldn't continue forever. The magic spell was broken by the crew making ready to depart. The engines sprang into life, and the anchor chain clanked in rhythm with every link, as it wound its way back onboard.

We waved goodbye to Saint-Tropez as we gently made our way back towards Monte Carlo. Alexei pointed out various places of interest as we progressed along the Riviera, but all too soon we were approaching Monte Carlo. The bay-shaped harbour has a backdrop of high-rise buildings, and beyond them the almost mountainous hills rise steeply beyond. That day, the clouds were draped over the highest peaks. One side of the harbour is dominated by Le Rocher (the rock) with its elegant buildings perched on the top. There was little conversation, I think we each wanted to absorb every detail, not wishing to forget any of it.

We dropped anchor outside the harbour, and the crew made ready the rather large tender. Alexei insisted we keep the clothes we were wearing, and so all we had to do was to step into the tender, where our clothes from the night before had all been beautifully packed by the steward. I felt so sad saying goodbye to Alexei. Unbeknown to them both, his path had crossed with Charlie's all that time ago. Now it felt as though I was saying goodbye to so much more. We eventually stood on the quayside, and I kissed him goodbye.

"I've missed you, my adorable friend. I can't wait another five years to see you, Alexei. Why don't you come to Washington to see us soon?"

Alexei smiled his irresistible smile. "I will, my darling, soon." He tightened his grip around the slender waist of his child bride, who smiled adoringly up at him, and said how pleased she was to meet one of Alexei's older friends.

"Yes, of course you are, dear," I said.

It was not far to walk back to our hotel, but it felt a lot further than it was.

"I know we're all tired, and it's a bit of an anti-climax after our time with Alexei," I said, "but this is our last night. Let's all get changed and make the most of the evening."

There was general agreement, and so we made our way back to our respective rooms to get ready for the evening. I sat momentarily on my bed, feeling quite dreadful. Eventually I went into the bathroom and looked at myself in the mirror. What stared back at me reflected my mood perfectly. I didn't have long to transform myself, but whatever time I had, it wouldn't have been long enough.

We met in the foyer and Sylvia and Audrey both looked wonderful. I still felt tense, I wanted to avoid looking for conversation, so we wasted no time in setting off to find a nice place to eat. Walking around Monte Carlo in the warm evening air is impossible *not* to like. We walked along Place du Casino enjoying the spectacular views in all directions, and the wonderful food smells wafting out from the restaurants. There was laughter and chatter coming from the pavement cafés and bars. The lights and reflections dancing across the harbour provided an enchanting backdrop. I still could not believe Sylvia's transformation; she was just a different person. She walked with Charlie, but I could see the habits of a lifetime were not going to be easily changed.

We settled on a lovely looking little restaurant and sat outside. As soon as we had organised ourselves and placed our orders, I said what I had to say.

"Tell me what you're thinking, Charlie, however unkind it is about me."

"I'm still lost for words," he said, "I feel like a fool, really. Everything you said about Sylvia is true, I know that. I wouldn't have achieved a thing without you, Sylvia."

"Did I do the right thing, Charlie?"

"I know you have another life to go back to, Joanna. I know it's all just been a dream; I accept that. I also know I can't exist without Sylvia. I'm such an idiot when it comes to women, there's three of you at this table who know that! The only thing I know for sure is that I could never blame you for anything."

Sylvia took Charlie's hand and smiled at him.

"It's not only you, Charlie. I'm an idiot for saying nothing all these years. I just came to accept that I was a part of you, but couldn't have you, so I settled for the next best thing."

Our first course arrived at an opportune moment, as we were suddenly lost for words. As the evening progressed, the atmosphere lightened considerably, and we laughed again. Charlie's endearing preoccupation with song lyrics provided us with entertainment; he even had the others doing it. As we dined, a lovely young girl walked past, one of a great many young girls that walked past. This one, however, was wearing a beautifully embroidered lace top. She also had a ponytail.

Charlie just can't help it; he said, "Is that Chantilly lace?"

I fell for it. "No Charlie, Chantilly lace is usually black, and finer detail."

Bill said, "She's got a pretty face though, hasn't she?"

Harry then added, "*And* she's got a ponytail."

"Not only that, look how she *walks!*" Charlie said.

The next thing we knew, they were each singing a phrase from the 'Big Bopper' song which culminated in us all joining in with the last line. We laughed and laughed. Things were never going to be the same again, but for this moment at least, we were our old selves. Sylvia did not let go of Charlie's hand all evening. The smile had returned to her face, and I felt that, after so long living in the shade, she had finally felt a ray of sunshine.

"Who was it who sang that song?" asked Sylvia.

"Never *ever* ask who's singing a song," Charlie said, pretending to be cross. Everyone laughed. Sylvia asked what the problem was, so Charlie explained.

"We used to spend hours submerged in memory loss, trying to remember who was singing a song. It drove us nuts. Now we have Shazam, and we've vowed never to ask that question again. But it's not so much fun now."

"You and your songs, Charlie, you're incorrigible." I said. "Watch out, Sylvia, don't listen to music with Charlie. It always ends with him singing to you."

"I've heard Charlie sing; it's not good, is it," Sylvia replied.

We were laughing and having fun again. It was dark now, but tomorrow it would be sunny again. Our day continued well into the evening; I was not sure how I was managing to stay awake after the night before. It had been an incredible trip; there was so much to talk about. I wanted to show them that there was an alternative to the Village or a B&B in Southwold. I think Monte Carlo, Roberto's restaurant, and Alexei's hospitality had done that beyond my wildest expectations. We ended our evening walking back to the hotel with the six of us locked arm in arm.

The time in Monaco was an hour ahead of the UK, so when I got back to my room, I phoned Molly as I had promised.

"How did it go? What did Sylvia say?"

I told her the story, about Roberto's and about Alexei; I told her everything, she could not believe it.

"Only you, Mom, could take your friends to a restaurant and end up cruising the French Riviera with one of the world's richest men."

I had to agree; it had been quite a day. Molly asked me how I was; I said I was fine.

"I don't believe you, Mom, how are you *really?*"

"I know I've done the right thing, but it just doesn't feel like it."

Molly was concerned for me, but this was not a conversation I wanted at that moment. As soon as I asked her about Giles, her enthusiasm was self-evident, and it was abundantly clear things between them were progressing extremely well.

"Is this about Giles, or the business?" I asked.

"It's both, Mom; well, maybe it's more about him."

"Are you sure he feels the same?"

"I told you I was sure before; he loves me, Mom. He just can't hide it."

"Oh sweetheart, I'm so happy for you, but please be careful."

"I just know I can trust him, Mom, but you're right, that's why I need Charlie in my corner."

"Love you, Moll."

"Me too, Mom. I'll speak to you tomorrow. Bye, Mom."

"Bye, Moll."

When we finally ended our call, it left me with more questions than answers. Charlie was now a permanent part of Molly's life, and therefore of mine. The prospect of the double life I had created for myself suddenly terrified me. Not only had I done this to myself, but I was also asking Molly to live a double life as well. What of Charlie and Sylvia's relationship?

The last thing they needed was me to be a permanent presence, like the Ghost of Christmas Past. Could I really keep up the pretence of a double life with Alan and the boys? I had not fully thought this through, and now the prospect of what I was proposing terrified me.

I slept badly again, but we met for breakfast as arranged and everyone else appeared to be in high spirits. Charlie and Sylvia were acting differently together. I was so used to seeing her playing her supporting role, but now not only did she look radiant, suddenly she *was* radiant. I was genuinely pleased for her. We had a couple of hours before we needed to get our taxi back to the airport, so I suggested a final stroll around Monte Carlo. Charlie walked hand in hand with Sylvia, while Bill and Harry were busy talking together. Audrey and I walked behind arm in arm.

"You're not yourself, Joanna, do you want to talk about it?"

"I do, and you're the only person I can talk to, Audrey."

"I know, you're wondering whether you've done the right thing; will Charlie hit it off with Sylvia; will he ever be able to push you out of his mind, and what on earth are you going to tell your husband?"

"Oh, my God. You really *do* know me, Audrey, don't you? Tell me what you think."

"I just don't know about Charlie; it's not Sylvia, it's you. I am not sure she'll be able to replace that part of Charlie that he gave to you. As for your husband, only you can make that decision, but it's going to be a difficult one."

"Don't spare my feelings, Audrey, it's best to tell me like it is."

"Okay, I was lying; it's going to be far worse than that."

I have a wonderful relationship with Audrey, despite the short time I had known her; we are closer than any female friend I've ever had. I put my arm around her.

"I really need you, Audrey."

"Well, that's good. It's far more difficult to be envious of someone who needs you."

"There's nothing to be envious about Audrey, I'm a mess right now."

"That's true, another bad night? Just don't forget who brought us here, who got us a table at Roberto's when none were available, who whisked us off on that wonderful yacht? You might feel a bit low, but you're still the most amazing woman I have ever met. If anyone can get through it, *you* can."

"Oh, Audrey, what a lovely thing to say, do you really mean that?"

"Of course I mean it, it's true. Your life is so different to ours; I understand now why you felt you had to move on from Charlie."

"I wanted it all Audrey, but you can't have it all, can you?"

"No, Charlie is not Alexei, is he? I can't see you settled down in a nice house in Bristol driving the kids to school each day."

"That's the doubt which has tormented me for thirty years."

"Are you telling me you have been thinking of Charlie for all that time."

"I have, I can't help it."

"You're as bad as each other aren't you. You know you have to move on Joanna."

"I know, I've taken a big step in that direction, haven't I?"

"You certainly have."

We walked on, enjoying the sights; there's something about the place. Perhaps it's the climate, the affluence, or maybe because it personifies the kind of lifestyle which drove me on to leave Charlie behind. Right now, I wasn't sure it was what I wanted. When the time came for us to head back to the airport, I was not sad to leave. Everyone else was excited in the jet on the way back; we had so much to remember and to talk about. They didn't stop talking, I don't suppose they even noticed that I was quiet.

"The look on your face, Charlie, when you saw that bottle of champagne," Sylvia said.

"I couldn't help it, I never dreamed I would drink a wine as rare as that."

"The food in Roberto's was wonderful," said Bill. "I've heard of the place, but like Charlie, I never dreamed I would dine there."

"I've always wanted to cruise on board a superyacht," said Sylvia. "I never thought it would happen to me."

"It's all been like a dream to me," said Audrey. "I think we all know who to thank for it."

"What's *your* memory, Harry?" asked Sylvia.

"Oh, being re-united with a chemical toilet."

We all laughed, and they could not stop thanking me.

Chapter Twelve
HELLO DARKNESS

The flight was short and sweet, and they laughed all the way. They would be at the Village with plenty of time to unpack and prepare for the evening. I knew Molly would be back in time for dinner, so I suggested we all dine at my hotel. The prospect of us not being together never entered my head. The taxi dropped me off first, and they would all come back to join me later. I unpacked and showered, then went to a lot of trouble to get ready for the evening, not wanting anyone to see how deflated I felt.

Molly arrived back in good time and came straight to my room. From the moment she walked in, she was irrepressible. It was Giles this, and Giles that; she was so happy. If you can't be happy yourself, then sharing your daughter's happiness is surely the next best thing. Her excitement was contagious, and everything she said reminded me of those early days with Charlie.

"I really love him, Mom. I've never felt anything like this before."

"Have you told him that?"

"No, I don't want to risk changing anything between us. He's married; it's all too complicated."

"Please don't do what I did, sweetheart. I so wanted to tell

Charlie I loved him, but I didn't say it. I regret that more than anything else in my entire life. What about his wife; will he leave her?"

"He says he will, when the time is right."

"Do you believe him?"

"I know that's been said a thousand times before, but yes, I know he means it. I just hope they can work it out. I want him, Mom."

"What's her name?"

"Andrea; she looks a lovely woman. I've seen a photograph of her. They just don't get on, that's all there is to it. They don't hate each other or anything, I don't think they ever had much in common. It's little Jimmy that's the problem."

"I can see how happy Giles makes you, Moll, so *make* it work. Tell him you love him."

"Oh Mom, what would I do without you?"

"Well, you could get ready for dinner, because we're meeting the others in fifteen minutes."

They all arrived in good spirits, and if I had created tension between Charlie and Sylvia, they did not show it. I watched their body language for some sign, although I didn't really know what I was hoping to see. Charlie asked Molly numerous questions about their venture, some of which she couldn't answer. He was interested in the proposed business structure going forward, and Sylvia wanted to know the details.

"It seems to me that what you need, Molly, is the advice of an experienced company executive," Bill said. "Someone who's been involved with high level mergers and takeovers. You also need someone who really understands how to bring these things together. Perhaps, someone like an experienced company secretary and finance director. Do we know anyone like that?"

Molly laughed. "I'm ahead of you Bill. I *do* know people like that, and I've already signed them up."

Charlie hugged Sylvia. "I guess we do make a pretty good team."

He was right, they did make a good team. They built a business between them and have a lifetime of memories to share. Sylvia knew Annie well. She used to babysit the little girls and picked them up from school when Charlie couldn't make it. She saw Sally and Debby get married, and saw Annie finally leave it all behind. Of *course,* they make a good team; she is an essential part of Charlie's life.

He and I didn't build anything between us, and the only part of Charlie's real life that I ever stepped into was his office on that dreadful day. I know nothing about his girls, and doubt they even know that I exist. Charlie knows nothing about my boys; they certainly don't know he exists. Charlie and I share nothing between us, other than ourselves. The only thing we shared beyond ourselves is Molly, and even that I had to deny for so long. I knew I could never compete with Sylvia in any way.

"Are you all right, Mom? You look miles away."

"Oh, sorry, sweetheart, I drifted off a bit there. I'm not sleeping well, I'm really tired."

Our meal went well. I said very little, and perhaps that contributed to the success of the evening. The conversation was all about Molly, and about our trip to Monte Carlo. Finally, it returned to Molly again, and it was agreed that Charlie and Sylvia must meet Giles, hopefully the next day.

"You don't mind, do you, Mom? Perhaps I can get Giles to have dinner with us in the evening."

"No, I don't mind, you three set it up with Giles, I can ….."

Audrey interrupted me. "Excellent, that's settled then. We can go out for the day, Joanna."

They were busy discussing the next day, and I really had nothing I could contribute.

"Do you mind if I retire for the evening? I'm really feeling very tired."

Charlie was as gallant as always. "Can I escort you to your room?"

I loved that about Charlie, but obviously I declined his kind thought. Audrey didn't give me any say in the matter, wishing me goodnight, saying she would pick me up in the morning. When I finally got myself to bed, I felt dreadfully depressed. I tried to reason with myself. Why did I feel like that? But it's impossible to see your toes when your head is enveloped in a black cloud.

-oOo-

Next morning, Molly woke me, knocking on the door, obviously excited.

"I can't wait, Mom, I'll just have a cup of coffee and shoot off. I've told Charlie where to meet us later. I'm sure it will be okay with Giles."

With that she was gone. I got myself ready for some breakfast, looking forward to seeing Audrey. She was bright and cheery when she arrived, driving her Mini.

"What's the plan, where are you taking me?"

"I'm going to take you somewhere that's rather special to me. I think you'll enjoy it." Audrey said, obviously wanted it to be a surprise. We set off on what proved to be quite a long drive.

"You looked so down last night, Joanna. You're usually so full of life and happiness."

"I'm sorry, Audrey. I tried not to be. Do you think they noticed?"

"Of *course,* they noticed. How could we not notice that you stopped smiling?"

"Charlie always used to notice if I stopped smiling. He

would put his arms round me, and whisper an appropriate song lyric in my ear, something like '*The Sound of Silence*'. I love that about Charlie."

"It wasn't just Charlie, it was both of you, Joanna. He never whispered those words in *my* ear, and we both know why."

"I'm so sorry, Audrey. I didn't know I came between you and Charlie, though I knew I came between him and Sylvia. Can you imagine how that makes me feel? I managed to turn something which was so beautiful into something that destroys everything it touches. That's why I *had* to tell Charlie."

"I've never seen you so low, Joanna. This is all about Sylvia and Charlie, isn't it?"

"It's just made me realise what they share together. All the wonderful ordinary little things that he and I never shared. He disapproved of my lifestyle, he used to quote the words from that damned song to me. Charlie used to say he knew where heaven was; it was anywhere that we were together. It's taken me all this time to realise he was right."

"It's too late, Joanna; we all make terrible mistakes in life. Look at me, look at any of us. Stanley said we are all the product of our past lives, but we have to live in the *present,* not in the past. You have to let him go."

She was right, of course. My life had become complicated enough, and I had to give him the chance he so deserved. We said little for the rest of the journey. Every so often, Audrey would glance at me. I could see in her eyes how concerned she was for me. After what felt like an eternity being stuck on the M25, and later held up again on the A40, we finally pulled into a leafy lane. As we rounded a corner, a rolling vista opened before me, and there standing in the middle of this beautiful landscape, was a magnificent house. We approached two heavy wrought iron gates, supported between stone pillars. There was a house name carved into a stone on the right-hand pillar – Belmont.

Audrey stopped the car at the gates. Neither of us said

anything, but then she took off her glasses and reached for a tissue.

"What's wrong, Audrey?"

"This is where all my memories are stored; this is my ancestral home."

She was clearly overwhelmed. Having stepped out of the car, she just stood at the gate, holding the railings. I intuitively knew she wanted to be left alone. Several minutes elapsed before she reached for a key to open the padlock. Audrey pushed the heavy gates apart, which swung open with an audible creak. She got back into the car without saying a word, and we drove down the long entrance drive as the impressive house grew larger with every second, until finally we stopped at the door to a rather grand entrance porch.

I was overwhelmed, both by the house and by Audrey's reaction. She unlocked the door and we went inside. My initial impression was that everything was furnished and functioning, as if Audrey had just left there. She could see I was puzzled.

"I didn't sell the estate when I moved to the Village. I let this wing of the house, and the tenants have recently left."

"Very sensible, Audrey, but why have you never mentioned it?"

"We had a discussion once at the Village. I remember it was the day that Stanley arrived. We talked about leaving our 'stuff' behind and starting a new life. I didn't say anything, because I wasn't ready to walk away from my life; I just needed a break from it."

Audrey went on to say that she had few happy memories of that place. Her childhood was very unhappy, and when she returned with her handicapped father after their bankruptcy, she lived a life of guilt and regret.

"So why didn't you want to sell it, together with those bad memories, so you could move on?" I asked.

"I can't. I made my father a solemn promise, virtually on his death bed. You see, this really is my ancestral home.

Calcut's have lived here for well over 200 years. My father was born here, just as I was. He could remember when this house was filled with joy and laughter, and his last wish was that I would ensure the house remained in the family and would once again echo to the sound of laughter."

"That's quite a responsibility, Audrey."

"I have sad memories here. I just needed to get away from it, but I can never leave it behind."

"You know what Charlie would call it, don't you? '*Hotel California*'. So why don't you and Harry live here?"

"I haven't told him about it."

"Why not?"

"It's far too big for two people, which is why my daughter Fiona doesn't want to live here. But also, it's full of those bad memories for me, and I didn't want Harry to be part of those memories."

"What are you going to do? It sounds like you're trapped."

"This is why I've brought you here, Joanna; it's because of you, really. I was happy in the Village with Harry, but then you came along and changed everything."

"I don't understand, Audrey."

"I think you do. Look at me, I don't recognise myself! You did this! And look what has happened to our nice, contented life in the Village. Suddenly we're jetting off to the South of France and sailing on board a superyacht. You did this to show us another life, didn't you?"

"Are you cross with me? I just don't feel people like you are ready for a retirement community."

"I'm not cross with you, Joanna, I love you for it. I've had an idea ever since Harry and I got married, but I felt it was all too much to consider. Now, thanks to you, I think we can do it."

"Do what, what are you talking about?"

"I've made a decision. I want Bill and Charlie to always be a part of my life; we share Stanley's bond between us. Harry feels the same. We aren't short-lived daffodils in full bloom one week and gone the next. We still need room to grow, so why don't we all grow old together? *Here?"*

"Wow! That's a really big idea!"

"It can work, Joanna, look at the size of this place, each wing is as big as a family-sized house. Imagine what Charlie would say if I asked him how it could be converted."

"You *have* thought it through! You're right, it could work."

Audrey showed me around the house, which was enormous, and full of family history. I could see why she wanted to retain it.

"I'm sorry this place holds such bad memories for you, Audrey, because I can feel what your father felt here, and it's like a house full of joy to me. I think it's wonderful."

"I'm so pleased you like the house. I don't know if the others will think it's a good idea, but I'm going to suggest it."

"I've got a better idea; you said it yourself. Why not just bring them all here and ask Charlie how to convert it? I think they will suggest it *for* you."

We smiled at each other. Audrey talked for the next hour or so, describing some of her less unhappy memories there. As we walked round, she would quite unconsciously reach out and touch a chairback, or a banister rail, as if communicating with it. I could see this house would be quite impossible for her to sell. She was a part of its ancestral memory, inhabiting the very fabric of the building. Most of us don't have an ancestral home like that. It hardly applied to my parents' little rented house in High Wycombe. This house and its memories were uniquely special.

Our house in Washington DC is magnificent; it's relatively new, certainly compared to Audrey's house. The walls are adorned with photographs of all the great and good of the Washington establishment who had over time graced our home. There are two American presidents, four chairmen of the Federal Reserve, presidents of the World Bank, as well as numerous world leaders. This wonderful old house of Audrey's had probably never seen such luminaries, but it seemed to be so much more. It imposed its presence upon you. The people have come and gone, but the house seemed to retain their spirit. My house only retained their photographs.

"I love this house, Audrey, and I can see why you could never leave it."

"I know, but I can't afford to keep it as it is. I *have* to do something."

"Could you really see it converted into separate dwellings?"

"It might sound silly," Audrey said. "I'm sure the house wouldn't like it, but if I can honour my father's wish to bring joy and laughter back here, then maybe the house will forgive me."

"I think it will, Audrey."

Finally, and reluctantly, we left there and headed towards the local pub for a late lunch. We discussed Audrey's plan in detail, and although it was radical to say the least, it was possible. The question was: would Fiona, Harry, Bill, and Charlie like the idea? Audrey added another name.

"Sylvia would have to like the idea as well."

She was right, I was still not used to thinking about them as a couple. Here I was, enthusiastically discussing my friends' possible future, when it belatedly occurred to me that this was *their* future. I would not be a part of it.

"Thanks for bringing me here today, Audrey. I needed this."

"I know you did. Even you can't smile all the time; it's such a giveaway."

"I'll get over it, I'm very rarely depressed. I just don't know how to deal with it."

"You're talking to an expert, Joanna. My poor mother was depressed most of her life and I thought I was going the same way when I lost everything. It took me two years to even start to feel better."

"What did you do to get over it?"

"That's the problem, you lose the will to do anything; it's like drowning, with no incentive to struggle to the surface. You convince yourself that your problems are the cause of your woes, when in fact it's a nasty chemical imbalance in your brain which is causing the trouble. I learned from my poor mother; I took all the medical help offered me. I tried to concentrate on those nasty chemicals, not on my problems."

"I can't imagine you depressed, Audrey, you're so strong."

"Look at you, Joanna, how can someone who never stops smiling be depressed? Not that I think you are, you're just feeling low, and in the circumstances, I don't blame you, but you *will* rise above this, trust me."

"When you tell me that, Audrey, I believe it."

We drove back in much better spirits. Audrey's an invigorating person to be with at any time, but especially so that day. I also think I managed to erase any doubts she had about her plan. It was crazy, but I agreed with her; it *could* work. We went over it all again on the way back and a decision was made. She would tell Harry about the house and explain why she had not mentioned such an important thing before. Then, at the right opportunity, she would invite them all down to Oxford to ask their advice about how she could overcome the maintenance costs and retain the house. At the first mention of possibly converting it into different apartments, Charlie would be in his element, and the dye would be cast.

By the time we arrived back at my hotel, Audrey's plan had become an exciting project, exactly what I needed. I thanked her for saving me from myself that day, but she dismissed the whole thing. She really is a wonderful friend. I commented that I was half expecting Molly to bring Giles to the hotel that evening for dinner, and she wished me luck with that.

Chapter Thirteen
THE BUSINESS PLAN

I hadn't heard from Molly all day. She didn't say she would phone me, but I had assumed she would. Perhaps the meeting with Charlie and Sylvia had gone so well that they had no time. Just as I was starting to feel even more left out, my phone rang; it was Molly.

"Hi, Mom. Are you OK for dinner tonight at the hotel?"

"Of course, will Giles be coming?"

"That's great, see you soon."

I didn't know if Giles was coming or not. I thought Molly must be rushed off her feet, so I got ready and sat in my room waiting. Then my phone rang again.

"Where are you, Mom? We're in the bar waiting for you."

"Why didn't you tell me you were here, I'm sitting *here* waiting!"

"Sorry, Mom. There's just so much going on, I don't know if I'm coming or going."

I went down to find them all together in the bar, including Giles. I had met him twice back home. He is extremely polite, immediately standing up to greet me as he offered me his hand.

"Hello, Mrs Wright, it's lovely to see you again."

I smiled back. Having long since decided that I liked him, I put my arms around him and kissed his cheek.

"Enough of Mrs Wright, it's Joanna. And it's lovely to see *you* again, Giles."

"I've got to say it, Molly looks so much like you. The two of you look just like sisters. No, I *mean* it!"

"It's not me you need to flatter, Giles; it's these two, Sylvia and Charlie."

I decided not to admit that his flattery had worked, but I did kiss him again. Everyone smiled, obviously all were in good spirits. Giles asked me what I would like to drink and rushed off to the bar. He didn't need to; the waiter would have brought it for me, I suspected he did it intentionally to give me a moment with the others. He is such a considerate man.

"Well, how did it go?"

"My head's still spinning." Molly said. "We've gone through so much together. Charlie and Sylvia have been brilliant."

"Is Giles happy with that?"

"He is, let him come back and we'll tell you all about it."

Giles returned and sat down. There was a silence as they all looked at each other.

"You tell Mom, Charlie."

Charlie sat smiling, so I assumed it was good news.

"It's a long story, so let's go through to the restaurant first," he said.

I was intrigued and waited patiently. As soon as we sat down again, Charlie began. The first thing he made clear was that he knew nothing about artificial intelligence, but he said he didn't need to; that was Giles' job. He also didn't know anything about specific applications, or the marketing of AI, but he didn't need to, because that was Molly's job. What he *did* understand was that Molly's company, Intuitive, had put an awful lot of work into this joint venture with Giles' business. Sylvia had combed through the reports and contract which Molly had been sent over with, and it was apparent to Charlie that this was not really a joint venture. It was a straightforward buy-out of Giles' intellectual rights!

Furthermore, according to Sylvia, the price they were prepared to pay, for a business such as Giles', was not in line with his last three years' accounts. Charlie said they must know something that made Giles worth much more than face value. Molly, despite being a senior executive of Intuitive, had come here not realising anything about this, which all indicated a high-level conspiracy.

"In my business," Charlie said, "our secret of success was working hard, year after year, building houses. That was not a piece of information my competitors would pay a penny to know. However, when an insider told me about a building company which had overstretched itself just as the interest rates were rising? Well, that was information *worth* paying for!"

Charlie made his case very logically. Giles had explained to him that he had made ground-breaking progress in the field of artificial intelligence, including several patents. Most AI programs rely upon a self-learning algorithm, a laborious process of recognition, classification, and elimination, all of which requires ever more processing power. Giles had a way to short cut that procedure. Almost! There was just one, albeit large, obstacle holding him back. Charlie was sure that Intuitive, with all their resources, would be able to piece together just how close Giles was by looking at his patents.

"The thing is, there are lots of clever people like Giles searching for the holy grail of artificial intelligence, so why is Intuitive so desperate to buy *his* idea? It can only be that they are certain Giles' idea *is* indeed the holy grail. Now here's the thing, they can only be certain of that if they already have the missing piece of the jigsaw puzzle. Their piece of the puzzle is worthless without Giles; this is the ultimate high-stakes game for them."

"I don't need to understand AI." Charlie went on. "*You* know what's holding you back, Giles. And Molly, you know the kind of research your company has been involved with.

You two are the brightest people I know, so you'll figure it out between you."

"He's wonderful, isn't he!" Molly said.

"I've always thought so," Sylvia replied.

"Charlie says I should walk away from Intuitive and join forces with Giles."

"What do you think, Giles?" I said.

"Charlie put me straight on that as well," Giles replied.

"What did you say, Charlie?"

They all laughed and looked at Charlie.

"Well, I said you're an IT geek, Giles. You might be a genius but what do you know about building a business and marketing? Without Molly, you'll probably just become a footnote in history."

"Charlie! You didn't!"

"He did, Mom. I didn't know what to say!"

"I'm sure you know I'm right," said Charlie. "You've got something really special going on between you two, and to-gether you just might change the world."

"They don't need to worry about finance either," Sylvia said. "They can manage without the Intuitive money. Charlie and I would like to invest in the business, and if Giles succeeds, then everyone will want to invest."

"Are you sure you're happy with all this, Giles?" I asked. "This is obviously not what you were anticipating? And it's a big step for you, Moll, to just walk away from your job."

"It's an enormous step! But I trust Charlie implicitly. I would trust him anyway, even if he weren't my father!"

"Charlie's your father?" Giles said.

"Oh, I'm sorry! I didn't mean to say that. Oh dear."

"That's okay," Giles said, "I understand; your Mum and Charlie are divorced."

"Actually, Giles, we were never married," I said. "It's a long story, I'll leave Molly to tell you later."

The look on Molly's face said it all, but she was not to

blame; it had become impossible to keep Charlie a secret. It suddenly felt ridiculous that we had entertained the prospect in the first place. This raised an obvious question. How on earth were we going to keep this from Alan and the boys? I had managed to do exactly that, for thirty years, but now everything was different.

Giles was very tactful, seeming to sense that the subject was best avoided for the moment. The situation was helped by Sylvia and Charlie, who were on good form. Being involved in business again was obviously the adrenalin they needed. The two couples bounced ideas off one another all evening.

It did at least give me the opportunity to be an observer. Sylvia was radiant, no longer the wallflower, and clearly blossoming in her new role. Charlie seemed content to let her shine. I think he enjoyed seeing the new confident Sylvia. He certainly enjoyed seeing Molly vibrant and engaged, as she was that evening. Every time she smiled, so did Charlie. And every time Charlie smiled, she smiled; they were remarkably close. I wanted to hug them both!

It was also impossible not to notice the spark that existed between Molly and Giles. They were completely infatuated with each other, Giles so reminded me of my young builder. As Charlie said, Giles is a genius, which can make him a little unworldly. He is incredibly polite and considerate, but like my builder, a bit shy and awkward, yet in the most endearing way. I suspect in some circumstances his intellect might distance him from some people. He certainly wouldn't suffer fools gladly, but in Molly he had found a beacon of light shining as brightly as his own. He's tall, and good looking with fair hair, rather like Charlie. I was biased of course, but they did seem to be made for one another. I was won over, and I had the impression Charlie was too.

The evening concluded with Giles and Molly both saying they needed time to think about Charlie's advice, but my impression was that their minds were probably already made up.

We said our goodbyes in the foyer, and I said I would wait for Molly as she walked with Giles to his car. Charlie and Sylvia walked hand in hand together toward his car. I couldn't help noticing that Molly and Giles stood next to his car, locked together in a kiss. Even after all this time, whenever I find myself standing next to a car in a hotel car park, I think of Charlie. It never was just a kiss; it was always something else entirely. I have never seen another couple so blissfully unaware of their surroundings as Charlie and I used to be. Not until that evening.

It must have been twenty minutes before Molly came back to where I was sitting on one of the chairs in the foyer.

"I'm sorry I was so long, Mom."

"Never apologise when a kiss takes a long time, sweetheart. That's exactly how it should be."

"He's lovely, isn't he, Mom."

"He is, sweetheart; in fact, I think I would go a bit further, I think he's gorgeous!"

We laughed. We both knew Charlie was always embarrassed to be told he was gorgeous and Molly understood the comparison I was making. Not that she needed my approval of Giles, but she was clearly delighted. It was written across her face in large letters; I was truly overjoyed for her. We all want the best for our children, but above all I wished her love, and she had found it.

We walked upstairs to our rooms.

"I'm sorry for that slip about Charlie. I just didn't think."

"I know what you mean, Moll. Can you imagine how I feel? Every time I see you and Charlie together, I just want to put my arms around him and kiss the father of my daughter. I don't want to deny him."

"I know you don't, Mom, so what are we going to do?"

"I don't know, but at least Charlie's on this side of the ocean. If your Dad finds out, it will turn his life upside-down. I just want to protect him from that."

"I agree, Mom. Charlie was right when he said I just had to decide which was the greater good."

Chapter Fourteen
AUDREY'S GAMBLE

Molly's excitement was contagious when we met for breakfast, She was rushing straight back to Giles; they had so much to discuss. Charlie's words echoed in my mind.

"Together, you just might change the world."

Molly and Giles were both hugely capable people, Charlie was right about that. Together they were greater than the sum of their parts, and I felt they could achieve anything. Above all, they were so ideally matched that I felt they had each walked straight into the hands of destiny. I waved her goodbye as she drove off in our hire car. As I returned to my room, I was beaming with pride, wanting to shout aloud in the foyer - "that's my daughter, Molly! She might change the world!"

I hadn't made any plans for that day, and Molly had the car. However, I didn't have time to feel sorry for myself. My phone rang just then; it was Audrey.

"Where are you, Joanna? Why are you not here?"

"I don't have the car."

"Why didn't you say? I'll be there in half an hour."

"Audrey, you're wonderful, but no, I'll get a taxi. I'll see you soon."

She argued, but I insisted. I arrived at the Village just as they were having coffee. Charlie was full of apologies, saying he had promised to be my chauffeur but had manifestly failed in his duty.

"Will you ever be able to forgive me?

"No! I'm sorry, Charlie, you're fired!"

"Then I'm taking you to the industrial tribunal for unfair dismissal."

We all laughed, but I could see Charlie was genuinely upset that he had forgotten me.

Audrey's daughter Fiona was there. We had not met before but I had already heard so much about her.

"Hello, Joanna. It's good to finally meet you, Mum talks about you all the time."

I felt as if I knew her; I had heard them all talking so fondly about Fiona, and I knew Charlie was especially close to her. I gave her a big hug.

"It's really lovely to finally meet you, Fiona, and who is this?"

"This is my friend, Lorraine; my flat mate."

"Hello, Lorraine. I am delighted to meet you. So what brings you both here today?"

"I have no idea, Mum asked me to come over this morning; she's up to something."

"You'll all have to excuse me," Lorraine said, "I've just dropped Fiona off while her car is in the garage. Some of us have to go to work."

"Hang on," Fiona said, "I'll see you off."

Audrey smiled. She certainly *was* up to something. She had everyone sitting attentively while we waited for Fiona to return.

"I've got something to tell you," she said. "I've been telling Harry this morning. When I came here to the Village, I didn't sell up and leave my past behind. I've still got it!"

"Do you mean that house of yours that you described to us?" asked Bill.

"Yes, I do. My ancestral home, Belmont."

Everyone was surprised, but also interested. Sylvia asked why she hadn't sold it, and Audrey explained her obligation to keep the house within the family. All of this raised further questions. Why had she not told them before? I could see Audrey was embarrassed that she hadn't told anyone about such a significant part of her life, especially Harry.

Charlie, ever the gentleman, immediately saw Audrey's discomfort, and stepped in to help her.

"I know why Audrey didn't tell us. It's the same reason that I haven't told you that I still own *my* house. We all came here to get away from our past, and that is what one's house is; it's the custodian of all those memories that you want to get away from. If I were convinced the Village was what I wanted, I would have sold it, but there was a part of me that was still unsure. Stanley knew that. That's why he asked each one of us why we were here."

"Thank you, Charlie." Audrey replied.

"I'm glad it's finally out in the open," Sylvia said. "This is a wonderful place, and you're all wonderful people but *look* at you. You're like birds in a cage! It's taken Joanna to show us that we can still fly!"

"Sylvia's right, Joanna," said Bill. "You've opened the cage door and invited us all to fly. I think it's about time we did what you invited us to do; move on from the past and embrace our future. So tell us about your house, Audrey."

She was obviously relieved and told them about her commitment to her father. When she then explained about the onerous maintenance costs, her dilemma was immediately obvious. Audrey went through the many reasons why she could never leave Belmont and explained again why the memories were too painful to live with. Charlie immediately said it sounded like '*Hotel California*'. Audrey and I looked at each other; we had to work hard not expose our secret. Charlie was predictable, but I so love that about him.

Sylvia immediately suggested that we should all go and look at Audrey's house. "Charlie and I know all about house maintenance costs. Maybe we can come up with a few suggestions."

Again, I looked at Audrey, who smiled back at me.

"We've got nothing better to do, why don't we go right now?" I said.

There was enthusiastic agreement; only a week ago Audrey would have required a change of clothes and shoes, not to mention a face makeover! Now she said, "Wonderful, let's go then."

It was quickly decided that Harry and Charlie would drive their respective cars, and we would go in convoy. We had to stop on the way at a motorway service station for Bill to be excused, and while we were there, we decided to have an early lunch. I was unimpressed by the whole thing, as was Audrey, so we sent the boys to see what they could find. They seemed determined to make matters worse by demanding a proper tea service, and when Bill asked for a tea strainer, the poor girl had to explain that a tea bag in a mug did not require a tea strainer. I could now see how some of the hilarious stories I was told about, came to be. They seemed to delight in making complete fools of themselves, and the more fuss and confusion they created, the more they enjoyed it! Harry said he would like to see the menu for lunch; the young girl said he was looking at it.

"No, my dear. The a la carte menu," Bill said.

The girl must have thought she was dealing with a bunch of idiots. She walked away to get her manager, who started off being terribly polite, until Charlie asked her where the proper restaurant was, the one with tablecloths. The boys thought this was all good fun, but it had gone above the heads of everyone else. As the manager was asking them to leave, one of the queuing customers became extremely irate, threatening to throw them out.

"Can you have a word with this gentleman?" Charlie said to Harry.

Harry stepped forward. "You wouldn't believe this tray could fit into your mouth, would you?"

Audrey quickly moved forward to stand between them. "Come along, boys! I believe we were just leaving."

She tried to be cross with them, but my laughing didn't help. "Why can't you just behave yourselves? It was only a cup of tea!"

"It might only be a cup of tea, but these places need to be told there are some people left who can remember a *proper* cup of tea." Charlie said.

"Quite right!" said Bill. "It's bad enough that we all have to dumb down; you don't have to celebrate it."

"You lot are incorrigible. How do you put up with them, Sylvia?" Fiona asked.

"Give it time; they grow on you."

We laughed all the way back to the cars and continued our journey. The boys had the last laugh when we stopped again for lunch in Oxford. We went to a lovely hotel where they served us the perfect lunch, followed by tea served from a beautiful bone china tea set, not to mention the tablecloth!

Charlie looked gleeful. "I think we can rest our case, gentlemen. A civilised lunch! Would you ladies have preferred the tea bag in the mug?"

"Ok Charlie, you were right as usual, but you didn't have to embarrass us all like that," laughed Sylvia.

"Got to break a few eggs to make an omelette," said Harry.

I sat there enjoying their banter. No wonder Audrey didn't want to live without these people. I did not want to live without them either. We set off again on our journey, I was with Charlie following Harry's car, as we finally approached Audrey's house. Nearing the bend which would reveal the magnificent vista of Audrey's estate, I looked at the others to watch their reaction. Their eyes widened as we rounded the bend, and they each smiled. Belmont is the most beautiful estate.

We continued along the drive towards the house, and this time I noticed the overgrown grass verge and the fallen tree. Some of the wooden fence guards around the trees had also fallen, as well as a distant gate. I didn't notice any of these things the day before; I doubt the others were noticing them either. We entered through the heavy front door and stepped into the expansive panelled entrance hall.

"I know you described the house to us, Audrey, but you could never do it justice. This is magnificent," Charlie said.

Sylvia stood open mouthed. "Wow, I had no idea, Audrey!"

Harry stood with his arm around Audrey. "If this place holds unhappy memories for you then I understand. this an awful lot of memories."

Audrey gave us her tour of the house, including some rooms I didn't see the day before. Most of the rooms had been shut off and smelled damp and a bit musty. Finally, we entered the dining room. It was a huge room in proportion to the rest of the house, dominated by an enormous dining table. There was a central stone fireplace surrounded by oak panelling on all sides. The ceiling was embellished with intricate plaster work. Once it caught your attention, it was difficult to draw your eyes away from it, such was the detail. The windows were tall, with beautiful tapestry curtains and window dressings.

"This is the most beautiful room in the house, Audrey," I said. "Why have you kept this in such wonderful condition, while you've closed up some of the others?"

"This is the one room where I have happy memories. I just had to preserve it."

"I have happy memories of this room," Fiona said, "I always remember Christmas here. And do you remember, Mum, when you held that Conservative party fundraiser here? We had a power cut and no lights; it was an absolute fiasco!"

"I don't think we need to mention that Fi," Audrey replied.

"Oh, I don't know, it sounds rather interesting," joked Harry.

Audrey very quickly changed the subject and set off to show us the rest of the house. We must have wandered around for an hour or more; it was certainly a lovely old country house. The part of the house that Audrey had let to her tenants looked reasonably well maintained, but the rest of it was sadly neglected. Having completed our tour, we ended up back in the hall.

"This is just the main house, there are also the outbuildings."

"You mean there's more?" Sylvia exclaimed.

Next, we toured the outbuildings. There was an old tumbled down cottage that was once staff quarters, and then across the way, there were the stables. Eventually we made our way back to the main building.

"So, what do you think?" Audrey said. "What can I do to save this place?"

"This is nothing but maintenance," Charlie replied, "I can see your problem, Audrey. Is it of sufficient historical interest to open it to the public?"

"I looked into that once; it's of *some* interest, but it's not going to be a big attraction. Besides, it's not big enough to open it to the public and still leave a sufficiently large private section."

"Do you want to maintain a home here, Audrey?" asked Sylvia.

"Yes. I promised my father that, whatever else happens, Fiona must be given the opportunity to live here."

"Sounds like a poisoned challis to me," Fiona said.

"In that case, your options are really limited," Sylvia said. "The only thing I can think is that you convert it into separate apartments and retain one or two for yourself."

"Would that be possible, Charlie?" Audrey said, with a remarkably straight face.

I glanced across to her and she smiled the most beautiful

cheeky smile. I smiled back. Charlie said nothing but set off exploring the fabric of the building. He came back after some considerable time and made a pronouncement.

"It's perfectly possible. You have those out-buildings, they can be converted into dwellings. In the main house, you could have several self-contained flats, or you could have four self-contained apartments, each with its own side entrance, as well as a communal central entrance if you wanted. If you could find the right kind of people to either rent or buy some of the apartments, I think it could work very well."

"What sort of people do you think I would need to find, Charlie?"

"Well, obviously if you're going to live next door to them, they need to be people you can get on with. In the ideal world, you need some kindred spirits."

"Do you mean people like us?"

Charlie was obviously about to answer but stopped mid-breath. "Audrey! What *are* you up to?"

Sylvia caught on immediately. "What a wonderful idea, Audrey! You *are* clever, it's perfect for everyone."

Bill looked at Harry, and slowly they both began to smile. "It's a rare day when a complex problem throws up a perfect solution, but I think you've found it, Audrey," said Bill.

"I like the sound of it; what about you, Charlie?" Harry said.

"Well, assuming I forgive Audrey for tricking us all, I *love* it!"

Sylvia laughed. "It's not every day you get one over on Charlie. You enjoy it, Audrey."

"What do you think, Fi, will it work for you?" asked Audrey.

"You mean, I might have to live in an apartment here, with you lot?"

"Yes of course, we can have four apartments," Audrey said.

"*Me,* living in this old house with you lot? I love you all, but I'm not sure I want to live with you."

"You wouldn't be living with us, we would all have our separate apartments," Charlie replied. "I've seen lots of examples of large houses turned into separate flats and apartments, it can work well."

"Well I suppose you're right, it's not a lot different to my flat now."

"Oh, I'm so pleased, Fi," said Audrey.

Bill turned to me and said, "I bet you and Audrey schemed this plan between you."

I didn't get a chance to answer. Audrey said, "Look at us all, we're different people since we've met Joanna. None of this would have happened without you, Joanna."

I said I had nothing to do with it, but it did seem to be the perfect solution. We walked around the house again, with Charlie describing how the apartments could be created out of the existing rooms. In next to no time, Audrey's crazy idea felt as if it was an imminent reality. Everyone had some input; this was really going to happen.

All the way back in the car we discussed it. As far as the conversion was concerned, Charlie and Sylvia could see no problems. They had not discussed finance, and this project would cost an enormous amount, but again Sylvia didn't think it should be a problem. Each of them had capital to invest, and with the finance shared between them, the individual cost was not an obstacle for a group of people like that.

We talked so much that the long drive back to the Village just seemed to disappear, and I found myself caught up with their enthusiasm. When we arrived, it was already quite late, so I agreed to dine there with them. Fiona said she would not stay. She had to get her car back from the garage and Lorraine was picking her up soon. I went with Audrey and Harry to their apartment where I could use their bathroom. As soon as we arrived I phoned Molly to invite her to join us, but we could not compete with the lovely Giles! She did say she would see what he wanted to do. Harry was obviously keen to get out of our way, he was ready in no time. He hugged and kissed Audrey and said he would head over to the bar. It was quite the wrong thing for me to say to Audrey, but it just came out.

"You're so happy with Harry. Do you ever wonder what life might have been like with Charlie?"

"I used to think about Charlie every hour, then it was only every day. Then it was every other day, and then only once a week. Now I don't really think about Charlie like that at all, but I wouldn't want to live without him somewhere in my life. I know why you're asking, Joanna. It *will* get better with time, I promise you that, but he will always be a part of you."

I knew Audrey was right, but the black cloud was closing in on me again. I had only days left before I was due to go back to Washington, and I wasn't really looking forward to being home. At least it would put an ocean between me and Charlie. Seeing him every day was proving to be more painful than I could have possibly imagined. Audrey and I walked over to the restaurant together, while she did her best to raise my spirits. The others were waiting for us there, settled in their usual chairs.

"What would you girls like to drink?" asked Charlie. "Stanley's buying."

Alan came over to take our order, saying, "I've got a new single malt, Charlie; would you like to try it?"

He didn't wait for an answer and went back to the bar to assemble our drinks. The boys each had a glass of the new single malt and as is their ritual, Alan didn't tell them what it was. Charlie swirled the glass and held it to his nose, while the others waited attentively for his verdict. He swirled and sniffed, and finally tasted. His expression changed immediately; he just sat back looking at his glass. It was some time before he said anything.

"I've not had this whisky before. I think it's an Islay whisky, and Stanley described one that until recently has been very difficult to find. I remember he said it tasted of barbecue, and smoky bacon. I think Stanley's telling me this is Caol Ila."

Alan nodded in agreement without saying anything, and Harry just said quietly, "Well done, Charlie."

"Can I taste it, Charlie?" I asked.

He handed me the glass, and I was about to lift it to my lips, when Charlie said, "Don't rush! Just look at it, then smell the aroma, then wait a moment and see if it speaks to you before you taste it."

I did as he requested, knowing this was all about the description Stanley had given him. I didn't know Stanley, so I concentrated on the aroma, and I imagined Charlie's voice telling me about the flavours. Suddenly I was taking this seriously, and in that moment, my glass of amber fluid took on a new significance. I finally tasted it, and although it was not really to my liking, I could taste the flavours Charlie described. I have seen Charlie apparently deep in conversation with his glass of whisky on several occasions; now I finally understood.

"Thank you, Charlie," I said.

The mood lifted as they discussed the whisky, while Audrey, Sylvia, and I toasted the future with our gin and tonics. Audrey suddenly said, "Oh look! It's Molly and is that Giles?"

They had decided to join us after all. They walked towards us with their arms around each other. I introduced Giles to Audrey, Bill, and Harry. Giles was not his usual awkward self with strangers.

"I've heard so much about you all, it's a privilege to meet you," he said.

Audrey was immediately impressed. Following my lead, she threw her arms around him. Harry shook his hand, crushing it as he always does, while Bill the scientist greeted him as if he was the prodigal son. Giles is not generally good with strangers, but in just a few moments, he seemed to slip effortlessly into our little group. They were both dying to tell us their news, and it quickly became apparent that they had decided to take Charlie's advice. Molly was going to leave her job with Intuitive, and team up with Giles. He was pleased to accept Charlie and Sylvia's offers to become investors. In the space of just a few days, their futures had taken a new direction; this was a hugely significant moment for them both.

"Are you both quite sure about this?" I said.

"I've never been more convinced about anything in my life, Mom."

"What about you, Giles, are *you* sure?"

"The one thing I am completely sure about is Molly. If we can change the world of AI, then that's a bonus."

It took me a second to realise what he had just said, though Charlie was much quicker. He stepped forward and shook Giles by the hand.

"Giles," he said, "you've just made the best decision of your life, and I don't mean having me as an investor!"

I was so happy for them, but someone needed to say it. "I'm sorry to be the one to ask the question, Giles, but where do your wife and son fit in to all this?"

He was embarrassed. "You're right to ask, Joanna. I don't know how it's going to work out, but I can't see a future for me which doesn't include Molly, so I'll *make* it work."

That was the correct answer, but I still worried. I looked at Charlie and could tell from his face that he felt the same.

Giles is perceptive and he knew why I was worried for Moll. He squeezed Molly's hand and turned towards me.

"Molly's told me about you and Charlie; in fact, she's told me a lot about all of you. I hope you don't mind, Joanna."

"Of course not, we're pleased, aren't we, Charlie?"

He nodded in approval.

"All I can say is that we are determined not to make the same mistakes that you and Charlie made. Oh, good heavens! I didn't mean to say it like that. I'm so sorry."

I interrupted him, or he would have gone on apologising otherwise.

"No need to apologise, Giles. Everyone here knows the mistakes Charlie and I made. That's in the past now. Just be sure you don't make the same mistakes."

We changed the subject, deciding it was time to head towards the restaurant. Giles found a kindred spirit in Bill. The two were immediately engaged in a conversation which might as well have been in a foreign language, as far as the rest of us were concerned! Giles was quite the centre of attention, but then excused himself for a moment. I could see him in the hall talking on his phone. When he came back, he whispered something to Molly, who smiled and kissed him.

Towards the end of our meal, Molly quietly said, "We need to go, Mom. Can you get a lift back to the hotel with Charlie?"

"Yes, I'm sure I can, but what's the rush? I could go with you."

"I'm not going back to the hotel. I'm going with Giles," she whispered.

I didn't ask any questions; I didn't want to say the wrong thing. I just told everyone that they were in a rush to go. The pair of them could not leave our company quick enough.

"I'll be in touch; see you guys soon, bye," Molly said.

Harry turned to Audrey, "Was it something I said?"

"No, it wasn't something you said, Harry," I replied. "It was something *he* said."

"What do you mean, what did he say?" asked Harry.

"Be quiet, Harry! I'll explain later," said Audrey.

We finished our desserts and went to the lounge for some cups of coffee. Everyone seemed to be in high spirits, except for me. Molly and Giles have so much joy and enthusiasm between them; it was perhaps inevitable that it would remind me of the contrast with my own life. Audrey talked about her plan for Belmont, except now of course her plan had become *their* plan. Charlie and Sylvia talked about their investment in Giles' business. Charlie had to ask Sylvia how much he could afford, and which fund or account it would need to come from. Eventually the conversation turned towards Charlie and Sylvia's plans for the future.

"What are your plans?" I asked.

Charlie looked at Sylvia. "We're just going to take it a step at a time."

"There's so much going on, what with this new venture with Molly, and Audrey's house," said Sylvia. "We aren't ready to make big decisions like living together, we are just going to continue as we are, and let things evolve by themselves."

"I think that's very sensible," I said.

"What about Jack, your husband, Sylvia?" I asked. "Have you seen him recently; does he know about you and Charlie?"

"Jack's always known about me and Charlie. We were estranged even when we were living together, but I do need to tell him. I suppose we should get divorced."

"Why does life have to be so complicated?" Audrey said.

"You're right," replied Sylvia, "I think what Charlie said is best, we just take it a step at a time. Maybe if Audrey's plan for the Belmont apartments goes well, perhaps that might be when…well, who knows? We'll know more about that in the next few weeks. I've got one of our architects going over the house next week."

"Do we? I didn't know!" said Charlie.

"You should realise by now, Charlie, Sylvia only tells you what you need to know," said Audrey.

Everyone laughed. Charlie was so used to having his life managed for him.

"You don't know how lucky you are, Charlie Bartlett," I said.

"Actually, that's not really fair," replied Sylvia. "I know a lot of people, especially at work, who think Charlie takes me for granted, but it's not true. When I needed an operation years ago, Charlie paid for me to have it all done privately. Then he insisted I needed a holiday, and so he sent Jack and me on a two-week cruise. When my car failed its MOT, I came home from work one day to find a lovely new car parked on my drive. Then there was the time when I lost a necklace that belonged to my mother. I was so upset, Charlie rushed out and found me a replacement the same day. I could go on and on. People say he doesn't appreciate what I do for him, but you do, don't you, Charlie?"

Charlie was really embarrassed. "*You* know I do, that's the main thing."

I love that about Charlie; when *we* were together, he never missed an opportunity to be kind, he would have done absolutely anything for me. The only thing he didn't do was leave his wife. I don't think he is capable of doing an unkind thing.

Charlotte came over. "Come and join us," Bill said.

She sat next to Bill and joined in the conversation. I had noticed a few occasions when Bill and Charlotte have been chatting together, and Harry has now been told to stop calling her the 'commandant.' Charlotte's a bubbly character, always fun to be with, and tonight was no exception, so we ended our evening on a high.

Chapter Fifteen
THE LAST SUPPER

The next couple of days flew by, and I remained a supporting actor in this cast of players. Molly and Giles had two huge projects to contend with: their business, and their future life together. They were besotted with each other. I knew it would only be a matter of days before she could move into her new house, and I wondered if Giles would be there too.

My wonderful friends Audrey and Harry had their plans for Belmont, and I was in no doubt that they would make it a success. It was true that I had taken it upon myself to open the cage door that my friends had put themselves behind, but I could never have guessed that they might all fly away together!

Bill had become a dear friend, so kind and understanding. Sadly, this only served to make him a more tragic figure. He must have been so very much in love with his wife Sarah; she left a void which Bill struggled to fill. Everyone hoped that his developing friendship with Charlotte might be a new beginning.

As for Charlie and Sylvia, I tried not to dwell on it. The only thing I was sure about was that I loved being with these people. I was the outsider looking in at their lives. What would not I have given to be an insider, to be a part of it? This was my last evening with them. While Molly was still living in the UK, I would be coming back, but for the moment I felt terribly sad. We made the decision to share this last night at the Village. I had to admit the place had grown on me. Giles offered to drive us there, wanting to be a part of my last evening, which of course would not have been complete without him.

As soon as we joined the others, Audrey said, "I can't believe this is your last night with us! When are you coming back?"

"I don't know Audrey, but I'll be back. I *can* promise you that."

"We're going to miss you, Joanna, you're one of us now," said Bill.

"Enough of this, let's not have any speeches," I said. "We mustn't turn this into the last supper; let's have a happy evening together."

We did have a wonderful evening together; everything was so familiar, just as it should be. Charlie had a conversation with his single malt whisky, and we all raised our glasses in a toast to Stanley. Harry did his best to be a curmudgeon, and Audrey told him not to be grumpy, and then the next moment she hugged him. Bill said something, and everyone listened. Charlie said something, and everyone laughed. Sylvia was radiant as ever, but now everyone notices. We had a delightful meal and enjoyed a superb bottle of wine, courtesy of Charlie. It all came to an end far too soon, and we made our way into the lounge for some coffee.

No sooner were we sitting down than Harry said, "I agree about not having any speeches, mine will be the first and the last, so best get it over with! I just want to thank you, Joanna, for coming into our lives. Long before we met you Joanna, thanks to Charlie we all felt as if we knew you. You inspired us, especially me. You're everything Charlie said you were, you're not like other people, and you've shown us that *we* don't have to be like other people either. I want to thank you for that."

"Oh Harry! That's so kind!" I said as I hugged him.

Alan arrived with our coffee, and there was the usual rush for their favourite chocolates. The boys pretended to fight over them, while Audrey complained that their conduct was unseemly. Charlie did what Charlie always does, he ended up with the chocolates and offered them to the ladies, then the boys continued to squabble over those that remained. After much amusement, we finally settled down with our coffee and chocolates.

Audrey said, "I want to thank you as well, Joanna. You have changed the way I look. You have changed my outlook; you've changed my life. How can I thank you for that? I just wish you weren't leaving us."

I hugged her. "You're my dearest friend Audrey. I wish I weren't leaving, but I'll be back."

"Harry was right," Bill said. "Best get these things said and over with. So, I just want to say that you have inspired me too. I never thought I could replace what I lost when Sarah died. I didn't even want to. You've made me realise that I don't have to deny myself the joy of life and relationships. I may never find such joy again, but if I saw an opportunity, I would grab it with both hands, and that's thanks to you."

"Oh Bill, I hope you do!" I said. "That's so kind of you all, but enough of this. Look what you're doing to my mascara!"

"You've changed *my* life, Joanna," Sylvia said. "I've known you for thirty years, and all those kind things everyone has said are true. I need to add something to what's been said. Your relationship with Charlie *was* painful for me. You didn't mean it to be, but it was. I might have hated you for it, but that was always impossible; you've always been a dear friend. What you've done for me, and for Charlie, has been wonderful. How can I ever thank you for that? There are no words to express how I feel. All I can do is say *thank you*."

Through my tears, I said, "Oh Sylvia, that's such a lovely thing to say, but you don't have to thank me. Just please make him happy."

I was deeply moved by all their kind words, it was so unexpected, my mascara was running down my face.

"Look what you've done to me! I'm a mess!"

"You're right about the mascara, Mom," Molly said. "But while everyone is together, including Giles, I think this is the right time and place for me to say something. You know how I felt when we came here looking for Charlie. I am sorry I didn't understand then, but I do now. I realise what courage it must have taken to bring me here. You could easily have chosen not to tell me about Charlie. I think that would have been what most mothers in your position would have done. You didn't do that, you risked everything to bring me and my father together. I love you for that, Mom, and I love you, Charlie. I want to thank you both."

I tried to say something, but the words wouldn't come out; they comforted me as best they could. Charlie said nothing. I knew it was because, like me, he just couldn't utter the words. It was late and it was the time when I should leave anyway. This was when I had to say goodbye to Charlie and I dreaded the moment We all made our way towards the outer door. They each hugged me in turn, and then it was Charlie.

"Are you sure I can't drive you to the airport?" he asked.

"No, Charlie, that's kind, but Molly will take me."

"I don't know what to say, JoJo."

"We don't need words, Charlie, just give me a hug, and please don't kiss me or I'll make a fool of myself."

Charlie held me tightly. He didn't say anything, and he didn't kiss me. He then just turned away so that I couldn't see his face. Molly ushered me through the door and towards Giles' car. I was trying hard to stay in control, but it was a struggle which I was about to lose any moment. I sat in the back of the car with Molly.

"Be a darling, Giles," Molly said. "Can you give me a moment with Mom?"

Giles, the lovely man, immediately did as he was asked.

"You need a really good cry, Mom, and so do I."

It was the moment I so desperately needed. Everything about Charlie reminds me of that dreadful day when we came back from Bournemouth, when I turned and walked away from him. I constantly relive the pain of that goodbye, over and over, and this was another of those occasions.

"I can't hide it from you, Moll. You know what he means to me."

"How can it be wrong to love the father of your daughter? Don't apologise, Mom."

Giles was very patient and came back only to be waved away again. Eventually, with some composure restored, he was allowed back, and we set off for the hotel. I tried to apologise but Giles would not hear of it, also insisting that he would drive us to the airport in the morning. When we arrived at the hotel, I felt awful and just wanted to go to bed. I kissed and thanked Giles; Molly said she would catch me up.

"Is Giles not staying here with you tonight?" I asked.

"He can't, Mom, it's his wife."

I refrained from saying anything, but this was so like me and Charlie; I couldn't help but worry. Molly soon knocked on my door, offering to sit with me for a while, but I insisted I just wanted to go to bed. Predictably, despite being so tired, it was hours before I finally dropped off to sleep.

The next morning, I struggled up, looking terrible, and after my best efforts I still looked terrible. We had breakfast together and there were so many things we needed to talk about, but somehow it just seemed better to say nothing. Giles arrived on time and loaded my cases into his car, as Molly and I sat in the back again. It was quite a long drive to Heathrow Airport, and she did her best to make cheerful conversation.

When we finally arrived, Giles dropped us off at the terminal building, saying he would park the car and join us. Molly's particularly good at airports, knowing exactly where to go, and what to do. She had me checked in and free of my suitcases in no time at all. As we walked away from the check-in, there were five smiling faces walking towards us. I didn't know what to say when I saw them all.

"You didn't seriously think we wouldn't be here to see you off, did you?" laughed Sylvia.

I hugged them all again, and Harry joked that they had been there all night, waiting for me. We had some coffee together and they really lifted my spirits. Charlie was not his usual self, but I understood. When the time came to say goodbye for the second time, he was brilliant, saying they didn't want to upset me again. There were no hugs or kisses, they just waved me goodbye and left. It was a good try, but it didn't work! I said my goodbyes to Molly and Giles, and as I walked away, I consoled myself with the fact that we were only a phone call apart.

Chapter Sixteen
HOME AGAIN

My flight to Washington DC was dreary and uneventful. I arrived on time expecting that Alan would be there to pick me up as arranged. When I walked out of arrivals, it was the smiling face of Joe who greeted me.

"Hi Mom! Good flight?"

"Hello darling, I didn't expect you!"

We hugged each other. It was wonderful to see him.

"How's Carrie, still keeping you up at night?" I asked.

"She's getting better, Maria feeds her just the once now and she sleeps through the rest of the night."

"Oh, that's wonderful. Thanks for all the photographs, she looks gorgeous, I can't wait to see her again. So, where's your Dad? Busy, I suppose?"

"Yes, he asked me to pick you up. No problem."

We chatted about Carrie continually all the way home in the car. Molly had been sending him messages about her progress, and so eventually he had some questions.

"Do you think this business venture is going to work out for Moll?" he asked.

"Which part of it do you mean?"

"What other part is there?"

"Well, I might as well tell you, it's not a secret any longer.

It's not just the business. Molly and Giles are very much an item."

"Do you know, Mom, I guessed as much. Moll didn't say, but everything she sends me is about Giles. I was beginning to wonder. What's he like?"

"He's adorable, he really is. They're really serious about each other."

"I'm pleased for her; she's been too much work and no play for way too long."

"How's Mike?" I asked.

"Not heard from him for a while, but he'll be okay."

"You really should see more of your brother. I don't know what's wrong with you two."

Joe seemed to be keen to change the subject, asking about the mystery benefactor Molly had mentioned. I could tell Joe was a bit concerned about a total stranger investing money into his sister's venture.

"Who is this guy, anyway?

My heart jumped, I had never mentioned Charlie, for there to never be the need to deny him. This was an altogether new situation. Charlie was now a part of Molly's life, and how long would it be before he would be a part of my family's life?

"Oh, he's just someone Molly knows."

"Molly talks about him a lot, Mom, but she never mentions his name. Just who *is* this mystery guy? I feel maybe I should check up on him."

"You're being over-protective, Joe. Your sister can take care of herself; you know that."

I was trying desperately not to lie to my son. If this was a glimpse of my new future, then it was not a happy one. I did my best to avoid the subject. Joe and Molly are only fourteen months apart in age and have always been inseparable. Mike is four years younger than Joe, which is not a large gap, but despite everyone's efforts, he undoubtedly feels he is the odd one out. Alan and I tried hard, but it was always 'Joe and

Molly' in Mike's eyes. It seemed there was nothing we could do about it.

Joe carried my cases into the house and kissed me goodbye. He drove away but the mystery of Molly's 'benefactor' stayed with me, hanging over me like a toxic cloud. My housekeeper Sofia is a charming girl, she had been with us for three years then. For the first two years she called me Mrs Wright, now she calls me Joanna. Alan remains Mr Wright; I guess that says a lot about our relationship. As soon as she came into the room, she smiled and hugged me, as much my friend as my housekeeper. She wanted to know all about Molly. It seemed from what she was saying that the entire household had become her cheerleaders.

"Do you know when my husband is coming home?" I asked.

"No, I'm sorry, he left very early this morning, without saying anything to Mrs Garcia about dinner, so we're preparing for 7 o'clock."

"I'm sure that'll be fine, Sofia. I'll get unpacked. Do you know if we have any single malt whisky in the drinks cupboard?"

"You don't drink whisky."

"I know, I just thought I might try one when I've unpacked."

"You get unpacked and freshen up; I'll have a look for the whisky."

As I unpacked, my thoughts were all back in the UK. I sent a quick text to Molly, just to tell her I was home safely. I found myself wishing she would reply quickly; I needed to feel my connection with her. It could be a lonely house when only Sofia and I were there; sometimes it could take me several minutes to find her! On that occasion, I went back downstairs to be greeted by Sofia holding two bottles of single malt whisky.

"Would you like to try one of these?" she asked.

"Well, it's past the yardarm, so I think I will."

"What do you mean? Past the yardarm?"

"Oh, don't worry, it's just something the Brit's say! Let me see the bottles."

We had a bottle of Macallan and a half empty Glenmorangie. I had not heard of either of them.

"Don't open the new bottle, pour me a glass of the other one, and can you get me a small jug of water."

"Do you want another glass for the water?"

"No, what you have to do is to add just a drop water to the whisky until you find what they call the 'sweet spot'."

Sofia just smiled, looking bemused. I did exactly as Charlie had shown me, just looking at the glass for a while, then swirling the golden fluid around a little, before wafting it under my nose. With some scepticism, I waited for the whisky to speak to me, and to my complete amazement, it did! Charlie's voice filled my head.

"What is the matter, Joanna? Is there something wrong?" Sofia asked.

"No, I'm just being silly, it's nothing. Will you be an angel, next time you're shopping, could you try to find me a book about malt whisky?"

"Of course, I can't imagine why, but I'll find you one."

Mrs Garcia appeared, looking as cheerful as ever. She asked how my trip was, saying how pleased she was that I was back, and was Miss Molly really staying in the UK?

"Yes, she's got her own house now, and will be moving in any day."

"Will she be all right; is she by herself? Will she feed herself properly?"

Mrs Garcia worried about everyone, but especially Molly. I had to work hard to convince her that she needn't be concerned. I thought I would be helping by mentioning that Molly was not alone, telling her about Giles. That might have been a mistake! Then she was worried that Giles might not be an appropriate suitor.

Lots of my friends grumble about their domestic staff; apparently loyalty is in short supply these days. I was more concerned about how we would take care of Mrs Garcia when she needed to retire! I can't imagine being without her or Sofia. Mrs Garcia said dinner would be prepared for 7 o'clock, despite not knowing when Alan would be back. I was hoping he would at least telephone or text me, to let me know his plans, but I heard nothing. He finally arrived home just before seven.

"You're back," he said.

"Yes, the flight was on time. Thank you for asking Joe to pick me up."

He kissed me abruptly on the cheek, saying he would quickly get ready for dinner. With that he was gone! I hadn't seen him for three weeks, and his only words for me were, "You're back." As soon as he reappeared, we sat at the dining table, me at one end, him at the other, and it's a long table.

"So, tell me all about Molly. How's this deal going?"

I told him all about it, every detail; well, nearly every detail. Finally, I came to the part about Molly and Giles; he was not pleased. He came to the not unreasonable conclusion that mixing business with personal relationships was potentially disastrous. I agreed with him in principle and tried to explain why I thought this was different.

"It's never different; she hardly knows the man!" Alan said.

"I know how it sounds, but you haven't seen them together. They really love each other, it's as simple as that."

"What's that got to do with it? He could still be using her."

"You don't understand, Alan. When people really love each other, they're not capable of betraying that trust."

"And how would you know that?"

"At least I *know* what it is to love someone! I'm not sure *you* have the faintest idea."

"Perhaps I *don't* have the faintest idea, and whose fault would that be?"

"Let's not go there again, Alan. I've been away for three weeks. Can't we just be civil towards each other?"

"This *is* me being civil! What else do you expect?"

"I expect to be treated with at least a bit of respect. I try to fulfil my role with a smile; I just ask you to do the same."

"Well, you can do that next month; we've got the World Economic Forum to attend."

"What have I done, Alan, that I come home to this? I hoped you might at least have been a little pleased to see me."

"That is the point, isn't it! You've been away for three weeks, but nothing's changed, has it?"

For the rest of our meal, if we spoke at all, it was about Molly and Giles, but mostly we said precious little. Alan and I had a mutual understanding; we both know we didn't marry for love. He needed a wife who could charm and influence world leaders, bankers, and politicians. I needed a husband who could open the door to the kind of life I had always coveted. We had both succeeded in fulfilling our respective roles in the marriage. It's not that our roles had changed; I think it was our expectations which had altered. Alan's not an unkind or thoughtless man; he is probably typical of a lot of highly ambitious and driven people who get to the very top. The fog of ambition clears, and the inevitable question looms large. 'Is there nothing more to life than this?'

We had tried to discuss it on several occasions, but little good came of it. Maybe it is simply that a marriage based on convenience is not strong enough to stand the test of time. For my part, I had always felt a terrible burden of guilt. We both knew ours was a marriage of convenience, but we both hoped something more would grow out of it. I wanted to love Alan, and he in turn tried hard in the early years; it was not his fault that Charlie came between us. Towards the end of our relationship, Charlie said something that has haunted me ever since.

He said, "Whatever happens to us in the future, I want you to know there's a part of me that is forever yours."

When Charlie said those words, he had no idea that what

would happen to us in the future would be Molly. I have thought about Charlie every day of Molly's life. Alan rightly wanted more from our marriage; it wasn't his fault that I was never able to give it. Now that we have grown further apart, it's my guilt that tries to hold us together. We even talked about divorce once. Alan said it would ruin his career, and my guilt made me do everything I could to hold us together. We enjoyed a couple of glasses of wine each with our meal, perhaps it was four. I unwound a little and so did Alan.

"I'm sorry about earlier," he said. "I've had a bad day. I shouldn't have taken it out on you. This financial crisis is just not going away."

"That's okay," I said, "it's just as much my fault. You know how much I hate flying; it makes me bad-tempered."

"That's quite true, it does, but I think on this occasion it was me who was bad-tempered, so why don't we start again tomorrow?"

"I agree. I just need to go to bed, it's been such a long day."

This was typical of our disagreements. We had our problems, that's for sure, but we didn't hate one another. Neither of us can deny the empty space in our marriage, but we also have much that holds us together. We walked up the stairs together. Alan kissed me on the cheek, and we went into our separate bedrooms.

Chapter Seventeen
RETURN TO THE BRIGHT LIGHTS

I went downstairs for breakfast just in time to see Alan leaving for work.

"I'll try to let you know when I'll be home tonight. See you this evening."

This was a perfectly normal event for me. If I see Alan at all in the morning, he will just say goodbye. I cannot remember the last time he kissed me.

Normally, I never thought about it, but that morning was different. I allowed myself to imagine a different kind of life, a life with Charlie. In that life, it was impossible to imagine Charlie ever leaving my side without a lingering goodbye kiss. I tried to step back into my normal life as if nothing had happened, but of course something had happened.

The days went by as before, eventually turning into weeks. I met with friends for lunch, played golf and tennis, and saw as much as I could of my new granddaughter, Carrie. It was as if I had two lives; one there, and another life which existed in my laptop or my phone. Molly would phone or email me most days. Audrey and Sylvia both sent me regular texts or emails. Bill sent me an email one day to tell me he was seeing more of Charlotte; he thought I would like to know.

Above all, Molly was uppermost in my mind. Her work with Giles was going well, and she always sounded so enthusiastic. They constantly appeared to be on the brink of a breakthrough, but so far it was eluding them. The only consistency was their love for each other. Whatever our topic of conversation, I could always feel the presence of Giles in her voice and was so happy for her. I realised that through Molly, I was reliving my time with Charlie. Their relationship was so like ours, in some respects far too similar. Giles was still living with his wife, so their relationship remained in the shadows. We talked about it constantly; Molly needed me to confide in. I didn't need to make the comparison with Charlie, she was only too aware.

I rarely missed an opportunity to ask about him, and Molly knew exactly what I was asking. One moment we were talking about Giles, and the next we were talking about Charlie; we four were inseparably bound together. It seemed that Sylvia and Charlie were getting on simply fine, they decided not to live together for the moment, but in all respects, appearing to be very happy.

My life eventually settled into a kind of equilibrium, my mind and body in America, my heart and soul in England. It was not the happiest position to be in, but I did my best to be content. I needed a distraction and one conveniently came along.

I had to attend the World Economic Forum at Davos with Alan. I have attended dozens of these and similarly high-level meetings. I confess in the early days it was everything I dreamed of. Alan's social skills are not his best attribute, that was my job. In the early days, when we walked together into a room full of world leaders and bankers, they immediately stopped what they were doing, and Alan would become the centre of attention. It wasn't Alan who had caught their attention, it was me, and I loved it. Alan appreciated the advantage I gave him. He was clever enough to keep me by his side as much as possible. I would take notes, keep his documents in order, and generally appear to be indispensable.

The meetings are no longer the same. Many of the leaders and bankers I knew so well have now gone, replaced by an unknown face. My biggest and best ally was of course the President of the United States. Frank became, and still is, a genuine friend. Nothing made the other delegates pay attention quite like entering a room with the President. I had met the current President, but I could not imagine the same rapport would develop.

The prospect of the current Forum was a welcome distraction. Alan gave me a list of the delegates, highlighting those he particularly wanted to talk to. He went over some of the specific issues he wanted to discuss. This was what our marriage was all about; in this context, at least, we were a good team. We flew by private jet and arrived at our hotel in Davos the afternoon before the Forum was due to start.

The informal social meetings before these events are especially important; this is when a lot of the groundwork is done. It's also an opportunity for influential people who are not delegates to be a part of the process. I asked Alan once how they decide who is influential enough to be there. He said if they are there, they're influential enough. This was how Alan first met Alexei, at one of these meetings. For some strange reason, as we went into one of the hotel reception rooms that evening I wondered if we would see Alexei again. We did!

I saw him across the room and he caught my eye. His face lit up when he saw me, and he immediately came over to us.

"Joanna, my darling, a friendly face at last! And Alan, how good to see you both again."

He threw his arms around me, and then shook Alan's hand with great enthusiasm. Alan was a little taken aback by the warmth of Alexei's greeting.

"How are your friends, Joanna? How's Charlie?

I was momentarily reduced to silence; just the mention of Charlie's name in front of Alan sent my heart racing.

"They're all fine, I think, but I'm not with them now. I'm back in Washington."

"How do you know Joanna's friends?" asked Alan, "and who's Charlie?"

My heart sank to new depths. Alexei was oblivious to my consternation.

"I told you Alan, I met up with my friend Sylvia in the UK. Charlie and the others were her friends. We met Alexei on that trip to the South of France I told you about."

Alan takes little interest in the things I do, so I hoped this would continue to be the case. Fortunately, an important delegate from South America was keen to talk to him; Alan excused himself for a moment. While he was gone, I immediately mentioned to Alexei that it might be best if he didn't mention my friends again.

"Silly girl, Joanna," Alexei said, "why didn't you tell me before? I understand."

"No, you don't understand, Alexei. It's nothing like that; it's just complicated."

"My darling, everything about you is complicated. Do you think I didn't notice that look between you and Charlie? He's a lucky man, I liked him."

"Honestly, Alexei, it's not what you're thinking. This is *so* complicated, even for me."

"Whatever it is, for you, Joanna, I've already forgotten all about it!"

Alexei's a sweetheart. If I were ever in trouble, whatever it was, wherever I was, I know I could rely upon him to be my knight in shining armour. Alan returned, and my thoughts returned to the here and now. Alexei and Alan talked about oil prices, currency rates, and areas of dangerous indebtedness. Alexei wanted any information that might affect his oil and gas interests. Alan is always extremely careful about privileged information. Sometimes with people like Alexei, privileged information can work both ways; the two of them spoke quietly away from the crowd.

I mingled with some old friends and was introduced to the German Chancellor; we hadn't met before. According to Alan, the evening was a great success. I was never sure what constituted a success with those things, but this had been one. The actual meeting that started the next day went very well. I did my usual networking on Alan's behalf, happening to mention the correct topics into the correct ears. I also made sure various delegates did not stray too far before Alan had approached them. The public statement at the end of it all made it sound like an exercise in underachievement, but Alan assured me it was successful. The whole trip was just what I needed, taking my mind off everything else.

In the jet on the way home, Alan thanked me for my contribution. He was always appreciative of my efforts on his behalf. I thought he had forgotten about it but he mentioned Alexei's comment again; he had obviously been brooding on it. He asked me about the South of France trip, and how did it come about. I felt very awkward. During our marriage, I had never lied about anything. I might have been 'economical with the truth' but hadn't lied. After all, there was nothing to lie about before, Charlie was my only indiscretion.

I tried hard not to, but I had to make up a story, a reason for us all going there. The obvious one was that they were going anyway and asked me to join them. Oh, what a tangled web we weave, the very second you contrive to deceive! It was very unlikely Alan would notice that I had paid for most of the Monte Carlo trip, despite it being a lot of money. Bankers never look at their own bank statements. He then asked again who Charlie was? I said he was Sylvia's partner; it all sounded plausible because it was true. It was going to be impossible to keep it secret about Charlie and Sylvia's involvement in Molly and Giles' business. Joe had already mentioned the mystery investor to his Dad. I hated the subterfuge, so I said these were the same people who were investing in the business.

I should have known Alan would not just accept that at

face value, insisting he check into 'these people'. I said he would have to get the details from Molly. As I said it, I could feel my world closing in on me. I felt as if every word I said was being scrutinised. It wasn't, but that's what guilt does to you. As soon as we returned home, I sent Molly an email to warn her. There's a 5-hour time difference with the UK, so she telephoned me the next morning, when I apologised for including her in my ghastly game of guilty secrets.

"It's not your fault, Mom. I agreed to keep Charlie out of it. I'll play along. Don't worry, I do understand, really."

"I'm not sure anyone can understand the awful position I have created for myself. I hate it Moll, I'm not sure if I can keep doing it."

"We agreed it's best for Dad. If it ever became public knowledge, it would be awful for his position. I do understand how you must feel, and don't forget I'm in love with a married man as well."

"I didn't like to ask you Moll, but why hasn't Giles left his wife, like he said he would?"

"We talk about it, but that doesn't make it any easier. I have met her now, it was awful, but it couldn't be avoided. I had to make up stories and play the role of the secret other woman. I don't want to be that woman, Mom."

"What's she like?"

"She's a charming lady, very timid and reserved. She's not a strong self-sufficient woman, quite the opposite. Little Jimmy is her world, and there seems to be no place in it for Giles. But I can see why he is reluctant to tell her. They don't get on together, but she won't cope well with it."

"What about his little boy, have you met him?"

"Yes, I met them both together. You know me, Mom, I'm not a kiddie person; maybe it's just that he's Giles' son, but I thought he was adorable."

"If this all works out for you, that might be just as well."

"I know. We have talked about that; it's all so complicated."

"You're not having second thoughts, are you?"

"No, Mom! He's all I think about, night and day. Do you remember when you described how you and Charlie felt together, and I said I hoped I would find that same thing one day. Well, I have, Mom! We are you and Charlie all over again!"

I didn't say anything for a while, I just couldn't. Eventually Molly realised what she had said and tried to make light of it.

"You see, Mom, I really *do* understand. Not only would your shoes fit me, but I also feel as if I'm wearing them."

"That's a lovely thing to say. I'm going to go now, and that's a lovely thought to end on."

"I'll ring you tomorrow."

"Bye, Moll."

"Bye, Mom."

The next few weeks were uneventful for me, but not so for Molly. Giles and his team seemed to be getting closer to the breakthrough they were searching for. Molly met Giles' wife and son again. It was becoming an increasingly strange situation; every conversation we had rang alarm bells for me.

I decided I had to do something and made the decision to ring Charlie. I did not take that decision lightly. We hadn't discussed it at all, but I think we both felt it was probably better if we didn't telephone one another. He was surprised to hear from me, but immediately I sensed a warmth in his voice.

"JoJo, what a nice surprise!"

Charlie's the only person who has ever called me JoJo, it was something particularly special between us.

"Hello Charlie, how are you?"

"You're ringing about Molly and Giles, aren't you?"

"You know me too well, Charlie, you're right, I am."

"You don't need to tell me anything, do you want me to talk to Giles?"

"Do you really know everything I think, Charlie?"

"Yes, pretty much."

"How are you Charlie, really?"

"I'm good, Sylvia's good. I know what you're asking, I think it might work out. We have effectively been married for years. I just didn't realise it! What about you, are you happy, JoJo?"

"Oh yes, I'm back where I belong. You know me, Charlie; I need those bright lights."

"Let me ask you again. Are you happy?"

"When someone like us asks the other if they are happy, what they are really asking, is are you happy without me. I am not sure I can be truly happy without you, Charlie, but this is how it is and I'm doing the best I can. You didn't think I would admit that did you?"

"No I didn't, you've caught me out this time. I think you crossed a line there."

"You crossed it first Charlie, when you called me JoJo."

There was an awkward silence between us. I had no idea why I allowed myself to cross that line, I suspected Charlie felt the same.

"Tell me about Audrey's house. How's that going?"

"You've changed the subject, but yes, that's going really well. We've obtained all our planning permissions and it's actually going to happen."

"Will you all live there? Will you live there with Sylvia?"

"That's the plan; everyone is really excited about it."

"I'm not surprised, Charlie. It's a really exciting idea; you're all so lucky."

"Anyway, getting back to Giles, I know what your concern is. Leave this to me. It's a difficult one to deal with, but I'm not having our girl doing what we did."

"That's my fear, Charlie, they're so like you and me, but this time I want a happy ending."

"Leave it to me, Mrs Wright."

"Thank you, Mr Bartlett. Let me know what happens."

"Bye, Joanna."

"Bye, Charlie."

I put the phone down and burst into tears. I would have

given anything to know if Charlie was doing the same. Life can be so unkind, even when you are where you have chosen to be. I would do anything to protect Molly from the way I felt at that moment.

Chapter Eighteen
THE BRINGER OF HOPE

Alan did get Charlie and Sylvia's particulars from Molly, obviously determined to check up on them. He was only being a caring father, of course, but anything to do with Charlie made me nervous. I didn't like to ask what he found; I didn't want to appear concerned. A week went by and I could wait no more, so I asked him.

"Did you ever do a financial assessment on Molly's investors?"

"Yes, I had them checked out; a clean bill of health, I'm pleased to say. It seems they are exactly who they say they are. He was Bartlett Homes, a publicly listed company, in fact they are one of the largest house builders in the UK; he is still the largest shareholder. The woman was company secretary as well as finance director, they are both consultants now. She is also another large shareholder; between them they own 27% of the company. I suppose you knew that."

"Well, I knew he was Bartlett Homes, and Sylvia's an old friend."

"Where did you know her from?"

"I knew Sylvia when I lived in the UK."

Alan seemed content and I was pleased to end the conversation. The other matter about the cost of the Monte Carlo trip was never mentioned. I was still consumed with guilt, but my load was just that little bit lighter. Alan and I settled back into our well-worn rut. I knew from my emails and conversations with Molly that things with Giles had not changed, Charlie had obviously not found the right moment to talk to him.

Audrey kept me up to date with the house conversion; they were close to starting the work. We agreed Charlie would be in his element. Just as I was feeling I could wait no longer to hear from him I had an email from Charlie. He had found the right occasion and had a lengthy conversation with them both. He was hoping it might have the right effect. That was all it said. I was desperate to know more, but it was clear that Charlie preferred not to go into detail.

Within an hour of receiving Charlie's email my phone rang; it was Molly.

"Hi, Mom, you'll never guess what Charlie's just done."

"Actually, I think I can; tell me what happened."

"We went out for a meal together, and he's really given Giles a lecture. I couldn't believe it."

"Is it okay; he's not upset you, has he?"

"Of course not, he's Charlie, he's my father. *You* know what he's like; and now Giles does too!"

"Well, what did he say?"

"We got onto the inevitable subject of our future and Giles' wife, and Charlie was amazing. He said, 'Let me tell you a story Giles, and you tell me if you can identify with it.' Then he told Giles your story, Mom, how you met, and how much you two were in love, and how eventually he lost you. He said, 'Annie wasn't happy with me, but my fear was that she would be even more unhappy without me. The same applied to my girls. I couldn't bear the prospect of destroying their lives, but I got that completely wrong. I didn't just sacrifice my happiness, I sacrificed theirs as well. I didn't give Annie the chance of a new life, nor my girls the chance of a happy family. It was the worst decision of my life. I have never stopped paying for it'."

"What did Giles say, when he heard that?"

"He said he felt exactly as Charlie had, that it could destroy his wife. Then Charlie said, 'I'm sorry Giles, but I have to tell you this. You just do not realise the gamble you are taking. You haven't the faintest idea what a lifetime of heartache feels like. It's a pain that eats into your soul, it just closes in on you and never sets you free. What your wife will suffer will be short-term; she'll soon recover. If you aren't careful, you will lose this beautiful daughter of mine, and trust me, you'll never have known pain like it, and it will never go away.' Giles just looked at me with tears in his eyes. I don't think he had ever realised that he could lose me."

"Charlie said that?"

"He did, I couldn't believe it."

"Charlie's right, you know, about that pain. I never want you to experience that, Moll."

"Well, when Charlie left, we talked some more about it. Giles really respects everything that Charlie says, the prospect of us breaking up really did upset him. He said Charlie had made him sure that he wants to spend the rest of his life with me, he's going to tell Andrea."

"Oh, sweetheart, that's wonderful. I feel so sorry for Giles' wife, but Charlie's right, she will eventually start a new life. She might even thank Giles in the end."

"I hope you're right, Mom, but that's not all. I promised not to say anything just yet, but I have got to tell you! Can you guess what Giles said next?"

"No, tell me."

"He said, 'You know what Charlie's made me say, don't you: I want to spend the rest of my life with you. I don't have a ring or anything; I didn't plan this but Molly, as soon as I'm divorced, will you marry me?' Oh Mom, he's asked me to marry him!"

"Oh, my goodness, what did you say?"

"You know what I said! I said 'yes'."

"That's wonderful. Oh, I'm so pleased for you!"

With that I burst into tears, and Molly did the same. We sobbed and laughed in unison. It was one of happiest moments of my life. Giles was true to his word; the very next day he told his poor wife. I can only imagine the terrible hurt and anguish they both must have felt. I'm sure Charlie's advice was of little consolation to either of them that day. I so much wish I had been there to hug them both.

The next day, Molly phoned me again to say that she had told Charlie everything, albeit against Giles' wishes. Giles wanted to do things properly. He wanted to introduce Molly to his parents, he wanted an engagement ring, and then he wanted a proper announcement. Molly was so excited. She said she simply *had* to tell Charlie, and she *had* to tell me, and would I tell her Dad, Joe, and Mike?

As soon as Charlie heard the news, he apparently rushed to drive over to them, going straight into their research facility, finding Giles, and hugging him in front of two of their team! He congratulated Giles and then when Molly threw herself into his arms, it was obvious what was going on. The two researchers clapped, and Giles almost died of embarrassment! I love that about Charlie.

Then as we talked, I suddenly realised what Charlie had done. I told Molly another two people now assumed Charlie was her father. Molly hadn't thought about that, and I'm sure Charlie hadn't either.

"Oh, my God! You're right, Mom! What can we do?"

"I've got to tell your Dad. I can't go on like this."

"But Mom, he's the President of the World Bank. If it got out, it would be terrible."

"It would be even worse if he finds out some other way."

"Don't do anything yet, Mom, let me think about it, okay?"

"I've got to go Moll. I've got another call."

"I'll speak to you soon. Bye, Mom."

"Bye, Moll."

My other call was Audrey.

"Isn't it wonderful, Joanna, Molly's getting married!"

"It's supposed to be a secret, Audrey. How do you know?"

"Charlie, of course."

I told her about Charlie's little mistake, and Audrey understood my dilemma immediately. She felt the same as Molly; we had to consider Alan's career and position.

"That's easy for you to say, Audrey! Can you imagine what it's like living with a secret like this? It's really terrible."

"You're right, I can't imagine. I wish I could do something."

"You have, Audrey, you're there for me. There is one thing you *could* do; tell Charlie what he's done but tell him I've already forgiven him!"

"Is there anything you wouldn't forgive him for?"

"No, nothing."

Audrey and I talked some more about Belmont; I could really feel the excitement in her voice. Reluctantly I said I had to go; I needed to tell my sons the news. I phoned Joe, and Mike, who were really delighted, both asking when they would be meeting Giles. When Alan came home that evening, I told him the wonderful news about Molly and Giles. He was a little taken aback, which was my fault, as I had not fully explained how close they were, and obviously Molly hadn't either.

He wasn't too happy that Molly was going to marry someone he hadn't even met. I perfectly understood that, so I suggested that the pair of them should fly over to Washington for the weekend. Alan liked the idea, then said it was not possible that weekend, as we had guests coming for the day. Then he changed his mind, saying if they *could* make it at such short notice, they should come anyway. I sent Molly a text immediately. I did not have to mention anything about Charlie, she understood. It was a nice idea; I wanted Alan and the boys to meet Giles.

I asked Alan to remind me who our weekend guest was,

and he said it was the President, and the former First Lady. It was yet another graphic reminder that my mind was elsewhere. How on earth could I forget that the President was coming for the day. I have known them since before he was elected; his position has never affected our friendship. Molly and their daughter Lucy are great friends.

Molly came back to me, saying she would love to bring Giles. He would have to be dragged away from work, but he would be there. He would know what to say, and perhaps more importantly, what not to say! I quickly got in touch with Joe, and Mike; if they could both come, it would be the perfect weekend.

I love last-minute plans like that. I asked Sofia and Mrs Garcia to get things ready. They couldn't wait to see Molly and Giles; they were so excited. Normally I would be looking forward to the President and his wife coming, it is always great fun mixing them with other company. This would be that rare occasion when they wouldn't actually be the principle guests.

-o0o-

The weekend arrived in next to no time, and I have never been looking forward so much to seeing my family. Both Joe and Mike could come, but Mike's wife Patricia couldn't make it; she's a paediatrician and was on call. We were all at the Ronald Reagan Washington National Airport waiting for Molly and Giles to arrive. It was silly really. I was in tears even before they appeared; I always am.

"I thought this was a happy occasion," Alan said.

"It's not for us to understand these things, Dad," Joe replied.

When they appeared at arrivals, it was as if Molly had been away for years. We all hugged and kissed; poor Giles was overwhelmed. Alan greeted him warmly, the boys both hugged him. He could not have received a warmer welcome. When we finally made our way back to the house, Sofia was as pleased to see Molly as the rest of us, and Mrs Garcia hugged Molly with a handkerchief clutched in her hand. I felt Giles was a little flustered by it all, not being at his best in a crowd of strangers. I changed my mind about telling him the President was coming for lunch the next day, feeling he was already sufficiently overwhelmed. It was a lovely family day. Baby Carrie tried to steal our attention, but Molly and Giles remained centre stage. I knew Giles' work was important, but I'm not sure I had yet realised quite how important.

"If you crack this problem, Giles, do you realise you will be in line for a Nobel Prize?" Alan said.

"Never thought of that, but don't forget there are hundreds of people researching this field. So far, the industry is approaching AI one step at a time, and each step requires more processing power. There are only a few of us trying a radically new approach."

"When you crack the problem, Giles," Joe said, "what will be the major impact of AI?"

Molly answered for him. "Everything will be different; Dad, your job will change beyond recognition, and as for your job, Mike, I'm not even sure we'll *need* lawyers."

"Oh, thanks, that's encouraging!" said Mike.

Alan was extremely interested. The world of finance was already run by computer algorithms, and he understood only too well the effect AI would have.

"How close do you think you are, Giles?" he asked.

"Honestly? I think we are awfully close, but that must remain within these walls."

"Will you do me an enormous favour, Giles, as your future father-in-law? Will you give me the heads-up if or when it happens. This could have an immediate effect on world finance. The World Bank will need to be ready."

I overheard Giles whisper into Molly's ear, "What should I call your Dad, is he Mr Wright or Sir?"

"Alan, he's just Alan."

"If I were you, Alan, I would prepare now. Molly knows more about the effects it will have than I do. I just work on the basic science."

Giles seemed to blossom; so often he finds himself on a different level to most people, but my family seemed to be asking the right questions.

"You're quiet, Mom," said Joe.

"Oh, this is all above my head. I just like looking at his handsome face!"

Everyone laughed. I had been doing very well until Alan said the words father-in-law. Any little thing which brought the matter to my mind made my heart jump. When I looked at our family gathering, I wondered how on earth could I tell Alan?

We had a lovely afternoon and evening. Giles looked relaxed, I felt he was already a part of the family. The next day, Sofia and Mrs Garcia prepared for our lunch. Giles was aware that there was another guest, but no one told him who it was. We probably should have done, but we all wanted to see the surprise on both their faces.

When it was time, the cars arrived, and the security people came into the house. We were completely used to it, and they were used to us, so the whole thing was done with the utmost discretion. The President's senior protection officer is Tom. He has been in the position since day one and we know him well. It is against protocol but Tom's a good friend. Giles looked on in amazement, but Molly knew immediately what was going on. She didn't say anything, just smiled at me. We do not greet the President outside; the procedure is that he leaves his car and comes into the house directly, which reduces his exposure time to the minimum. Finally, he and the former First Lady walked into our large reception room. I was the first to greet him.

"Frank, how are you," I said, "and Olivia, wait until you hear our news!"

"You know I always feel better for seeing you, Joanna," the President said, "and what's this, the entire family! I know you're not here to see me. What's the occasion?"

He greeted everyone and had an especially big hug for Molly. Frank has always had enormous charm. He held Molly in his arms when she was only months old, now he just stood looking at her.

"Molly, I swear you're more beautiful today than ever."

"Frank, you say that every time I see you."

"That's because it's absolutely true, and who is this young man?"

"Mr President, I would like to introduce you to my fiancé, Dr Giles Simpson."

"Your fiancé! Do you mean you're marrying this young man?"

"That's exactly what I mean."

"Giles let me shake you by the hand, sir. It's not every day I get to shake the hand of the luckiest man in the world."

Giles was almost speechless. "It's a great honour, Mr President."

"The honour is entirely mine, my boy, I can assure you. I have watched this young lady blossom over the years, and I've often wondered what calibre of man might one day prove himself worthy of her. I'm assuming, my boy, that you *are* someone pretty special!"

Giles did not know what to say, but Molly did.

"Giles has changed my life, Frank, and when I say he might also change *your* life, I'm not kidding!"

"That's a relief, I would hate to think he was just lucky! Mind you, I too have been lucky in love. Let me introduce you, Giles, to my lovely wife."

In next to no time, it was as if Frank and Olivia were a part of the family, which is how Alan and I regard them. Giles had to explain the nature of his research yet again, and Frank was seriously interested.

"What's this going to do to our military capability?" the President asked.

"It's only going to be limited by your imagination," Molly replied.

The President looked thoughtful. "When Oppenheimer realised what he had created in the atomic bomb, he said something pretty profound. He said, 'Now I am become death, the destroyer of worlds.' What are you going to say, Giles?"

"Mr President, I'm a scientist. It's not my job to philosophise, but I would sooner be the bringer of hope."

There was a long period of silence, the seriousness of the conversation having struck everyone. Baby Carrie awoke at a very opportune moment, and normal family conversation resumed. We had a wonderful lunch together, Mrs Garcia excelling as always. The President has a long line of banter with Mrs Garcia which goes back at least twenty years. He offers her a job on his staff, she refuses, he says he can't manage without her. That day was no exception, except of course Giles didn't understand.

"Mrs Garcia, your talents are wasted here! Why don't I have my driver take you home with us?"

"Mr President, I've told you a hundred times, you just can't afford me," Mrs Garcia said, barely suppressing her irresistible smile.

Giles looked at Molly and she just laughed. It was all a part of the most wonderful day. I don't think Giles could have been made any more welcome, we all came together as a family, and Charlie was not mentioned once. Unfortunately, Molly and Giles were booked on the late flight, so there was no option; they had to break up the party. None of us wanted the day to end, and finally it was all a rush for us to leave for the airport, but Frank and Olivia completely understood.

As we were saying our goodbyes to them, Frank said, "Have you two given thought yet about where you're getting married? I know it causes a bit of a fuss if I'm there, but I'll be there anyway, so just be sure we get good seats. And Giles, I still carry a bit of weight around here. If you ever need anything that I might be able to provide, you know where I am."

I so wanted that weekend to be a success, and it had been perfect. Mike had to shoot off but the rest of us went to the airport, bringing an end to a wonderful couple of days. When we had seen them off, Joe, Maria, and Carrie went their own way; Alan and I went home alone.

"What did you think of him?"

"He's a very impressive young man. I like him."

"You approve, then."

"I certainly do. Frank was impressed as well."

Chapter Nineteen
THE RED DRESS

Molly phoned me the next day, just to let me know they were safely back. She said Giles had not stopped talking about it, that he had no idea he was marrying into Washington royalty. We laughed. She said Giles had taken on board very seriously the President's comments about the military implications. Her next hurdle was to meet Giles' parents.

"Where do they live?"

"Near Bristol; it's quite a drive from here."

"How funny. I used to live in Bath, that's not far from Bristol, and Charlie came from Bristol. What a small world."

"Now that Giles has met my family, he's keen for me to meet his. We might even do it next weekend."

"I'm sure you'll get along fine. Keep in touch, Moll."

"Bye, Mom."

"Bye, Moll."

My week was uneventful. Alan and I had a few words over something trivial, which was normal. I had a nice lunch with Anita, the wife of the chairman of the Federal Reserve. I needed to keep busy; by myself, I would inevitably end up thinking about Charlie, so tried not to do that. I couldn't wait to hear how the meeting with Giles' parents went, and found I was counting the days. Finally, I received a brief text on Sunday, saying that the meeting had gone well, and Molly would ring me the next day. I just sat by my phone waiting to hear from her and the second it rang, I answered it.

"How did it go?"

"They're lovely, Mom. We got on really well. I met Giles' sister Abigail, she's great. Are you sitting down, Mom?"

"Yes, why?"

"You're not going to believe what happened."

"For goodness sake, just tell me, Moll; is it something bad?"

"No, it's amazing! I'll start at the beginning."

Molly told me about the discussion she and Giles had about wedding venues. Giles was determined he did not want to get married in a church, saying he was neither religious nor a hypocrite. He was adamant; he wanted a simple registry office. If the President were coming that might be a problem, so Giles' mother Margaret suggested they could get married in a hotel which could offer everything. So far so good, but then the bombshell.

"Are you ready, Mom? Margaret said they knew a local hotel that specialises in weddings, a fabulous place, but guess what it's called?"

"Well, I don't know; tell me."

"It's the Poppies Hotel, Mom! She actually said we should think about getting married in the Poppies Hotel!"

I was reduced to complete silence; I did not even know the hotel was still there. I had no great belief in fate, or anything like it, but everything about Molly and Giles felt as though Charlie and I had been given a second chance. So much of their relationship was a mirror image of ours, except it was all working out for the better; and now this. Of all the hotels in the UK, Giles' mother recommends the Poppies; it just left me speechless!

"I don't know what to say, Moll. You know what that place means to me and to Charlie. This is amazing. You don't have to, of course; it's up to you and Giles."

"But Mom, don't you see, it's perfect. I know Poppies holds a special place in your heart; it's where you and my father started your love affair. What better place could there possibly be for me to get married?"

"When you put it like that, actually, you're right. That place holds all the dreams that we never fulfilled; it's perfect that you two should complete those dreams for us. It is a very special place to us, Moll, and will become special for you too. My only worry is the effect it might have on me, and on Charlie."

"Oh, I'm sorry Mom; I was only thinking of us."

"That's how it should be, don't worry about us. You have months before Giles' divorce comes through; just think it over. Talk to Charlie about it."

"I intend to, I'll see what he says. I've got to go, Mom."

"Bye, Moll."

"Bye, Mom."

Not unexpectedly, I could think of nothing else for weeks. I wanted to talk to Charlie about it, but somehow that didn't quite feel appropriate. Molly kept saying their minds were not made up, so I just left it at that. Audrey phoned me several times, as well as emailing. Her house conversion was underway, Charlie and Sylvia were fully involved, and by all accounts they were enjoying every second. A lovely piece of news was that Bill and Charlotte were now considered to be a couple. I was so pleased and sent Bill an email congratulating them. He sent back saying it was all because of me; he saw the opportunity and grabbed it with both hands. I wrote back saying I hoped Charlotte didn't take offence at being grabbed like that, and he came back to me saying he'd had no complaints so far! It was wonderful news.

I asked Audrey about Charlie, as I always do, and it seemed that he and Sylvia were happy together. I wished I could have said the same for Alan and me. We seemed to be finding fault with each other almost every other day.

Giles' wife Andrea apparently took the news of their

divorce very badly indeed. I was not surprised. I didn't know the woman but I instinctively felt for her. I tried to discuss it with Alan, but he just turned it around against me. We ended up talking about the hypothetical situation of us divorcing. He said it was impossible for us to divorce while he was Bank President. I replied saying that I didn't know we were even thinking about it, but maybe he had?

Molly was excited, Audrey was excited, everyone was excited, except for me. I felt very much as if I was on the wrong side of the ocean. This immediately changed when Giles finally managed to divorce his wife. Suddenly, the planning became serious. They visited the Poppies Hotel together, and they loved it. Molly phoned to ask my permission to go ahead. I told her not to be so silly, it was their decision alone. I had to admit my first preference would have been a high society wedding in Washington, but the more I thought about the Poppies, the more it seemed like a wonderful idea.

Molly asked me about wedding dresses; it's every mother's dream to discuss wedding dresses with your daughter. I needed to be with Molly to help her look at them and try them on. I decided as I hadn't seen them for several months, I would fly over to England.

Giles was now living with Molly in her little house. She had a spare room and tried to insist I stay with them. However, I would have felt in the way, so I accepted Audrey's offer of staying with her and Harry. All the arrangements were made at the last moment, perhaps it was just as well, it left me with no time to worry about anything.

When I arrived at Heathrow the following week, I was so excited, expecting Molly to be there to greet me. When I turned the corner at arrivals I was confronted by the usual sea of humanity, all waiting for friends, colleagues, or family.

Despite the hundreds of faces, I immediately picked out Molly, but not just Molly. Everyone was there to greet me! I immediately made a fool of myself by bursting into tears. I felt as if I had come home. We stood there huddled together like a colony of Emperor penguins sheltering from a storm.

It was such a joy to be with them all. Charlie grabbed my cases and we made our way to the short stay car park. Giles found his car immediately, but Charlie and Harry provided us with endless amusement as they searched the vast car park with no success.

"Which zone was it, Harry?" Audrey asked.

"Well, that's the problem. I didn't make a note of it."

"I remember we parked close to the fence," Charlie said.

"But there's miles of fence, Charlie," I replied.

"I blame it on Harry, he's our navigator."

"I just followed you, Charlie."

Giles drove around looking for the cars, and returned to say he had found them, not far away, in the middle of the car park. Obviously, they were *not* close to a fence, so Charlie was on the receiving end of some terrible ribbing. All the way back to the Village, Audrey and I didn't allow him to forget it. I am sure Bill and Charlotte in the other car made quite sure Harry's part in the fiasco wasn't forgotten either. All of this did cause us some delay, but when we finally arrived, there was just time for me to go to Audrey's, unpack, change, and have dinner with them in the Village restaurant. We sat in the bar in the usual chairs.

Charlie said, "What will you all have? Stanley's buying."

Alan greeted me warmly, as he placed the empty glass in front of the empty chair. Charlie had a conversation with his whisky, then he looked up and smiled at me. Nothing had changed. He reminded us all that the work on Belmont was progressing well; there wouldn't be many more evenings like this here in the Village. They looked at each other with a momentary sadness, soon to be replaced by broad smiles.

I was just so pleased to be a part of it once more. It was wonderful to see Molly and Giles looking so happy together; Bill and Charlotte held hands and smiled at each other. Giles had lost a lot of his reserve. When he hugged and kissed me at the airport, I could tell he really meant it. Charlie on the other hand had been practising his reserve.

We had a wonderful evening together, and all the talk was about the wedding. They had made up their minds about the venue; it was indeed to be the Poppies Hotel, but they hadn't yet mentioned our distinguished guest. I had mixed feelings about Poppies. In so many ways it was perfect, but it was quite a small hotel, so the guest list would have to be very carefully managed. When I mentioned this, Giles said that was the best part about it; he really didn't want a big wedding. I mentioned some of the people who we would ideally want to ask, which amounted to a list of the great and good of the Washington establishment.

Molly had the final word, saying it was all about them and she agreed with Giles; it had to be the Poppies. Charlie was a little apprehensive, as I was, and I was not sure Sylvia was entirely happy. As the evening progressed and we discussed it, I think any doubts disappeared and Poppies started to sound ever more appropriate.

The first thing was to set a date. The owner of the hotel had personally given them a short list of possible dates to choose from. Three of them were quite distant, but one was a cancellation, in two months' time. We all looked at each other. Surely two months was too soon? It amounted to just nine weeks. But Molly made the decision; nine weeks it was.

The next morning, Molly and I had planned to go and look at wedding dresses together, but I had a surprise up my sleeve. I had been in touch with Antony, Emma-Jane's personal style guru, or as he likes to say, fashionista. One mention of a wedding dress for my daughter and Antony's exuberance entered the stratosphere. I obviously said we would meet him in London, but he would have none of it, insisting he would drive all the way to us first. I would admit as soon as I finished my conversation with Antony I was filled with excitement. He just had such enthusiasm; it was impossible not to become embroiled in it. Plus I really liked him, he was such a character, I couldn't wait to see him.

As soon as Antony arrived, his greeting for me was somewhere north of enthusiastic, possibly just south of excessive! He is truly one of a kind, and positively wonderful. He was dressed even more flamboyantly than at our previous meeting. I had already explained everything to Antony, suggesting he try not to be too overpowering when Molly arrived.

When she first caught sight of him, I could see she was taken aback. I very quickly explained, but nothing can prepare you for Antony. I just had time to say, "Trust me, Moll."

"Molly, my *darling*! Your mother told me you were beautiful; she said it would take an incredibly special dress to make your day complete. Oh my goodness! She's *right*; I am speechless and I'm *never* speechless, am I, Joanna! My darling, you are exquisite; let me look at you."

Antony walked around Molly, his silk scarf trailing in the air behind him. I suggested to Molly that she should brace herself. He pushed, prodded, and stroked. Poor Molly, standing there in the middle of the Village reception, looking absolutely mortified.

"You are *divine*, darling. A heavenly body sent here for me to dress. The angels will *weep!*"

Molly looked at me. "Trust him, Moll. When you see what he can do, it won't be the angels who'll weep!"

We left in Antony's car, and he drove all the way back to London. We went into a specialist shop in a road just off Bond Street where the assistants swarmed over us.

Molly tried on one wedding dress after another, but nothing was good enough for Antony. He dismissed every dress out of hand.

"Seriously, darling. You are *so* fabulous, you put the dresses to shame. We need something different. I need to excel. When I find the right dress darling, we will all know *instantly,* trust me."

With that he threw his scarf around his neck, adjusted his orange beret, and marched out of the store, his floral silk culottes flapping in the breeze. We followed like sheep as he hailed a taxi and we next pulled up at the same fabulous boutique where we had been before. The same lovely staff gathered round us immediately; Antony always seems to have that effect. He walked around the place looking at everything, then came back to us carrying a red gown.

"We're looking for a wedding dress, Antony," I said.

Molly was sceptical but tried it on. It was a stunning gown and she looked positively wonderful in it.

"This is amazing, isn't it," she said, "could I really get married in red?"

"My darling, you could get married in a *track* suit, and you would *still* be the most beautiful woman in the building. I want to raise you to the level of a goddess, and a goddess can wear *whatever* she likes."

It was totally unconventional, obviously it would not be appropriate for a church wedding, but this was a private hotel. To my surprise I loved it, only Antony could suggest such a thing. Molly was at least considering the idea, though Antony was hesitant.

"It's *almost* perfect," he said, "for the unconventional to work it has to be beyond perfection."

There was something that I had not told anyone. I had long held a silly notion that just maybe, one day, when the occasion was right, perhaps Molly might wear my famous Red Dress. I had become so obsessed with the idea, I think it was the prospect of the dress and the Poppies Hotel repeating history together. However ridiculous the idea, I brought it with me from Washington. I hesitated to mention it, but I took Antony to one side and asked him if he had heard of Sally Cummings' famous Red Dress. He instantly went into raptures about it.

"One of the most famous dresses there has *ever* been, the *perfect* creation!"

He looked closely at me, and we stood in silence. He presented an unfathomable expression. That expression gradually changed, his eyes widened, and a look of joy spread over his face.

"Of course, it was *you!* You modelled it, the picture on the front cover of Vogue!"

He clasped his hands to his mouth, as if suppressing a scream.

"What if I told you, Antony, that I have that dress in Audrey's apartment. What would you say?"

"I wouldn't believe you, darling! That would be a *miracle.*"

"Believe it, Antony. It's *my* miracle!"

"Ladies, we're leaving! Get that dress off, Molly, I'll find a cab."

We got the cab back to Antony's car, and all the while he was irrepressible, then driving far too quickly all the way back to Cambridge. Molly asked what on earth was going on; I just said Antony and I had an idea. There was such an air of excitement, despite Molly having no idea what was going on.

We arrived outside Audrey's apartment, and when she greeted us, she was enthusiastically hugged by Antony. I wasted no time in finding the dress. It had always been stored in perfect conditions, carefully wrapped with acid-free conservation tissue paper between all the folds. It looked the same as the day that Sally placed it in that same box. As I lifted it from the box, it shimmered in the light and caught everyone's attention.

Antony gasped aloud. "Let me *see* it! Let me *touch* it!"

He saw Sally's label, and looked at its perfect condition, then went into a complete swoon. He was genuinely overcome with emotion, touching, and stroking it with a mixture of reverence and desire. Molly had heard the story of my red dress at Poppies, and immediately guessed what it was.

"Is this the dress that you told me about, the famous Red Dress?"

"It's only been worn twice, once for the front cover of Vogue, and once for Charlie, at the Poppies Hotel," I said. "It's priceless, Moll; a dress fit for a goddess."

No one said anything, I'm not sure Antony could speak. Molly slipped her clothes off and stepped into it. Antony fussed around her, first one arm and then the next. So far, so good; he stood behind her and fastened the back. We continued to stand in silence. I knew Molly was the same shape and size as I was all those years ago. I so hoped it would fit her, and it did! The dress is timeless, that was Sally's genius; it could have been designed today. The fabric, the cut, the detail; it's truly exquisite.

Antony was so genuinely emotional, for once he wasn't his usual exuberant self. Audrey and I stood in silence, waiting for a comment from Molly. I doubted I was capable of saying anything. Looking at Molly in that dress was like looking at myself, thirty years ago. I found it deeply emotional. Audrey was equally lost for words.

Finally, Molly said, "Oh my God! I have never seen anything like it. Could I really wear a dress like this, it's so revealing?"

Antony finally spoke, "My darling girl, there are but a handful of women who could wear a dress like this, and *none* would be as radiant as you. I've waited all my life for this; I will *never* surpass this moment."

"I need to see it all. We need a larger mirror," Molly said.

"Follow me," Audrey said, "I've got a full-length mirror in my bedroom."

Antony had disturbed his beret with his flailing arms, so he adjusted his dress and then followed us, as we marched into Audrey's bedroom.

"Oh, my goodness!" Molly said, "I know you described it Mom, but you could never do it justice. I can't believe it, just look at it."

"We *are*, my darling," said Antony. "The Gods are looking down, and the angels *are* weeping! What did I tell you?"

Just at that moment Harry appeared, walking in our direction. Audrey was on the job immediately. "That's far enough Harry, turn around and go back where you came from. Come along, off you go."

We all laughed. It was a convenient diversion.

"Well, Moll. Do you like it?" I asked.

"Do I *like* it, Mom! It's the most beautiful dress I have ever seen, and it fits me. If I can make my entrance wearing this dress, just as you did, I can't tell you what that will mean to me."

"This dress is so important to me, Moll. It's been in its box for so long, just like Charlie and me. I've dreamed that, one day, somehow, it would come out again, and this is perfect."

It was a shame to put the dress back in its box, but Antony folded it with such reverence, we all felt that we should say au revoir. When it came time for Antony to leave, we all became quite emotional. He invited himself to the wedding before I could invite him.

"I'll be there for you, darling, on the morning of the day. I'll have my seamstress with me; we will need to make just slight alterations in my pursuit of perfection. Then there is my hairdresser; she will leave you looking divine. Trust me, my darling, you are to become my greatest *ever* creation!"

"Of course, Antony. I couldn't face the day without you," Molly said.

When he was gone, it was like the eye of the storm had moved directly over us. There was a strange calm as we three sat back to reminisce.

"You're right, Mom, Antony's amazing."

Audrey and I told her the story about Sylvia and Antony in the changing room, and him shouting out 'Bras please for Sylvia'. We laughed; what a good day it had been. I stayed for a couple more days, very much enjoying my stay with Audrey and Harry. Molly had so much help with the wedding arrangements; in a way it was reassuring that I was redundant. When Molly left, she looked so happy.

They all took me to see the progress being made on Audrey's house, Belmont. It was already starting to look quite different. Seeing it for myself brought it home to me that they really were going to leave the Village to live there. Audrey confirmed that Charlie and Sylvia were using this as a starting date for them to live together. That evening Audrey and I had a chance to talk together.

"Most couples would give anything to be like Charlie and Sylvia," I said. "They have so much in common. They know each other's minds, and neither of them could exist without the other."

"I have to admit it appears to be working out well for them," Audrey replied. "Are you okay, Joanna? Do you think you'll ever be able to leave Charlie behind?"

"I'll go back to Alan, but Charlie is always there in those dark recesses of my mind. My life will go on, and Charlie and Sylvia will no doubt marry eventually, but it doesn't stop me thinking about him."

"He's never going to be more than a memory, is he, Joanna?"

"No, I accept that, and I'm sure Charlie does as well; it's just the living with it that's difficult."

"All of our lives will change when we move into Belmont. It's a new beginning for us; you *will* visit us, Joanna, won't you? I mean regularly; I really miss you when you're not here."

"I miss you, Audrey, I miss all of you. I often wish I were a part it."

"It couldn't be more different to your life in Washington. I'm not sure you could leave all that behind."

"Maybe you're right."

Chapter Twenty
THE BIG DAY

When I flew back to Washington the next day, everybody gave me the customarily wonderful send-off. I was elated about the dress and Poppies Hotel but leaving them all behind upset me. Once again, Alan wasn't there to greet me; it was my ever-dependable Joe who picked me up. He was full of questions about the wedding plans, and I told him the venue and the dress were sorted but said no more than that.

When Alan came home, he was keen to hear about the arrangements, but asked nothing about me. I began to wonder if he had some suspicions, but nothing was said. Perhaps it was my attitude which had changed. There was certainly a large part of me that was on the other side of the ocean; maybe that was it.

The remaining seven weeks to the wedding went by incredibly quickly. I was in constant touch with everyone. Special arrangements had to be made for the President, which put the hotel into a tizzy. The guest list was also an enormous challenge. Alan had a list of eminent people who would be offended if they were not included. I had a list; everyone had a list! Eventually I passed a proclamation. Molly and Giles would prune the list - after all, it was their wedding.

The joy of the hotel wedding was that all the logistics could be left to them. They had a liaison manager, and when he was told who was coming, it was amazing just how accommodating they were. I was a bit concerned that my family had not met Giles' family, but it seemed there was little to be done about that. My other enormous concern, obviously, was Charlie. It was impossible for him to give his daughter away. He and Molly discussed it many times, and Charlie understood, of course, but I felt so sorry for him. The one thing I could be sure about was that he wouldn't let us down, and neither would anyone else. Nevertheless, I approached the day with enormous concern.

A part of me was so looking forward to it. Another part was dreading the moment when Alan and Charlie would meet. I just could not comprehend the two of them, together in the same room. Maybe I was being offhand, perhaps it was all my fault, but whatever it was, Alan and I seemed to be growing further apart. I determined not to mention anything; my priority had to be the wedding. Those final days went by so quickly.

-oOo-

We all arrived at Heathrow the day before the wedding. We were being driven directly to the Poppies Hotel. My fears were growing with every mile we travelled. It was not just Charlie; it was the Poppies as well. I was about to relive that most precious part of my life, but how could I relive it with Alan! The moment the taxi pulled up outside Poppies, the memories came flooding back; so little had changed! We went inside and it was the same layout as before, the décor had changed; if anything, it was even more impressive.

The heavy old oak door to the lounge bar had been replaced but was in the same position. I vividly remembered that night when John the maître d' escorted me to that door. I asked him to wait a moment, to which he said, 'Of course, Madam. When you're ready.' As I was standing there in the Red Dress, my heart was bursting out of my chest, but I pretended to be calm. He opened the door for me, and I walked into the room, and into Charlie's arms. It was a moment in time I shall never forget.

I walked over to that same door and opened it. I almost expected to see the room already full of people, with one special face smiling at me. The room had changed a little; I wasn't quite sure how, but the feeling was the same. I didn't go in, I thought it best not to. Turning back towards the reception, I saw Tom, the President's PPO smiling at me. Tom had to arrive early to do the usual checks; even a former President receives quite a bit of protection. Frank and Olivia would not arrive until tomorrow morning to attend the wedding and the reception, and then they would be whisked away by helicopter to stay with the American Ambassador at Winfield House, in Regents Park. It seems that even the President couldn't get enough rooms there.

Molly and Giles planned to stay at the hotel on the night of the wedding; it was something Molly wanted to do. They were going away for just a couple of days' honeymoon in the morning. I specifically asked Molly to be quite sure that she and Giles booked the principal suite for themselves. The memories may be more than thirty years old, but I did not want to find myself back in our usual room. We were shown upstairs, and it was all so familiar that the memories came back to me as if it were yesterday.

The last room at the end of the hallway was the principal suite which Charlie and I shared so often; I caught my breath as we were being taken straight towards it. In those days, the hall was half panelled, with a deep-piled heavily patterned red carpet. Now it was lighter and brighter, but to me it felt the same as before. When we stopped short of the principal suite,

I breathed a sigh of relief. It felt as if this old building was toying with me. Alan asked me if I was all right; apparently, I looked a little faint. I said it was just the journey, I did so dislike flying.

Molly had arranged for us to have dinner at the hotel with Giles' parents and sister, so we had plenty of time to make ourselves ready. Alan and I were so used to staying in large impersonal hotels, I think he quite liked the atmosphere of the Poppies. He didn't grumble once as he put his clothes into the wardrobe. It all felt slightly strange, because we had not shared a room for quite some time, we were no longer in the routine of sharing facilities. For his part, Alan was making a special effort to be nice to me, which I appreciated, and made a similar effort in return.

When it was time for us to go downstairs, I had no doubt we would present as the perfect couple. Molly was supposed to be there with Giles's family so she could introduce us. Alan and I walked into the lounge bar expecting to see Molly, only to be met by complete strangers.

"Are you Giles' family?" I asked.

We introduced ourselves. Giles' parents are both academics, and I could see where Giles gets his reserve from. His sister Abigail is the complete opposite, extremely outgoing, and full of fun. It was a little awkward at first. I think they were a bit overawed at meeting the President of the World Bank, not to mention the prospect of meeting the President of the United States. Margaret, Giles' mother, was especially worried about how she should address the former First Lady. I reassured her that Olivia wouldn't mind what she was called, and to just call her Olivia.

"The President's not here officially," I said. "We've known them both for thirty years. They're good friends and are just like anyone else."

Margaret was reassured, while Abigail was really excited about meeting all of us. They obviously adored Molly, and

I said we were more than impressed with their son. Gerald, Giles' father, said he thought they made the perfect couple; on that we were all in agreement. It was just a little awkward at first, but I think we soon realised that as parents of the bride and groom we had a lot in common. Then the liaison manager found us and showed us the room where the ceremony would take place; we even had a little rehearsal. Any doubts I might have had about a hotel wedding were quickly dismissed. Everything was wonderful - Poppies was wonderful.

Molly eventually arrived, full of apologies, she had been held up. At almost the same time Mike and Joe appeared with their wives, and our family was complete. Other guests who were staying the night before the wedding started to appear. I knew Charlie and Sylvia were staying as well and found myself constantly looking over my shoulder in case he was there. I could feel my tension growing.

Inevitably they arrived. I didn't know what to do; suddenly my past had caught up with me. Alan and Charlie were in the same room together! Molly understood my predicament, immediately welcoming Charlie, and Sylvia, and introducing them to everyone. Alan and Charlie shook hands, then Joe and Mike and their wives, and Giles' parents greeted them. Charlie looked far more composed than I was, but I was in no doubt his heart was racing like mine.

"It's nice to meet you, Alan. I've heard a lot about you from Molly," Charlie said.

"Likewise, Charlie. I understand you and Sylvia are putting a lot of money into Giles' business."

"They may not need us," Sylvia said, "but if they do, we'll be pleased to help."

The conversation continued. I thought Alan was probing and that Charlie was defensive. In more rational moments, I tried to convince myself this was merely my guilt affecting me. We ordered our meals and relaxed with a drink, Charlie having his usual, and I had the same. The Poppies whisky selection did not compare to the Village bar, but nevertheless Charlie found the Dalwhinnie. He sat looking at it, as he always does, and was about to make a pronouncement.

"Did you know, Charlie, this whisky is produced in the Highlands. It's the highest distillery in Scotland, I think the altitude is about a thousand feet."

Charlie looked at me in complete amazement. "How do you know that?"

"Oh, it's just something I remembered. I thought it might come in handy one day."

Charlie smiled at me. I could not help smiling back. I felt sure Alan noticed, and once again my guilt was all-consuming. I wondered how long this awful charade could continue before my secret world came tumbling down on me. I tried to avoid conversation, for fear of saying the wrong thing. I glanced around to see a waiter just about to enter the room, but he stopped at the door and turned back as someone else walked in. He was thirty years older, but I instantly recognised John the maître d' from all those years ago! He was superbly dressed; he always was an elegant man. As he came over to us, he gestured to the waiter at the bar with nothing more than a raised finger, and the waiter immediately picked up a tray.

"May I introduce myself, I'm John Palmer. I'm the owner, may I welcome you all to the Poppies Hotel."

I broke out into a cold sweat, knowing he would recognise us. I looked wide-eyed at Charlie, who also appeared to be in shock. John only looked at me for a second before a smile radiated across his face as he took my hand. It was obvious to everyone that he recognised me. My heart sank like a stone; what an absurd way for my terrible secret to come to light. I simply gave up, and just reverted to a nervous politeness.

"I'm Joanna Wright, mother of the bride," I said, "and this is my husband, Alan Wright." John stopped in his tracks. He looked at Charlie, who he also quite obviously recognised, then he looked again at me. I just sat there waiting for my life to change irreparably.

"Of course, Mrs Wright," John said. "I assumed it must be you, the resemblance with your daughter is amazing."

I didn't know whether to laugh or cry; I found myself doing both.

"Are you all right?" asked Alan.

"I'm sorry; it's a big thing being the mother of the bride."

I'm not sure I had convinced anyone. As I wiped my eyes and smudged my mascara all over my face, I just wanted to run away. We always had a wonderful relationship with John. He was so correct in everything he did, and would only ever allow himself to be maître d', and yet we both felt we had an unspoken friendship with him. Here he was, now the owner of the hotel, and still just as wonderful.

"Perhaps, Madam, you would like to freshen up in the powder room? It would be my pleasure to escort you."

"I think that would be a very good idea, thank you, Mr Palmer."

I followed him out of the room, and the moment we were out of sight I said, "Thank you, John, you were marvellous. It's all so complicated, but it's really wonderful to see you again."

"How could I forget you and Charlie? May I call you Joanna?"

"I wish you would."

"Joanna, you're still the most beautiful woman who has ever graced this hotel, and you and Charlie were so perfect together. And now your daughter is getting married here. Forgive my self-indulgence, but this is simply perfect!"

"Oh John, you were always so kind to us." I hugged him for a long moment. "It didn't end well for me and Charlie."

"I know, he came in for a final drink one evening. I've never seen a man so completely broken. You two made such an impression on me, I have never forgotten you. I couldn't imagine either of you without the other."

"It's a long story, John. Maybe we can come back one day; we would both love to talk to you."

Just at that moment, Margaret appeared and saw me standing awfully close with my hand on John's arm. I am sure she thought it strange, but she didn't say anything. We both used the powder room, and I did my best to look reasonable again. We went back to join the others and immediately went in for dinner.

"He's a nice man, isn't he, the owner. Do you know him well?" Margaret asked.

"Oh no, not at all. He's just very personable."

"You looked as if you knew each other, that's all."

I quickly changed the subject, asking Abigail about her plans for the future. As she was talking, I was sure Alan was suspicious about John. I really didn't know how many more of these scares I could endure. Charlie was quiet; I think like me he was beginning to think the evening was a mistake. I hadn't planned for him and Sylvia to be dining with us; it was obviously something that Molly wanted. I knew Alan must have thought it strange that friends of Giles and Molly should be a part of this family gathering. I could see Molly seemed awkward as well, or was I just becoming paranoid?

Giles was driving over that evening and staying at his parents' house. I liked the idea that they were sticking with the old tradition in that regard. Antony had arranged to be at the Poppies first thing in the morning to dress Molly. He was bringing a hairdresser as well as a seamstress with him. He wanted to make some small alterations to the red dress which he deemed essential. I should have been so excited, but I felt all the time that I was walking a tightrope. Above all, I dreaded the prospect of anything going wrong for Molly; this *had* to be her perfect day.

When the evening finally ended, I found myself pleased that I had got through it relatively unscathed. I was looking forward to the opportunity of just closing my eyes. As Alan and I walked up the stairs, I was relieved that the first day was over. I was not used to sharing a bedroom with Alan. At least at home I could close the door on our relationship. It wasn't long before he asked about Charlie and Sylvia.

"Why did we have that couple with us tonight when they're not family?"

"I know, but it's obviously what Molly wanted. They're particularly important to the business."

"It all seems very strange to me, and you seem to know them well."

"Well I do, I've known Sylvia for over thirty years; we have always kept in touch."

Alan seemed to accept that, for the moment at least. I didn't have to pretend to be too tired to discuss it further; I was exhausted. I just had to get through tomorrow, then it would be over.

-o0o-

Tomorrow came all too quickly; I did not sleep well and was awake far too early. We went down for breakfast together and sat at a table for two. We had only been there for a few moments when Antony arrived. I especially asked him to be as soberly dressed as he could manage, but I should have known better. He came into the breakfast dining room looking as flamboyant as ever.

"Good God! What on earth is that?" said Alan.

Antony rushed over to me with enough speed to send his silk scarf streaming out behind him.

"My darling, you can't *imagine* the traffic. The *ordeals* I suffer for my art. Oh my word, you must be Joanna's husband. What a responsibility, to be married to a goddess!"

Alan sat silently, seeming to sink into a catatonic condition. Matters only got worse when, moments later, Molly appeared.

"There she is, my *angel.*"

The pair of them hugged and kissed as Alan sank deeper

into his unfortunate condition. Antony's exuberance knew no bounds. The prospect of the Red Dress had elevated him to a new level.

"Let me introduce you, my darlings, to these two heavenly creatures. This is my beloved Penny, and this is Patricia. This gorgeous girl is the finest seamstress in the world, and I do mean the *entire* world! I couldn't possibly work with anyone else. I feel faint when she's not by my side. This wonderful creature is my gift from heaven. There is Patricia, and then there are the *rest* of the world's hairstylists."

We all said hello to the ladies. "He's quite something, isn't he," Penny said, "but don't worry, you really are in safe hands."

"I never doubted it," I said.

We all had breakfast together and Antony's enthusiasm was contagious. He could not wait to get started, waxing lyrically about dressing Molly. As soon as they all left for Molly's room, Alan slumped back into his chair.

"Are you telling me that man is going to dress our daughter, in her bedroom?"

"That's right."

"How can you be happy with that?"

"Antony only sees women as bodies to dress; it's nothing like you're thinking."

Just at that moment Charlie and Sylvia appeared, and came over to us. I told them about Antony.

"I know, I've just seen him!" said Sylvia. "I've been dressed and undressed by Antony, it's quite an experience."

Everyone laughed, except Alan, who had difficulty coming around to the idea. When I realised the time, I said I had to go and get ready myself. Sylvia agreed; everybody needed to get ready. As we headed back towards our room, John was nearby and took us to one side.

"I don't want you to worry about a single thing; we're very experienced at doing this. I have issued special instructions to all the staff. I intend this to be our finest ever wedding."

"Oh, bless you, John," I said, "it's reassuring to know you have it all in hand."

"The pleasure, Madam, is entirely mine."

As soon as we stepped into our room, Alan said, "How come you're so friendly with the owner?"

"For God's sake, Alan! This is Molly's day."

He was unable to pursue it, because when we were almost ready, I heard the distinctive noise of a helicopter.

"That must be Frank; we must go down to greet them," I said.

We both hurriedly made ready and went downstairs, Alan attempting to fasten his cufflinks as he went. The staff were busy falling over themselves, but I knew this was not what the President wanted. I greeted them in the foyer, followed by Alan.

"Goddamn it, Joanna, you look wonderful. Molly's got a lot to compete with." the President said.

"If only that were true, Frank. How do you put up with him, Olivia?"

"It's not easy, but I guess he's got a certain charm about him."

We hugged and greeted one another; they are such good friends.

"Now, Joanna, who's in charge here?" asked the President. "Apart from you, I mean."

I gestured for John to come over. "Now listen, John," said the President, "this is Molly's day, not mine. I am just another guest here, okay? I do not want any special attention. I want nothing to detract from Molly. Are we understanding one another?"

"Yes, Mr President, loud and clear."

"Good man! I like your place here; get this right and the CIA will make sure you only get good reviews on Trip Advisor from now on."

"We only get good reviews *now*, Mr President!"

We all laughed, and the President put his arm around John. "I believe you. I think I'll be coming back."

I introduced Frank and Olivia to Giles' family, and to Charlie and Sylvia. It was all going extremely well. People began arriving in increasing numbers; some of them were people I didn't know.

Then a group of very friendly faces appeared. It was Audrey, Harry, and Fiona, followed by Bill and Charlotte. I introduced them to Frank and Olivia. Audrey looked amazing; she was an immediate hit with the President.

"I love that accent, Audrey. Are you a member of the British aristocracy?"

"I often get confused about that myself, Mr President," Harry said.

It was wonderfully reassuring to have my friends with me, especially to see them getting along so well. Audrey asked me how it was going; I knew exactly what she was asking. I said I was walking on eggshells but so far, so good. Charlie and Sylvia joined us, and I felt I could deal with anything now.

We joined Giles' family who were deep in conversation with Frank and Olivia. Suddenly, I found I was standing next to Charlie. He was looking at me as only Charlie can.

"You look absolutely beautiful, Joanna. It's going to be quite a day, isn't it?"

"You look pretty gorgeous yourself, Charlie."

I wanted to say so much more, but this was not the time. Just then, Giles arrived, accompanied by his best man, Roger. Giles can give the impression of being quiet and reserved, but he also has a reputation for being a practical joker, especially with Roger. Giles shook hands with the President.

"It's good to see you again, Mr President."

He gave Olivia a hug. "I can't thank you both enough for coming all this way. It's such an honour for us to have you here."

"There's nothing that could keep me away, Giles. You know how I feel about Molly," the President said.

"May I introduce my best man, Mr President? This is Roger Jenkins."

Poor Roger, it was obvious that Giles deliberately hadn't told him about the President.

"I'm impressed, that's very convincing," said Roger, "what will you do next? Do you sing The Star-Spangled Banner?"

Frank has a wonderful sense of humour, and this was too good an opportunity not to play along with. "Well, my boy, if you sing God Save the Queen, we have a deal."

Gerald and Margaret rushed over, looking terribly embarrassed. They obviously knew Roger very well; I had never met him before. Gerald took Roger to one side, while Margaret apologised to the President. Giles could not contain himself any longer. He laughed, and everyone laughed with him, including Frank and Olivia. It took a few moments for it to sink in for Roger, which only added to our amusement.

"Oh, my God. What can I say, Mr President? I feel ridiculous, I've never made such a fool of myself in my entire life!"

"I think there's a good reason for that, my boy. You were ably assisted by Giles here. I thought the best man was supposed to poke fun at the groom."

"I'm never going to live this down, am I?" said Roger.

"I don't think anyone here would allow that to happen," replied the President.

Frank had wanted to be just one of the guests, and here he was laughing and joking with everyone. It was perfect. Gradually all the guests arrived, and the big moment was rapidly approaching.

Chapter Twenty-one
LADY IN RED

Antony appeared at the door, beckoning for me to come. "There's not a problem, is there?" I asked nervously.

"*I'm* in charge, my darling! How could there be a *problem?* My goddess only seeks your approval."

We went upstairs and walked to the end of the hallway, towards the principal suite. I stood motionless for a moment. This was entirely Molly's day, but I was in fear of that part of me which still existed, on the other side of that door. I knocked and entered. Nobody said a word; they had no need to - Molly stood there in the Red Dress. I was completely speechless. During my years in the fashion business, I worked with the most beautiful women in the world, wearing the most beautiful clothes, but nothing could have prepared me for this. I simply burst into tears quite uncontrollably. Molly did the same and we just hugged each other; neither of us could say anything. Even Antony was silent as he put his arms around us both, while we tried to compose ourselves.

"Eventually he asked me, "Does this mean that you approve, Joanna?"

"I do! I can't imagine there has ever been a more beautiful bride."

We both looked at Molly.

"It's this dress. The moment I put it on, it just seemed to take me over. I know what you mean now, Mom. This dress is amazing."

"It's not just the dress, sweetheart; it's you."

Antony suddenly looked at us both in horror and went into a tailspin. "Look at you both, look at your *faces!* Girls, we have two faces to repair, quickly now!"

Antony and his ladies really were as good as he said they were. Between them in no time we were both restored. In my case, they did a far better job than I had done myself that morning. We were awfully close to time, so we hurriedly made our way back downstairs. Everyone was assembled in the wedding room, the registrar was ready, and Alan was waiting for Molly in the adjoining room. Antony and the girls prepared to stand by the door.

"What are you doing out here, Antony?" I said. "All of you, go in and find yourself seats."

Giles and Roger were in their places. I looked to see where Charlie and Sylvia were sitting; I caught his eye and smiled. Quickly I took my own place. No one else other than Audrey knew that Molly would be wearing the Red Dress. I worried in case I should have told Charlie, but it was too late now. It was certainly not a conventional dress for a wedding. I found I was worrying about everything.

The moment arrived. My heart was racing! Molly walked into the room on Alan's arm, as everyone twisted round in their seats to see her. Their favourite piece of music was being played on the sound system, but there was still an audible gasp as she made her entrance. Everyone just looked wide-eyed. My daughter looked absolutely sensational. Antony's words were ringing in my ears. The angels surely *were* weeping! The look on Giles' face was something to behold. It so reminded me of Charlie's expression the last time the dress was worn, in this same building. He could not take his eyes off Molly for a second. Then he stepped forward to take his place next to Molly, and the ceremony began.

I turned around to look at Charlie and saw that he had tears in his eyes. I should have told him about the dress. Everything went like clockwork, and in what felt like no time at all, they were husband and wife. Alan and Gerald attended the signing, while everyone else wanted to talk about Molly. Roger rushed over to me.

"Mrs Wright, can I have a word?"

"No, Roger, you may not. You can have a word with Joanna, though!"

"I'm sorry, I've made such a fool of myself today. I'm frightened of saying the wrong thing."

"Oh, dear boy, just get on with it."

"Well, you see, the thing is, Joanna, they have a piece of music planned for when they leave the wedding room."

"Is there a problem, Roger?"

"No, but Giles didn't expect Molly to be wearing a red dress. No one expected Molly to be wearing a red dress, and well I don't understand these things, but that dress, it's a bit special, isn't it? Well, the thing is, I think we should change the final piece of music. There's still time. I can stream it from my phone."

"They went to a lot of trouble choosing their music. Are you sure that's a good idea?"

"I'm quite sure, Joanna, trust me."

"What is it you want to play?"

"Isn't it obvious? It's got to be 'Lady in Red'."

"Roger, come here, I'm going to kiss you!"

I didn't tell him about the lipstick, he rushed off looking rather silly.

When the moment came for them to leave the room, Roger could not have been more correct. As the music started, Molly and Giles didn't expect to hear 'Lady in Red', so their reaction was genuine surprise. It was simply one of those exquisite moments in life. In fifty years, when they think back on their wedding day, that moment will be the one they will remember. I think the same applied to us all.

I got a little lost in all the congratulations, but all I wanted to do was to see how Charlie was. Eventually I caught sight of him. Sylvia was with a huddle of people on the other side of the room surrounding the newlyweds. I went over to him and held his hand.

"How are you, Charlie?"

"It's all a bit emotional if I'm honest. I just didn't expect the dress."

"I should have told you. I'm sorry."

"It's not just that, I've just watched her get married. You can't imagine how much I want to shout out loud 'Molly's *my* daughter and I adore her'."

"I *can* imagine, Charlie. I do so wish it were different."

I squeezed his hand tightly, and he did the same. At that moment, Sylvia beckoned him over, to kiss the bride. Neither of us said anything, but I knew this would be difficult. Molly's attention was suddenly directed towards Charlie. As they looked at each other, the whole room noticed the expression on both of their faces. As Charlie walked towards her, the guests all stepped back. It was like the parting of the Red Sea. Molly held her arms out and Charlie walked into them. They just stood there, holding each other for ages, neither of them saying a word. I couldn't blame either of them; this was how it should be. But they could not have broadcast it any louder, that theirs was a special relationship. Alan must surely have noticed; indeed, everyone must have noticed. At least I was confident that Alan wouldn't say anything, at least not on that day. I just knew my darkest secret had finally moved out of the shadows, and into the full light of day. Audrey rushed over to me.

"Did Alan see that?" she asked.

"He must have done. This is it, Audrey. It had to come one day."

This was everything that I didn't want to happen, not that day of all days. I felt my entire world closing in on me; my legs were shaking, and I needed to sit down. Fortunately, the wedding breakfast was ready, so I slumped into my seat. Alan came into the room and sat next to me. Appearing to be extremely happy, he didn't stop talking about how wonderful Molly looked. I couldn't help but admire his self-control; he must have been in such turmoil.

Alan, of course, is a very accomplished public speaker. His father-of-the-bride speech was everything it should be, but for me every reference to his daughter felt like another knife in my chest. He finished to great applause. Giles was extremely nervous about making a speech; this was way outside his comfort zone. He apologised in advance, saying Molly didn't marry him for his public speaking abilities, to which Roger said, "What *did* she marry you for, then?"

Giles was lovely, thanking everyone, especially Alan for his speech. "How can I possibly follow that?" he said. "We have two Presidents in the room, I can't compete with that. I can only tell you how I feel about this wonderful lady. The first time I saw Molly was during a video conference, and I could not believe what I saw. From that moment, I could think of nothing else but Molly. Then, when we finally met, it all happened so fast. Molly smiled at me, and I smiled back, then somehow, she just reached out, and took a part of me to keep for herself. I knew it immediately; unless I was with her, I would never be a whole person again. So, you see, Molly's given me no option, I can't exist without her. I have to love her every second of every day for the rest of my life."

He had planned to say a little more, but at that point, he couldn't say another word. There was a momentary silence in the room before everyone stood up and applauded him. It was another of those wonderful moments in time. Roger stood up and gave a very funny speech; he was wonderful. He started by saying he had already insulted the President of the United States, so he couldn't possibly look more idiotic than he did already. Frank asked him if he was talking about the lipstick on his face. Someone handed Roger a mirror, and everyone was in fits of laughter even before he started his speech!

"Thank you for pointing that out, Mr President. It seems there are no limits to my idiocy. When my mother told my father she was expecting me, he said, 'You're having a joke with me.' This is the story of my life, and Giles keeps on reminding me of it."

He reminisced about their university days, and how he was always one step behind Giles. Then he progressed to when they were PhD students together.

"I was studying the possibilities of electrically powered flight. This was when lead acid batteries were the only economic option. Giles was studying artificial intelligence. Needless to say, my idea didn't take off, but Giles' idea certainly did."

Then he had enormous fun recounting some of their escapades together, the consistent theme being how Giles always came out on top. When it came to girlfriends, he said it was even worse.

"I don't understand it, *look* at him, he's a computer nerd! And yet, whenever we were introduced to girls, they would say, 'Oh, you're Giles's friend'. I can't even get my dog Monty to come back to me, and now I've got *this* to contend with. He can't just marry anyone. Oh no, somehow, he finds Molly. Look at her, has anyone ever seen a more beautiful woman? Even that's not enough for Giles; she's not just beautiful, she's smart, I mean, she's *really* smart. Not only that, but she's also wonderful, and she loves him to bits. I can't even get Monty to like me; is it any wonder I end up making a fool of myself? And now, to rub salt into the wound, I have this duty to propose a toast to wish Giles well for the future. Here is a man who's married the most wonderful woman in the world, and he's about to change computing for ever. It's highly likely he'll become a billionaire mogul, and he will probably be awarded a Nobel Prize for doing it. So please, raise your glasses to the happy couple. Let's hope things pick up for you in the future."

When he finally sat down, he was met with rapturous applause, and Giles immediately gave him a hug. When everyone had settled down, which took quite a while, Frank tapped on his glass.

"I'm sorry, folks. I just have to say a few words; it's what us Presidents do. I have got to tell you, Roger, that's a hard act to follow. You were so right about these two wonderful people. I first met Molly when she was about five hours old; I've watched her grow into this wonderful woman that we see today. She is as special to me as my own daughter. I have always known this day would come, and I often wondered what kind of man would eventually win her heart. I knew it would have to be someone very exceptional.

She has found that man, and as Roger has so ably described, Giles *is* pretty damn exceptional. We all recognise that glint in their eyes when they look at each other; I cannot tell you how happy that makes me feel. These two good people are made for each other, but first they had to *find* one another. They might have spent a lifetime searching; call it fate, or call it what you will, their paths crossed, and here we are today. Let me tell you the one big thing that life has taught me. We all go through this life searching for something; sometimes we are not even sure what it is we are looking for. Then one day, if you're lucky, you'll stumble across it, and trust me, you'll recognise it immediately. If you are lucky enough to find that special person, my advice to anyone is the same, hang on to them, never let them go. I would like to wish everyone here good fortune, and so may I propose a toast to serendipity."

It was a wonderful afternoon. Everyone was asking about the dress, and Roger had become a star. Frank and Olivia enjoyed themselves. I knew nothing would have stopped them coming that day; he adores Molly. Alan appeared to be fine, which I couldn't understand; he must have seen Molly's reaction to Charlie. I would never have credited him with that much self-control and admired him for it. I did the best I could to appear happy and normal, but Alan's reaction was all I could think about. Molly knew how I felt and took me to one side so we could discuss it. She was sorry for the way she had reacted, but I quickly put her as ease on that issue.

"Charlie wouldn't be Charlie if he had not reacted in the way he did. He's your father, Moll. You both reacted exactly how you should, and it was a wonderful thing to see. It's *my* problem, not yours."

Harry and Audrey came over to me; Audrey was looking concerned. Harry didn't understand what the problem was, and when she explained he just smiled.

"I'm not sure you need to worry about that. As soon as the crowd parted to let Charlie through, I noticed the owner of this place looking at you, Joanna. I can't remember his name, but he seemed to know what was going on. As Charlie walked towards Molly, the chap caught Alan's attention, and effectively turned him away from looking at either of them. He led Alan out of the room for some reason."

I questioned Harry, but he was adamant about it. This would explain a lot. Audrey was as relieved as I was and hugged me. Bill and Charlotte joined us.

"I've seen hugging going on, what am I missing?" he said.

We all laughed. I was so relieved I just hugged everyone. I found Molly and told her; like me, she breathed an enormous sigh of relief. Then, seeing my apparent delight, Charlie and Sylvia joined us, and I told them. He too was very relieved; we didn't know whether to jump up and down for joy, or laugh, or cry. I said I needed to find John and talk to him, so I excused myself and went to look him. He was at reception and I took him to one side.

"When Charlie walked over to kiss Molly after the signing, I'm told you distracted my husband, Alan. Why did you do that, John?"

"I just happened to be standing next to him, it was pure chance, but I saw that expression on your face. I've seen how you and Charlie look at each other. I've seen how Charlie looks at Molly. It's not rocket science, Joanna. It's not my place to assume anything, but I just thought it would do no harm if your husband didn't see it."

"I don't know how you could have been so intuitive, and so quick to react. You're a class act, John Palmer, you always were. How can I ever thank you?"

"You already have, do you realise how much business I'll get with photographs of the President on the wall."

"I'll make sure you get a lot more."

I walked back to the others, and on the way, I noticed the musicians had arrived; they were setting up in the large room where the ceremony had been held. The afternoon had slipped effortlessly into the evening, and eventually it became time for Frank and Olivia to leave.

"I'm sorry we have to go, Joanna, but I'm told we must."

"First could you do me a big favour, Frank? Will you and Olivia pose for some photographs with the owner John and his staff?"

"Consider it done, my dear. They've been exceptionally kind to us."

Molly and Giles came over to say their goodbyes, and Frank put his arm around Giles.

"Take good care of her, my boy. I'm sure you will."

Everyone wanted to shake the President's hand, so it took a long while for them to leave. It was sad to see them go; Frank and Olivia leave a big hole when they leave anywhere.

Molly and I agreed that she should change before the rest of the evening continued. The Red Dress was so precious, and Molly was very conscious of damaging it. We went to her room together.

"This is a moment in history, Moll. This dress will never be worn again. In a hundred years' time, it might even be an exhibit somewhere. People will come from all around to look at it, and wonder what stories it could tell, but no one will ever know."

"It was perfect, Mom. It just seemed to take me over; I didn't recognise myself in it."

"That's exactly how I felt when I wore it."

"Everything has been perfect, I'm so happy, Mom. It was just that thing with Charlie when I couldn't help myself. You're sure Dad didn't notice?"

"I told you, sweetheart, it's not your fault. Charlie couldn't be a worse-kept secret, could he. If John Palmer saw through us as quickly as he did, then who else has put two and two together. I can't go on deceiving your Dad, just as long as it's not today."

We talked about the events of the day as Molly got changed. I said how funny I thought Roger had been, and Molly said how pleased she was that Frank and Olivia were there. Frank's little speech had made her think.

"Frank was right about spending your life searching for that one special person. I'm so lucky I found him. Why didn't you realise that Charlie was *your* special person, Mom?"

"This is your day, Moll. Let's not talk about me."

We went back down to join the others, where the evening was giving way to the night. Antony and his ladies were just leaving. Molly became quite emotional, saying goodbye to them.

"I'm ruined, you know," he said, "I'll never see a greater triumph than this; my life can only descend from here. Take me home, girls, before I go into a decline."

He left with the same flourish as when he arrived; we were all the poorer for his absence. Then there was music and dancing, and still more food. I danced with Giles, who had had a bit too much to drink. I danced with Roger, who had had far too much to drink. I really liked him; he was a lovely young man. I even danced with Alan. After I had danced with Bill and Harry, it was inevitable that I would dance with Charlie. He gestured with a hand, and I walked towards him with my hand outstretched.

Sylvia was not far away, dancing with Harry. I am always conscious of her feelings; no one understands my troubled relationship with Charlie better than Sylvia. Why she tolerates me, I have never understood. I clasped Charlie's hand and resisted the urge to hold him close to me. We shuffled around the floor, talking quietly.

"You've coped with today wonderfully, Joanna. I know how nervous you must have been."

"Nervous doesn't do it, Charlie, I've been terrified. You and Alan in the same room; that's the moment I've always dreaded."

"I wish you had told me about the dress. When I saw Molly, you can guess what my reaction was."

"I'm sorry, Charlie, you're right. It was amazing though, wasn't it? That same dress in this same place; it just felt so right. It was as if history had been given a second chance to finally get it right."

"I felt the same. Molly looked amazing, didn't she. And what about John Palmer, it was as if everything from the past had come back together."

"I told John I thought he was a class act. He really is, isn't he."

"We had a strange relationship with him, didn't we? It felt like he was a dear friend, but he never once failed to be the maître d'."

"He told me about the evening you came back here, Charlie, for a final drink. He said he had never seen a man look so completely broken. He said he couldn't imagine us ever being apart."

"Careful, JoJo, remember that boundary line!"

"I know, Charlie. I'm trying hard not to step over it, but it's difficult, when you're on the other side of it."

"You don't make it easy, do you? Do you think I don't struggle with this as well?"

"I'm sorry, Charlie, I know you do. I'm going to hand you back to Sylvia."

We danced over towards Sylvia and Harry. "He's all yours, Sylvia. I'll swap him for Harry."

We danced a few steps, then Harry suggested we sit down with the others. Audrey as always was concerned for me, but I assured her everything was fine.

"Does everyone know about Charlie and Molly?" I asked her.

"Mum's told me, Joanna," Fiona said, "she thought it was safer if I knew."

"That's why Bill told me, Joanna," Charlotte said. "I hope you don't mind."

"I'm afraid everyone knows except my husband and my boys. Can you imagine how that makes me feel!"

"No, I don't suppose any of us can," said Charlotte.

Alan and the boys came over to join us, soon to be followed by Charlie, Sylvia, and the lovely Roger. Moments later Molly, Giles, and his family, came over. We found some more seats and huddled together. We were all talking, laughing, and joking; it was a lovely but strange situation. This was my world, my friends and family, everyone who is dear to me, including Charlie. All those years ago, I never once allowed my world to mix with Charlie's. Now he was at the centre of it, but for how much longer? It was obvious that Charlie was the wedge which could split my family asunder. This gathering was the first, and it would probably be the last.

As soon as people start to sit together in groups at a function like that, you know the night is drawing to a close. Those who were not staying overnight now started to leave, and the usual round of goodbyes began. Everyone said what a wonderful wedding it had been, how perfectly everything had been organised, and the dress; everyone mentioned the dress. Roger kept falling asleep; it was time for us to call it a day.

In the morning, Giles had his car packed and waiting to whisk them away somewhere; Molly didn't know where. She was just casually dressed in her usual jeans and t-shirt, but she was radiant. Everybody kissed and hugged them both, and then last of all, it was Charlie. Molly hugged Sylvia, and then turning to Charlie, she just put her hands on his arms, and gave him a quick kiss on the cheek. We had a flight to catch back to Washington DC, so as soon as Molly and Giles were gone, the breakfast party broke up. We said our final goodbyes and headed out towards our waiting driver. I let the others go ahead and stopped to thank John.

"Bless you, John, for everything. I promise I'll come back to see you."

"I hope so, Joanna. You made quite an impression on me, all those years ago, and now this wonderful wedding. I think I should be thanking you."

I put my arms around him and kissed him.

"Is there a Mrs Palmer, John?"

"There is, we've been married for nearly forty years."

"Tell her from me, she's a lucky lady."

When I joined the others at the car, Audrey and the gang were there to see me off. We had already said goodbye, but I just knew they would want to wave goodbye again.

Chapter Twenty-Two
THE BEGINNING OF THE END

I slipped back into my Washington existence, seemingly effortlessly. It wasn't real of course; a part of me was elsewhere. They kept in contact with me, but I missed them all and desperately missed Molly. We would share texts or emails every day and talked at least two or three times a week. The rest of my life was the time spent waiting for one of those calls. Whenever we spoke, she was always so happy and full of enthusiasm; just the pick-me-up I needed. Molly would always mention Charlie.

I wasn't sure if it was the unusual circumstances of their relationship, or the fact that Charlie had become an important asset to the business. Whatever it was, the two of them were becoming closer by the day. They often dined together in the evenings. Charlie was always there as a friend, and as a mentor; above all he was always there as a father. I am not sure how I would have coped had the situation been reversed if either of them had rejected the other. It was self-evident that the greatest gamble of my life had been vindicated, it was everything I could have dreamed of. I should have been relieved and happy.

I was none of those things, I felt stressed and depressed. Molly's wedding should have been one of the happiest days of my life, instead I was on tenterhooks the whole day. And hanging over me like the sword of Damocles was the ever-present risk of Alan finding out about Charlie. I tried to conquer my demons, but every so often Alan would mention something Molly had told him about Charlie, and I would sink back into my morass of self-doubt and fear.

Perhaps it was inevitable that during the weeks following the wedding, my relationship with Alan was even more strained than usual. We had one of our normal upsets after he came home from work extremely late, tired, and stressed. It was entirely about nothing, as these upsets normally are, but nothing I did or said was right. He was just spoiling for an argument, something to relieve his stress. Mrs Garcia had left his meal in the warmer and the dining table was set.

"I take it you've eaten," he said.

"Well, yes. I didn't know what time you were coming home."

"Couldn't give a shit, more like. Why don't you just get on with whatever it is that you do?"

I thumped a bottle of wine down onto the table, next to him, and tossed him the corkscrew.

"Perhaps you can find what you're looking for in there."

"I'm not going to find it in *you*, am I, that's for sure. Look at you, the Queen of the Washington establishment; one look from you and everyone dances to your tune. Everyone thinks you're so wonderful - they have no idea, do they?"

"What do you mean?"

"You know what I mean. You've spent your life flashing your eyes at men, but there's nothing behind those eyes, is there? I saw how you looked at that man Charlie at the wedding, and at the owner of the place. You know, I'm past caring. Flirt as much as you like, it's what you do best, isn't it? Just don't do it in front of me."

"I wasn't flirting with Charlie."

"The man's nothing more than a filthy letch. He looks at Molly like he looks at you. He kept on dancing with Moll. He had his arms around her far too often. For Christ's sake, he's old enough to be her father! I've told her to have as little to do with him as possible."

"What did Molly say to that?"

"She listened, said she hadn't noticed a problem, but she would watch out for it."

My heart was about to burst out of my chest. If there was ever going to be a time for me to tell Alan, that was it. He was in quite some rage. My bad temper is buried somewhere deep inside me. It's a rare day when a situation digs deep enough to find it, but Alan seemed to be searching for it. I wanted to shout at him. I wanted to scream and throw things. For a moment, I wanted to hurt him like he had never been hurt before, and I had the very thing which would do it.

Either Alan didn't dig deep enough, or maybe I just don't have the capacity to hurt him. I poured myself an extremely large glass of the wine and walked out of the room. I knew if I didn't tell him then, I never would. It would destroy him, but it might also destroy my relationship with my boys, something I could not do. A little later, I went back for some more wine. Alan had already opened another bottle. I sat down, neither of us said anything for quite a while.

"I'm not sure I can go on like this, Alan. There is someone behind these eyes, and that person hurts."

"I'm not seeing that person. I suppose this is the problem, isn't it?"

"I'm sorry, Alan. But, yes, that *is* the problem. Maybe we should think again about splitting up."

"I've told you before I can't divorce you, not now. I hate to admit it, but in that respect, I need you, and let's face it, you owe me."

"What do you mean, I owe you?"

"You came to me with nothing, I made you the queen of Washington."

"No, you didn't! You gave me the platform! Whatever I am,

I made myself. I helped to make your career too. Do you think Frank would have nominated you for President of the World Bank, had it not been for me?"

I was waiting for Alan to shout back at me, but he just sat silently. He had already drunk too much, but then he poured himself yet another one.

"I'm just tired of it, Joanna. I'm tired of it all, at the moment. The whole world is locked into this financial experiment, and it's people like me who lose sleep over it. We've created so much money, if we have this wrong, you cannot even imagine the consequences. I suppose what I'm saying is that there are times when what I need more than anything else is simply the love of a woman."

I did not expect that for one moment. His comment cut through me like a knife. Alan didn't say it, but obviously I wasn't that woman. It was a horribly painful reaffirmation of what we both already knew. I put my arm around him.

"I'm really sorry, Alan. I wish I *were* that woman; you deserve it."

"Well, maybe it works both ways."

Something happened between us that night. Our problems hadn't gone away, far from it, but our understanding had changed. When Alan said he needed to be loved, it devastated me like nothing he had ever said before. It's so easy in the heat of the argument to forget that one basic requirement. It's something we all need. If we don't have it, none of us likes to admit we need it; it makes us feel vulnerable. Living without love in your life gradually diminishes you as a person. That dull empty ache destroys you from within.

All too painfully, I had come to realise that there was a part of me that was forever Charlie's. Poor Alan, he wanted the one thing that I no longer had to give. We both enjoyed a wonderful life together in so many ways, but all the while that dull empty ache was destroying us both from within. I felt terrible that night because I knew this was my fault. He blamed me for his aching heart, and he was right. The 2008 financial crisis had taken over his life. He worked incredibly long hours, and when he came home tired and stressed, he didn't really want to take it out on me; he just wanted to be loved.

We ended that day with an unspoken agreement. We agreed we could not continue the way we were. He agreed to be less bad-tempered with me, and I agreed to be more understanding with him. Nothing was said about the long term, but I think we kind of agreed we should concentrate on what we were good at, rather than go on grieving for what we didn't have. I suppose in truth it amounted to a kind of working arrangement. What I did not realise then was that it amounted to a cathartic moment for Alan. He agreed whole-heartedly with the working arrangement. What I did not find out for some time was that he also decided to let go of that dull ache which was destroying him. In other words, he finally gave up on me.

I spoke to Molly the following day. She was as full of life as ever.

"We're getting closer, Mom. Giles thinks he's almost there."

"Why am I not surprised, sweetheart? I believe in Giles, just like you do."

"I know you do, Mom. It's kind of wonderful, isn't it?"

"I hear your Dad told you to watch out for Charlie. He's got a pretty low opinion of him."

"I nearly died, Mom! You know what I *thought* he was going to say, I was so relieved. Are you ever going to tell him?"

"Not unless I have to. I have hurt your Dad quite enough as it is. I have made up my mind to protect him from it. It's not just your Dad; it's your brothers too."

"I agree, Mom. I think it's probably for the best."

"How are you getting on with Jimmy?"

"I can't believe it; I'm doing the mom thing. He's a lovely little boy, and he seems to really like me."

"That's wonderful. How about Giles' ex-wife? You must get to see her as well."

"It's good; to our surprise she's got a really nice boyfriend. I've met him too; we actually get on well now."

We chatted some more until she had to go.

"Got to go now, Mom."

"Bye, Moll."

"Bye, Mom."

It seemed that everyone's life was working out for the best, except for mine. A few months after our talk, Alan appeared to be very much happier, but I had no idea why. I stopped feeling tense when he came home late because he was being friendly and agreeable. In most respects, our marriage went back to what it had been a few years previously. We went out together to social functions, we hosted functions at home and seemed to be rubbing along simply fine. He was still working incredibly long hours but when he came home, he was a different man.

There was the occasional clue that I spotted. There were a few phone calls which ended abruptly when I entered the room. He started buying some new clothes, and perhaps the most obvious clue, I could smell the woman on him. She obviously wore expensive perfume, and the slightest trace was detectable. This was not different women; this was the same woman. I quite amazed myself with my reaction. I should have confronted him, shouting hysterically, throwing his clothes out of the window. But compared with what I had done to him, this was no more than I deserved. What I did not know was whether it was just a fling of some kind, or was it something else? And of course, I had to know - who was she?

Alan was in many respects a new man; whoever she was, she was fulfilling a need that I couldn't. I could have asked him outright, but that would have changed our relationship immediately, and certainly not for the better. I decided to say nothing to anyone. I certainly was not going to tell Molly. Paradoxically, I trusted Alan to handle this like a gentleman. I was sure he would deal with it one way or another. As time went on, I did inevitably become envious of this unknown woman; that was the problem, she was unknown.

Every social event we went too, I suspected everyone, but found no one. I began to realise that this was not a fling. Whoever she was, she was staying the course. I could have paid to have him followed; I could have found out, but maybe a part of me didn't really want to confront it. But it all came to a head when we were invited to a private dinner party by some good friends of ours. She is a Senator, and he's a banker, so we always expect an exciting guest list.

We arrived a little early and were among the first there. The other guests soon followed, all couples except for Lily Gomez. I was sure I had seen her before, but I wouldn't have known her name. We were introduced, and she was delightful. Extremely attractive, late forties, possibly early fifties, but she could pass for thirty-five on a good day. She said she was a corporate lawyer; for some reason I had already made that assumption. She asked me what I did.

"My husband is the President of the World Bank, so I'm kind of full-time hostess."

Lily's eyes widened; she was frozen to the spot.

"Is Alan here?" she asked in a shaky voice.

"Yes, he's over there. Let me ask him over."

She said nothing as I beckoned to Alan. He immediately caught Lily's eye, and a look of abject horror appeared on his face. I had only been in this situation once before in my life. On that occasion, I was the other woman standing in Charlie's office. Alan came over, and before he could make an even bigger fool of himself, I put him out of his misery.

"I've already been introduced to your mistress, Alan. I think she's charming."

They both just looked at each other.

"Don't worry, I'm not going to make a scene. We don't want all these people to know, do we?"

"When did you know?" asked Lily.

"The second you walked through the door. You must tell me what your perfume is."

"I'm sorry, Joanna," Alan said. "I didn't mean for you to find out like this. I'm so sorry."

"I think it best if I leave, Alan," Lily said.

"Everyone will talk if you do," I replied. "Alan doesn't need that kind of scandal; I think you had better stick with it."

"This is horribly difficult," Lily said, "I can't believe you're dealing with this so well, Joanna. We've wanted to tell you for some time, but these things are not easy, are they."

I was coping well with Lily, I could have coped well with Alan, but suddenly coping with them both as a couple was quite a different matter. That was something I had not considered, why it should make a difference I didn't know, but somehow it did. Perhaps it was the finality of the situation. It wasn't just that I was being replaced; that our life together, and our relationship was being replaced. My reaction surprised me, I thought I could take such an event in my stride, but instead I wanted to burst into tears.

"I'm not as tough as I thought I was," I said, "I need to go to the bathroom, would you excuse me."

"Let me come with you," Lily said.

Her suggestion was totally unexpected, I hardly knew how to respond. I neither accepted nor declined her offer, I just walked away. That was when I found myself in the strange situation of being escorted to the bathroom by my husband's mistress. Neither of us said a word, until we were both in the bathroom, I think we both simultaneously saw the pain in each other's eyes.

"Oh God, this is awful, Joanna, if only he had told you before."

"I knew anyway, I've known for a couple of months. I just didn't know who."

"I do feel awful Joanna, I'm not some sleezy other woman. I didn't set out to wreck your marriage."

"I know you didn't. My marriage failed long before you came along, I am not going to blame you. I'm not even going to blame Alan."

"When I asked Alan about you, he just said you were the most wonderful and amazing woman he had ever met. But you just didn't love each other."

This was really going to the heart of it, it took me a while to compose myself.

"Sadly, Alan's right. We didn't love each other, we like each other, we support each other, we do everything together, but he wanted more."

"What do you mean?"

"I mean he just wanted to be loved, we both did. It's nothing whatever to do with you Lily, it's my fault, I just couldn't be what he wanted me to be."

"I'm sorry for you both, I'm divorced myself, I know the pain you've lived with."

"I believe you do, you're not what I expected."

"I can talk with some experience Joanna; I really do know how you feel. What you can't realise is how I feel. You may not have noticed me but we have met in passing more than once. I've admired you from a distance, I have never met anyone who doesn't admire you. I sat once on the edges of a function and watched you dance with the President; it was as if you were the only woman in the room. The moment I met Alan and realised who he was, and who you were, I was terrified. I've always been in awe of you, look at me, I'm shaking."

"I can't think why you would be in awe of me, I'm a failure as a wife."

"We're both failures as wives Joanna, what you could never be is a failure as a woman."

"Just tell me, Lily, do you want my husband? I mean do you want him for the rest of your life?"

"Wow, I didn't expect that! Okay yes, I think so."

"In that case we both know where this is headed. This is

not easy, is it. I suppose I just have to do what I have to do; you must know better than I what that entails."

"Alan said you were an amazing woman, he's right."

"Well he hasn't told me anything about you," I joked, "I get the feeling we might be seeing a lot more of each other."

The rest of that evening was a surreal experience. Lily and I left the bathroom pretending to be old friends, while Alan was the perfect gentleman. I doubt anyone suspected a thing. I assumed if I were ever in such a position that I would loathe and despise the other woman. I will never forget Annie's reaction in Charlie's office that dreadful day. In reality there was nothing to loathe; Lily was compassionate and understanding. I did not doubt that she was a lovely woman. But it was hard to make the pretence of normality, I just wanted the evening to be over. Alan and I said nothing as we drove home. I felt quite strange, as if this were all happening to someone else.

The moment we got home, Alan said, "Okay, let's get it over with."

"That's not what I want, Alan. I know it's my fault."

"It *is* your fault. You've had affairs, and I've said nothing."

"What do you mean, I've had affairs?"

"Do you really think I don't know about your affairs? All your little secrets!"

I said nothing. What could I say?

"I know you're Alexei's mistress."

"What! I'm not Alexei's mistress! I've never *been* his mistress, I had a brief relationship with him, but that was over thirty years ago, long before we met."

"What about the others?"

"There *are* no others, Alan, honestly. You are being paranoid; I swear I've been faithful to you from the moment we moved here together."

"Can I really believe that?"

"I've got nothing to lose Alan. I can see Lily's going to replace me, but I will *not* have you believing I have been unfaithful when I haven't."

"Oh, my God! You're telling the truth, aren't you? I've been an idiot!"

"You have, you really have; it's just not true."

"I'm sorry. I'm sorry about all of it. I didn't want it to end like this."

"Do you love each other, you and Lily?"

"It's early days; it's only been four months."

"As long as that?"

"Truth is, I've forgotten what love feels like. Lily's divorced; she has experienced a whole world of pain. We've not mentioned it but yes, I think we do."

"I'm going to cry again, but before I do, I will just say this one thing. The moment you know you love her, tell her, and then never ever let her go. I'm going to bed now."

"My God, Joanna, if only you could have loved me!"

"I'll see you in the morning, Alan."

I sobbed for hours with my world crashing down around me. Losing Alan meant losing everything; I sank into a deep well of depression. I hardly slept at all and finally struggled downstairs at 9.30 assuming Alan would have been long gone. I was surprised to see him sitting at the breakfast table talking to Sofia. He asked her if she would leave us alone, which she did.

"I've never known you this late for work, Alan."

"I know, but these aren't normal times."

"No, they're not."

"They say you never know what you've lost until it's gone," Alan said. "It was never perfect, but we had a lot, didn't we? You were right, what you said the other day, about Frank nominating me. That *was* down to you; a lot of my career has been because of you. We've made a wonderful team, you and me. I can't believe I can be thinking of giving all that up for something as elusive as love."

"I understand, Alan; I really do. I don't blame you or Lily. I wish we had what you have found with her."

"I wish that too, but it just didn't happen did it?"

"I suppose not."

"I've no right to ask you, Joanna, but will you stay with me while we get this sorted out?"

"I've got nowhere else to go, Alan."

"No, I don't mean here; the house is yours if you want it. No, I mean can we stay together until this is all sorted out? This is all far too quick. I think we both need time to adjust, and I need time to get used to not needing you."

"That's a kind thing to say, Alan. I will do whatever you want. I would like us to stay together until it's the right time. Will you want a divorce right away?"

"I can't, you know how stuffy the bank is. Besides Lily's divorce has already caused a huge scandal. You know her husband was Senator Roberts?"

"Oh, my goodness! No, I didn't realise, poor Lily."

"Do you really think we can do this without animosity? No one else manages to do that."

"We're not anyone else, are we, Alan? I can do this if you can."

"We *are* a good team, aren't we?"

Alan finally left for the Bank, and I watched him drive off, something I have done for years. When your entire world is crashing down around you, it's something that nothing in life can prepare you for. It's not just the big issues, like your finances or where you will live. You worry yourself sick about all the small issues. How will my family react? What will friends think? Will I lose them, will I lose my social position? How do I actually pay the bills?

These are all considerations worthy of attention, but what really numbs your senses is the rejection, and fear of the unknown. Before Lily, I think it was very unlikely that I would have walked away from my marriage, despite its obvious inadequacies. Fear of the unknown is a stultifying emotion. Add Lily to that equation and you immediately add rejection, with all its attendant feelings of inadequacy. I needed to talk to someone; someone outside of my Washington circle. Audrey answered her phone almost immediately.

"Joanna, you've read my mind! I was going to ring you today, how are you?"

"I need a friendly voice, Audrey. I need a shoulder to cry on."

"Oh, my goodness. This is serious, isn't it? Just take a deep breath and tell me."

"He's leaving me. Alan's got himself another woman."

"Oh, thank heavens! You had me worried there, I thought it was something serious."

"This *is* serious, Audrey. This is my life, everything I know and love. I'm going to lose it all.

"This is *not* serious; some kind of hideous illness would be serious. This only amounts to an adjustment."

"An adjustment, Audrey I'm losing everything!"

"I'm sure it feels like that now, but remember I've been where you are today. Trust me everything you know and love, it's all just a pack of cards; all you're doing is shuffling the pack."

"How can you say that Audrey? My life in Washington isn't a pack of cards, it's real."

"Joanna, you're my best and dearest friend, you know I would do anything for you, but I wouldn't lie to you, not even to cheer you up. I've stood in that hole you're standing in. Please believe me, it really is like a pack of cards. You keep the same pack, maybe you throw out the joker, but then you turn the cards over afresh."

"You mean I just start again?"

"Of course, you just pick yourself up, brush yourself off; you start all over again. You're not walking into the sunset; you're walking into the sunrise. Your friends, like Frank and Olivia, they will always be your friends. There will be a few so-called friends you lose. Good riddance to them! And there will be some new ones you will gain. Your family's not going to change; your membership at the golf club is not going to change. The only thing that *will* change is Alan. How much will you miss him?"

"I *will* miss him. We didn't have a loving marriage and haven't shared a bedroom for several years, but he's basically a truly kind and decent man."

"I know you weren't happy with Alan in that respect, and I know you told me you often thought about separating, but did you ever expect another woman?"

"No, that's been a shock. When you don't really love someone, it's very easy to forget that they might love someone else. I should have realised that maybe it was always a possibility."

"Well, come on; tell me what she's like."

"If you met her, I think you would say she's really nice. I have to admit it's not her fault; she hasn't stepped in and broken up a perfectly good marriage. I think she's been an extremely cautious and slightly reluctant participant in all of this."

"This is not your typical other woman, is it, Joanna?"

"Well, she's typical insofar as she's the younger woman, but no, Lily's pretty special, really. I suppose in time to come, I will have to meet her, maybe quite often."

"There you are, you're talking about the future! That's the first step."

"Audrey, you're wonderful. How can you be so calm and understanding about this?"

"I've been there Joanna. Freddy didn't just leave me for another woman, he reduced me to bankruptcy, and destroyed my life. I don't mean to make light of your predicament, but honestly, you will come through this I promise you. You're talking about it, that's the first step."

I *have* taken a step, haven't I? I'm already not panicking quite so much. I knew I could rely on you. You won't mention this to anyone, will you? Especially Charlie. I really don't want him to know."

"No, I promise."

"Tell me about the house, Audrey. How's it going?"

"Oh, it's so exciting, it's really taking shape. My apartment only needs decorating, and the other three are at different stages. Charlie says we will be finished by Christmas!"

"Do you mean you'll all start the new year in the new house?"

"That's what Charlie says. We're all making plans, and we have given the Village notice that we're leaving."

"That's wonderful, I can't wait to see it."

"I bet you have got no idea what you're doing for Christmas, do you, Joanna? Why not come and stay with us? We could have Molly and Giles stay as well."

"Well, I don't know, Audrey. I have obviously not thought about it, but that sounds like a wonderful idea."

"It *is* a wonderful idea. Try to make it happen."

"Thank you, I will. I had best go Audrey, and let you get on. I'll phone you again soon."

"Bye, Joanna."

"Bye, Audrey."

Talking to Audrey really did give me a boost; I had taken a first step. It might have been an infinitesimally small step, but it was the one that all journeys begin with.

-oOo-

In the following weeks, Alan and I decided to tell the family, which was exceedingly difficult. We already had a lunch planned with both the boys and their families, so that was the obvious time. They were shocked and concerned but they accepted it far better than I had imagined. I was left to wonder if they understood more than I realised. I insisted that I should be the one to tell Molly, so having told the boys, I knew I could delay it no longer, I phoned her that evening.

"Hi Mom. How are you?"

"I need to come right out and tell you something, sweetheart."

"Oh, my God! Dad knows about Charlie, doesn't he?"

"No, it's not that, but he's leaving me anyway."

"Oh, Mom, what's happened?"

"You know it's never been perfect between us? Well, it's got a lot worse the last year or two. We agreed we would maintain a kind of working relationship, but your Dad's taken it a step further. He's got himself another woman."

"Another woman! Dad's gone off with another woman?"

"He hasn't gone off with her, he's being a real gentleman about it. We are avoiding any scandal and sorting it all out very sensibly."

"Oh, Mom, I'm so sorry, this is terrible!"

"It's not so bad, honestly. I've not been happy for a long time, and it's not too late for me to start again."

"How much has Charlie got to do with this, Mom?"

"Is it that obvious?"

"Of course it's obvious, I don't think you ever gave Dad a chance. I think it's only ever been Charlie for you."

"If that were true Moll, would you hate me for it?"

"Oh Mom, I can't hate you, I just feel so sorry for Dad, and for Charlie. I thought you and Dad had a good life together."

"We did, we were great together, but in the end, he wanted what I couldn't give him. I don't blame him Moll, it's not his fault, he just wants to love someone."

"This really is all about Charlie isn't it, even now?"

"I suppose you're right. How could I love your Dad when I was always in love with someone else? It was never fair on him, was it?"

"Oh, Mom, how could you be so stupid."

"That's my tragedy isn't it, Moll. When it comes to Charlie, I've always been stupid."

"No Mom, I shouldn't have said that I'm sorry. I know how

much pain you have been through with Charlie, and now you and Dad have got all this to sort out, I am so sorry. So who's this other woman?"

"Lily Gomez; that's a name to conjure with, isn't it! Smart navy suit, cream blouse, stiletto heels, long black shiny hair, lawyer."

"Don't tell me she's my age, please."

"No, she's not. To be honest, if I try hard enough, I will have to admit she seems to be a real class act. None of it's her fault; I think you'll like her."

"I don't know what to say Mom. I can't believe it. Are you okay, really?"

"Honestly, sweetheart, I'm going to be fine."

"What will you do, where will you go?"

"I don't have to go anywhere. I can just stay here, or I can do whatever I like."

"I'll book a flight over; I need to be with you."

"You will do nothing of the kind, Moll. I promise you; I am going to be okay. Anyway, I've got an invitation to stay with Audrey in their new home for Christmas. I'm sure you and Giles could come as well if you wanted to."

"I should phone Dad, shouldn't I, do the boys know?"

"Yes, we told them a few hours ago. They're being really good about it."

"Now listen, Mom. We'll talk every day, I want to know everything as it happens, and I can fly over any time."

"Please don't worry about me, and please do promise me you won't tell anyone, especially Charlie."

"I'm in the middle of something, Mom. I'll have to go."

"Bye, Moll."

"Bye, Mom."

It wasn't until all the family knew that it became a reality. We told the household staff of course; they would know anyway. Sofia didn't seem surprised at all. Friends were a different proposition. It was so important that Alan should avoid any scandal, and I respected that. If we told just anyone, everyone would soon know. It was exceedingly difficult. We decided to tell just our nearest and dearest friends, like Frank and Olivia. Then we had to face the obvious problem that we had given them. Who do they invite when we get together? When we told Frank and Olivia, he was brilliant.

"We've got several friends who have gone separate ways; we normally try to remain friends with both sides," the President said. "The only thing which prevents that is bitterness. When one side can't be in the same room as the other, or when the mention of the other woman or man, gets them reaching for the kitchen knife, well, those are the people you lose touch with. My advice to you, Joanna, is to get on with this woman, Lily. And Alan, when Joanna finds herself another man, because trust me, she *will*, I suggest you shake his hand."

Frank made us both think. He was obviously quite right in his judgment. A month went by, and it felt as if it had been a year. Everything seemed unreal, I felt as if I was trapped in somebody else's life, a strange hinterland, where I did not really belong. Alan and I were very civil to one another, I think he felt guilty for betraying me, he was trying hard. For my part I felt equally guilty for the way I had treated him. I was not sure that guilt was a very satisfactory basis for our mutual understanding, but it was all we had.

Alan surprised me one evening when he asked if I could cope with seeing Lily again, suggesting perhaps we could go out to dinner somewhere. I was more than a little taken aback, I assumed there was something important he wanted to discuss. This was a big step; I knew it would not be easy for any of us. I was apprehensive but agreed.

We went to a very smart restaurant and sat together; it was all terribly civilised. Lily was more ill at ease than I was; in fact, she looked terrified. After plenty of time to adjust to this new situation, some of my old confidence was coming back. I really didn't blame her for the failure of my marriage, and so with Frank's words still ringing in my ears, I thought for everyone's sake I should take his advice.

"This is so awkward Joanna; I hope we can do this," Lily said, "I'll be honest I'm terrified."

"Please don't be, I don't blame anyone but myself, and I think you have dealt with this situation admirably."

"Alan said you were remarkable; I can't imagine another woman who would be big enough to say what you have just said. If this all goes how we hope it will, then the fact is, there will be times when we shall have to see each other, perhaps with our families. I'll be the other woman in that situation, I'm the one who will be on trial when I meet your family. I need a friend Joanna."

"You're right, Alan and I will always share our children; our lives are forever bound, and he will always be a special person in my life. If you are a part of Alan's life, then you'll also a part of my life. I think we need to be friends Lily; I don't think it will be too difficult, do you?"

"No I don't, I would like us to be friends."

We both sat smiling. That had gone much better than I expected. Alan looked a little surprised but composed himself.

"The thing is, Joanna, Lily and I need to be together. What we want to suggest is that for the time being at least, I would like to move in with Lily. Obviously, I don't want to draw any attention to that."

"So, what you want me to do is to pretend you're still living in the house, not to tell anyone, and shout 'bye darling' out of the front door every morning!"

Alan looked alarmed, I quickly reassured him, "I'm joking! Of course, you need to be together. We can work it out."

I think I impressed Lily that night. I didn't set out to, but I'm sure I did. She certainly impressed me. She had it all - looks, brains, and personality. It was difficult crossing that divide, but when I took that step, I found I really did like her.

Audrey continued to be a wonderful support; she gave me

so much good advice. She knew how guilty I felt about Alan. When she pointed out that Lily was the key to me assuaging my guilt, I knew she was right. I wanted Alan to be happy.

The day that Alan effectively moved out was a big day for both of us. He was leaving his past behind, just as I was. We stood in the hall, and hugged each other, then I kissed him. We had already agreed not to make any speeches. I just stood there with tears rolling down my face. He also had tears in his eyes.

"I'm sorry for everything Alan."

"So am I, we nearly had it all, didn't we."

"We did, so much of what we had has been wonderful."

"Am I doing the right thing, Joanna?"

"Time will tell us both, Alan. Lily's lovely. Go to her."

He left, and for the first time in thirty years I was alone.

Chapter Twenty-Three
LAST NIGHT OF
THE OLD ORDER

L iving alone was frightening at first, but you adjust. I kept up my usual social engagements, played tennis and golf, and met girlfriends for lunch. What was more difficult to deal with were the invitations to us as a couple, most of which I declined. I attended a couple by myself, saying that Alan was busy at the bank. I couldn't see how much longer we would be able to keep our breakup a secret. Alan would have to make some decisions, and soon.

We were weeks away from Christmas and I also had some difficult decisions to make. We always used to spend Christmas together as a family, but this had gradually become more difficult for the boys, juggling time with their wives' families. We would always see each other separately, if not together. That year was going to be no different. Alan was going to Joe's for Christmas Day and was taking Lily for the first time. I was invited and Lily being there would not have been a problem, but I had instead decided I would accept Audrey's invitation, and go to England.

Christmas without my family felt like a giant step; it really troubled me. I am not sure they understood. I had no doubt that going to the UK would look like I was running away. They didn't realise how attached I had become to my English friends, and of course Molly was there. I tried to assure them all that I was *not* running away. I was accepting a kind invitation to stay with very dear friends, and it also meant I could spend Christmas with Molly. I just hoped the boys believed me. There was also the fact that in England I was just me; I was not Joanna-without-Alan.

It all seemed to happen so fast. One moment I could not decide what to do, wracked with indecision, and the next moment I was walking through Heathrow arrivals. Audrey said she would meet me, and I should have guessed they would *all* be there. All those smiling faces. I did what I always do and burst into tears. As we made our way outside, we all laughed at how ridiculous I was. They had hired a taxi, a people carrier, specially so that we could all travel together. All the way during the long drive to Belmont we talked nonstop, and no one asked me about my marriage because Audrey, true to her word, had not mentioned it.

As we drove the final mile towards Belmont, I felt as if I had drunk a couple of glasses of champagne. I was so pleased to be with my friends with their lively conversation; my head was spinning. Even as we approached the house, I could see how much everything had changed. The fallen tree was gone, the fence and gate were new, the border next to the drive was manicured. When we arrived at the front entrance, I just stood looking at it. The tired paintwork was gone, the house was resplendent in the bright afternoon sunshine. The trees in the surrounding landscape cast a long shadow in the winter sun. Even at that time of year when everything was dormant, this was a magnificent vista. Where else could I be possibly be but England.

Harry opened the door and we stepped into the central hall. Everything was redecorated; the tall ceiling was white; it had been grey and brown before, and the contrast was striking.

The oak floor that I remembered as uneven and hidden somewhere beneath a century of patination, was now glowing with pride. The imposing staircase had been completely restored; the handrails were like outstretched arms inviting me to touch them. There was a strong smell of paint, but above all there wasn't the damp smell I remembered; it was warm and welcoming.

"Come and see our apartment first, Joanna," Audrey said excitedly.

Harry proudly escorted me towards their door. As it swung open, it revealed a beautiful apartment with its own internal staircase, not what I expected at all. It was huge.

"Are all the apartments this big?" I asked.

"Audrey's is the biggest," said Charlie, "but if you don't include the dining room, it's only a few square feet larger."

Harry showed me round; it was wonderful. All the rooms had high ceilings, with a lot of the original decorative plasterwork. The principal rooms had tall windows enjoying magnificent views across the Oxfordshire countryside. They had retained the wonderful character of the old house, but now it was new and fresh. There was just one problem. There was hardly anything in it, and there were no floor coverings. They obviously saw the look of puzzlement on my face.

"I thought you were finished and had moved in?"

"We did too," said Bill, "but don't worry about that; come and see our place next, it's just over there, look."

"Let me show you the way, Joanna," Charlotte said.

I was taken aback for a moment. I knew Bill and Charlotte were a couple now, but I had not been told they were going to live together. That was another step entirely.

"You didn't tell me you two were living together, Bill, that's wonderful!"

I hugged and kissed him, and then the same with Charlotte.

"We're not quite living together yet. We don't have any furniture for the moment; it's all been delayed," Charlotte said.

"What's the hold-up?" I asked.

"We've had lots of last-minute delays," Charlie said. "Silly things really, but this is the building business for you."

"Some of our furniture arrived yesterday," Harry said, "and there's still more to come, but at least you've got a bed, Joanna."

"I know, it's crazy," said Charlie, "but the big problem is the Christmas deadline. The building work is finished now; we just need the carpet layers to finish, and for the rest of the furniture to arrive. Trouble is, it's Christmas, and everyone else is on the same deadline."

"So, *can* we all spend Christmas together?" I asked.

"Oh yes, we will," replied Sylvia. "I've organised for the carpet layers to come tomorrow, and we all have bits and pieces of furniture arriving here the day after."

"The day after is Christmas Eve; that's cutting it a bit fine," I said.

"It is a bit, but we'll triumph," said Charlie. "Audrey and Harry have just about moved in; the rest of us are still in the Village. If it goes according to plan, we all move in on Christmas Eve. How's that for timing?"

"I think it's wonderful," I said, "look at you all; could it *be* more perfect?"

I think they would have been equally happy sleeping on the floor in a sleeping bag. Their wonderfully ambitious project had come to fruition; the furniture was just the icing on the cake. Audrey showed me to my room. I had clean, albeit paint-splattered floorboards, a brand-new bed, a chair, and a temporary clothes rail. It was perfect. My bathroom was complete in every detail.

"Audrey, it's wonderful, could you possibly be any happier?"

"It's going to be perfect, isn't it, Joanna, and best of all, you're here to share it with us."

We decided to dine out that evening; actually, we had no other option. We left early for the restaurant. Charlie said that as it was a long drive back to the Village, they would have to leave the restaurant in good time. They were all excited and full of enthusiastic plans. I had forgotten what enthusiasm was; it was good to be reminded. It was the first time since my separation when I felt really comfortable with people. No one asked me how I was coping or was feeling sorry for me. I felt slightly awkward when they asked about Alan, but nobody made a big thing about it.

Charlie and Sylvia looked happy together. I found myself looking for signs in their body language and expression; I couldn't seem to stop doing it. They were all triumphant about the development, the whole evening had a party atmosphere about it. It was impossible for me not to be carried along with their enthusiasm. It was a really wonderful evening, but after my flight I was exhausted, so I was not sorry when the evening broke up early. I was looking forward to my new bed.

We didn't want to delay them, they had quite a drive ahead of them, so we quickly said our goodbyes and allowed them to be on their way. Charlie rushed towards his car as if it would hasten the arrival of the next day.

"We're like kids on Christmas morning, aren't we," Harry said.

"And why shouldn't you be?" I said. "I'm just so pleased to be a part of it."

When we arrived back at Belmont, just the three of us, the house without any furnishings felt very empty. The slightest sound seemed to be amplified, echoing around the empty space. Audrey said that, after all the hustle and bustle of the building works, it felt very strange. We found ourselves tiptoeing into their apartment. Harry suggested a cup of something before bed, but I graciously declined. Audrey made sure I had everything I needed and wished me a good night. I sent Molly a text, and then fell fast asleep.

-o0o-

The next morning, I was startled by the most appalling noise. It sounded like someone struggling to get out of a room they were trapped in. The loud bangs echoed everywhere. I jumped up feeling quite alarmed only to find Audrey had calmly made me a cup of tea.

"What on earth is going on?"

Audrey was evidently delighted. "That wonderful sound is generated by carpet layers."

Her excitement was contagious, I was keen to see what was going on. First, we had some breakfast in Audrey's lovely new kitchen, and I quickly got dressed. Their combined enthusiasm had obviously ratcheted up another notch. I rushed out to see what was going on. The hall was simply full of rolls of carpet, and men were moving around everywhere. Harry was rushing about with a clipboard, going from room to room.

As he rushed off again, he shouted, "Move your stuff into the bathroom, Joanna."

No sooner had I done that than my bed was being removed as well. I watched the guys nailing down the carpet strips; this was the cause of all the noise. This was followed by the underlay, swiftly followed by the carpet. The guys worked with such precision, it all appeared to be effortless for them. I was enthralled watching them. Before long it was finished, and a vacuum cleaner being run over it.

"Good heavens, what a transformation. One moment it was a room-in-progress, and now it's a complete bedroom." I said.

I didn't see that Charlie had arrived, suddenly finding he was standing behind me.

"We used to get this with customers all the time. We worked for months to build a house, then the carpet layer came along and got all the praise for it."

"You're right, Charlie," said the carpet layer, "no more than we deserve."

They carried my bed back in and my one chair. In a strange

way, I was thrilled. I had become fully caught up with the whole thing. Charlie later sent someone out to buy everyone a pizza, and we all sat on top of the rolls of carpet in the hall. Charlie obviously knew the carpet layers. It was almost a party atmosphere. I could 't help but think what that told us about Charlie. He was the CEO of one of the country's largest building companies, and yet he knew all their names. They called him Charlie, and there was nothing they wouldn't do for him.

They worked on into the evening to make sure every room was finished. We thanked them all when they finally left. Now the house and the apartments felt complete; everywhere felt like home. Charlie said they always opened a bottle of champagne to celebrate the completion of each stage of the house. They had previously consumed a demolition bottle, a first fixing bottle, a plastering bottle, and so on. Goodness knows what a first fixing was, but it was obviously worthy of celebration. Harry produced the bottle and passed around the glasses.

Bill proposed the toast. "The carpets."

I raised my glass and repeated, "The carpets," as enthusiastically as everybody else. "You're just so lucky, sharing this together. What a wonderful way to start your new life here."

"We know," said Audrey, "and if my father is looking down on us, he'll be smiling."

"That's a lovely thought, and I agree, how could he not be smiling?" said Charlotte.

"It's a shame Sylvia couldn't be with us today Charlie, she's missed the carpet celebration."

"Yes, it is, she had to go back to Bristol to sort out some last-minute things."

Bill said they really needed to go. It wasn't an easy drive back to Cambridge. I asked what the problem was and of course I was forgetting; London is in the way.

Bill smiled as they left. "This is the last time we have to leave here. We move in tomorrow."

Just as we were waving them goodbye, they passed Fiona coming up the drive.

"Hello, Joanna," Fiona said. "I'm so pleased you're with us for Christmas. You've met my friend, Lorraine, haven't you?"

"Yes, just briefly; you're Fiona's flat mate."

"I'm pleased to meet you again. This is really exciting, isn't it."

Charlie's got a special relationship with Fiona. They joke that he considers her to be his stepdaughter. She obviously adores both Charlie and Harry and hugged them both. I said quietly to Audrey that she must be really happy to see them all so close. She gave me a wonderful smile and nodded in agreement.

"When's Sylvia coming, Charlie?" I asked.

"Not until tomorrow; she's staying at Jack's tonight, it's too far to come back this late, especially with all this frost about."

I had never met Sylvia's estranged husband Jack, but felt a bit sorry for him, despite never meeting him. Then I had another thought.

"Where are Fiona and Lorraine staying tonight?" I whispered to Audrey.

"We're not as disorganised as we look, you know. Fiona and Lorraine have brought two of those blow-up beds with them. It's only for one night, they'll be fine. Not only that, but they also have tonight's supper with them."

"What about you, Charlie, what are you doing?"

"I got the last of my stuff out of my apartment at the Village this morning; it's in a delivery van, ready to be delivered here tomorrow. So I don't have much option. Besides, Fiona's brought me another of these blow-up bed things."

"Are you sad to leave there?" I asked.

"We've got some good memories there, all of us. But you were right, we went there for the wrong reason. All of this: it's because of you, Joanna; you and Stanley."

"I bet you'll miss the bar," I said.

"Do you know, that's one of the finest collections of single malt whisky in the country. How can I *not* miss it!"

We laughed, as they briefly reminisced about some of their antics together. Audrey, Fiona, and Lorraine went off to prepare the supper that Fiona brought with her, while I reminisced with the boys. They did share some good memories from their time in the Village. Charlie told me about the time they were stopped by the police when Harry had spilled beer all over them. Somehow Stanley got them out of a fix; it was hilarious. Then there was the time in a Chinese restaurant when Lizzy fell into some diners at an adjoining table, covering them in their coffee. Then they told me about when they entertained those same unfortunate people at the Village; it was all just so funny.

A little later, Audrey and the girls came back into the room, looking rather serious.

"I think the best thing, Fiona, is to just tell them, as you told me," said Audrey.

Fiona looked extremely uncomfortable, as did Lorraine. There was a very awkward period of silence. We looked at each other anticipating some dreadful news.

Finally Fiona said, "What I have just told Mum is that Lorraine is not my flatmate, she's my partner."

Everyone looked rather taken aback; it was embarrassing, nobody knew what to say. Okay, so they were gay. What was the problem. The silence was deafening, so I thought perhaps I should say something to ease everyone's tension.

"So you're a couple, that's lovely, how long have you been together?"

"It's eight years now," Fiona said.

"Eight years, and you didn't tell anyone," I said.

"Well no, we just didn't get around to it," replied Lorraine.

"Fiona, you silly girl, and you, Lorraine," I said, "you love each other and you didn't tell your Mother! The one thing that all us mothers wish for our daughters is for them to find love. Why would you deny your Mum that for so long? All the family things you two have missed out on. Your mother's wedding, Fiona, you should have been with Lorraine. You're a part of the family, Lorraine. Family is precious, you can't just ignore your family. What were you thinking of, not telling both your families?"

"Oh, my God, I've not looked at it like that," Lorraine said, "I'm sorry, Audrey, Joanna's right, I wish we had told you before."

I reached out my hands to them both, "Come here, you two, you're idiots, but I want to hug you anyway."

It was a lovely moment. I realised parting with a secret they had kept for so long was an extremely significant moment for them. It was obvious Audrey was having difficulty dealing with it, so I just hoped my approach would work. Moments later, it was obvious that it had. They all hugged the girls again, and went from accepting that they were gay, to being happy for them. That's quite a step to take in one go!

"What are your plans, then?" I asked, "can we have another wedding? I love weddings."

Fiona smiled. "You're incorrigible, Joanna! We had to jump this hurdle first."

"That wasn't a hurdle; that was just a lolly stick lying on the floor."

Everyone laughed. It had turned into a wonderful moment to add to this already wonderful day. We were soon sitting around Audrey's dining table in her kitchen, enjoying a meal together. If Audrey had any problems accepting Fiona's sexuality, then they soon evaporated. Lorraine was charming; it was impossible not to like her. I wondered if Harry with his military background might take a little time to come around to the idea, but not a bit of it.

Come the end of the meal, Charlie sat there looking very contented. He said what he would like now to end this wonderful day would be a really nice single malt whisky. The problem was they didn't have any, but I had a little present for Charlie which I had brought with me. I had intended it for Christmas Day of course, but told him I couldn't pass up the opportunity and I would give him his present early. I went into my bedroom and fetched the box. Everyone assumed it was a bottle of whisky and Charlie's eyes lit up as he unwrapped the Christmas paper. When he saw what it was, he was completely reduced to silence. He just sat looking at it. Audrey asked me what it was.

"I remember, Charlie, that time in the Village when you tasted a whisky you had not tasted before. You said Stanley had described a rare whisky, and that was enough for you to identify it. This is that same whisky, Caol Ila."

Charlie looked up at me with an expression that I could not describe. "This isn't just any Caol Ila, though, is it?" he said.

"No, it's not, Charlie. I remember you said that for a long time it was not sold as a single malt because it was the vital ingredient of some blended whiskies. This is 38 years old, and it was independently bottled by Douglass Lane, as a part of the Xtra Old Particular range."

"How do you know all this?"

"I've been swatting up, Charlie."

I could see Charlie was deeply moved; he knew precisely how significant that bottle was. He seemed undecided if he should open it or not. He looked at it intently, running his hands over it, before finally looking up at me.

"Should I open it?"

"That bottle has waited for you 38 years Charlie, can you think of a more fitting occasion."

He could not bring himself to answer, he just opened the bottle with extraordinary reverence. I mentioned to Audrey that he would want a tiny little jug of spring water, which she immediately fetched for him. The moment came when he poured a little into the glass. He looked at it, he smelled it, he swirled it around. He tried the tiniest sip, and then dribbled a small amount of spring water into it. Then he sipped it properly. Charlie sat blinking his eyes, not saying anything; nobody said anything. I handed him a tissue. He wiped his eyes, put the glass down and turned towards me, he put his arms around me and kissed me. After what felt like an age, I managed to whisper into his ear.

"Remember that boundary line, Charlie?"

Charlie somehow managed to make light of the whole thing. He just wanted to talk about the whisky.

"If only Stanley could have tasted this."

Harry and I had a tiny little glass each, and Fiona wanted to try it.

"I didn't know you liked whisky, Fiona," I said.

"Charlie's been working on me for ages."

I wasn't sure if it was the whisky which was the centre of attention or Charlie's reaction; it was a lovely moment. Fiona and Lorraine were relaxed and happy together. Their obvious love for each other filled Audrey and Harry with a joy they had not anticipated. And Charlie? Well he was just Charlie, feeling his way through life as he has always done. It was a sublime evening in every respect. There was not a hint that this was going to be the last night of the old order.

Chapter Twenty-Four
FIRST DAY OF THE NEW ORDER

The following morning was filled with excitement, and just a little trepidation. We waited anxiously to see the arrival of furniture vans and removal lorries. Bill and Charlotte arrived, their broad smiles broadcasting quite clearly that their furniture was following closely behind them. This was obviously a significant moment for them both, a crossing-the-threshold moment. We opened the door and stood together in the main hall to greet them. They stood by the entrance, Bill putting his arm around Charlotte. It was a bright frosty morning, without even the hint of a breeze. They kissed each other, and the angle of the sun was such that their condensed breath combined and just rose up above them, silhouetted against a shadowy background. It seemed to be symbolic of so much more.

"Hang on a second," I said, "let me get my phone. That will make a wonderful photograph."

I took the photograph, and we all agreed the light had created a memorable image. Audrey immediately rushed outside with Harry and stood in the same place, and I took their photo. I looked at Fiona and Lorraine and gestured outside.

They stood there, arms around each other, and breathed a combined plume of condensed breath into the air as I took another photograph.

Bill gave me a quizzical look. "They're a couple, Bill. Wonderful, isn't it!" I said.

He immediately smiled and said, "Why has no one told me this before?"

"I know, it's silly, isn't it?" I said. "They didn't tell anyone; I've already told them off."

We all laughed and smiled as we gathered back in the entrance hall.

"What about a photo of you and Charlie?" Audrey asked.

"No, it should be Sylvia and Charlie. What a shame she's not here yet."

"The sun will have moved by then. Come on, you two, let's have a photograph," Harry said.

Charlie and I stood together, and Fiona said, "Put your arm round her, Charlie, you've got to be close together."

Charlie did as he was told, and the photograph was taken. I knew it was one that I would quietly treasure. For the others, it was symbolic of union, and a new beginning. For me, it would be symbolic of *their* union, not mine, but it was still a memory I would cherish. Then it was time to do what the Brits do best; we had a cup of tea. We sat with our bone china cups and saucers, and our Rich Tea biscuits. I had come around to Charlie's point of view - the ritual of tea drinking is something to be enjoyed and savoured.

They had a few different teas, each appropriate for the occasion or the time of day. Our morning tea was Darjeeling from a favourite Indian estate. The correct brewing time in the teapot must be adhered to, and you quickly realise that sitting looking at the teapot is an essential part of the anticipatory process. Then comes the pouring ritual, requiring the use of both hands, one to lift the teapot, and one to hold the tea strainer. There is a momentary pause to consider the strength or otherwise of the tea, as everyone looks at the colour in quiet deliberation.

The addition of milk seems to be an open debate, appearing to be neither right nor wrong; it all depends on the tea in question. Milk before tea, or tea before milk is another conundrum which adds breadth to the experience. As for the end-product of this ritual, I had to admit there was not the slightest comparison to be made with the ubiquitous teabag. There was no question, I was a convert. I absolutely love every aspect of the tea ritual. The next time the boys complain about the tea in a motorway service station, they will have my full support.

Before our second cup, a furniture van arrived, and it was the start of a procession. The furniture which poured out of the back of these vans appeared to be out of all proportion to the size of the vans themselves. Piece by piece, they were carried into their appropriate positions. Item by item, this magnificent house was becoming a home, or more correctly, four homes. The entrance hall was graced with a low-level dresser, two hall chairs, a long case clock, and an oak settle. There were new items as well as numerous antiques.

"Where have all the antiques come from?" I asked.

"We all had various items in storage, things that we couldn't part with," Charlie said.

I was completely caught up with the whole thing. This was symbolic of a new start, in every respect the first page of a new book. The last van appeared at 3 o'clock, and by 4 o'clock the house was complete. The champagne was produced, and the last in a long line of event-toasts was proposed.

Charlie proposed the toast. "The furniture!"

Just as we raised our glasses, another van arrived. I asked if they had forgotten one.

"I know who this is," said Audrey. "It's the outside caterers for this evening."

They really had planned everything. We could not possibly

have prepared food with everything else that had been going on; this was perfect. The caterers made their way indoors with their arms full of boxes. It was all done with military precision, as they commandeered Audrey's kitchen.

"Where's Sylvia, Charlie? Have you heard from her?" I asked.

"No, to be honest I'm getting a bit concerned. I'll give her a ring."

Sometime later Charlie came back, saying she was full of apologies, she had been just about to phone him. She was still at the Bristol house with Jack. Apparently, she still had much to do, as well as things to discuss with Jack, and she had run out of time. It was a long drive to Oxford from Bristol, and she felt that with consideration for the frost and ice, it would not be advisable to drive over until the morning. We all agreed that was sensible, but Charlie was clearly disappointed. His disappointment was short-lived, however, due to the timely arrival of Molly and Giles. We all greeted them enthusiastically, and none more than me.

I hugged Giles, and then Molly, we stood holding each other for an age. I was overjoyed to be with them for Christmas and I took Moll to one side.

"We've just found out that Fiona and Lorraine are gay. They've been a couple for eight years without telling anyone."

I told Moll how I had dealt with it and suggested she might do the same. Molly smiled as she and Giles were greeted by them.

"Fiona and Lorraine are a couple, Moll, that's wonderful, isn't it?"

"How long have you been together?" Molly asked.

"It's eight years now," Lorraine replied.

"You've been together all that time, and you didn't tell anyone. You didn't come to my wedding, Lorraine! What on earth were you thinking, that's such a shame."

"I know, we've been really silly," Lorraine replied. "It took someone like Joanna to make us realise that. I never thought being told off could be so liberating."

We laughed and congratulated them all over again. We were now complete except for Sylvia. I felt so sorry for Charlie. That evening was much more than just Christmas Eve. This was the first real night at Belmont. Quite rightly they wanted two celebrations, one to celebrate the completion of the house, and one for Christmas Day. With consideration for the significance of the occasion, it had been decided that we would dress for dinner in true British tradition. Audrey said it was an essential requirement of dining in the grand dining room on this auspicious night.

Molly and Giles went with Charlie to his apartment, Fiona and Lorraine went to their apartment, Bill and Charlotte went to theirs. I returned to my room in Audrey and Harry's. We all made ready for what was going to be an eventful evening. In many respects, it was going to be an historic evening for that house. I felt so energised by their collective enthusiasm. My other life in Washington lay in tatters, but somehow, I was managing to stay away from those thoughts. Just occasionally, it would drift into my mind, and I would quickly dismiss it. I tried to be equally dismissive of those negative thoughts which reminded me this was *their* great new adventure, not mine.

I came out of my room to find Harry looking even more sartorially perfect than usual.

"I have to tell you, Harry, you carry a dinner suit better than most!"

"Between you and Audrey, I don't have much option, do I? Besides, look at *you*, what a vision you are, Joanna; you look simply amazing."

"I have to try a bit harder these days, Harry."

"May I be forgiven for saying so, but that's nonsense! In my opinion, you don't need to try at all."

Audrey appeared, and Harry and I both said in unison, "Wow!" She was dressed in one of the outfits Antony had selected for her and she looked absolutely wonderful. There were two entrances now into the dining room, the original entrance from the hall, and now there was also Audrey's private entrance, alongside the kitchen. There was still a lot of noise coming from behind the kitchen door, indicating that preparations for dinner were still underway. Audrey popped her head round the door to enquire whether everything was on schedule. The caterers suggested we should take our places in the dining room, so we made our way through. We walked in to find everyone was there waiting, except for Bill and Charlotte.

They all looked wonderful. The new lighting created the perfect atmosphere, and the huge open fire bathed us in a magical light which danced from one to the other. I'm sure I was not alone in feeling that the house was scrutinising us, making sure we were adequate to the task ahead. In that regard at least, I was confident. We stood behind our respective chairs, waiting for Bill and Charlotte, who duly appeared a moment later. Charlotte looked quite beautiful. Not normally one for dressing up, on that evening she looked wonderful. What was completely unexpected was to see Bill looking every bit as perfect as Harry.

"Good Lord, Bill, you didn't find *that* in a laundry bin, did you!" proclaimed Harry.

Charlotte laughed, saying that this was the new slimmer Bill, in his new clothes. Bill guffawed for a moment, and mumbled under his breath, saying how he had fallen under the influence of a good woman. Harry held Audrey's chair for her as she took her place at the head of the table. She looked positively magisterial. As we sat down, I found every aspect of the house, the wonderful dining room, and this group of people, deeply moving.

Bill stood up and gestured that he wanted to say something. "Before the caterers appear," he said, "can I just say a quick word. I would like to apologise to everyone for being a little late this evening. We were held up because I had an important question which I had to ask Charlotte. I got down on one knee and asked her to marry me, and I am delighted to say she said yes. What delayed us was that I couldn't get back up again!"

We rose to our feet in unison and rushed round the table towards them. They were hugged and kissed and hugged again. I said how delighted I was. Bill was very generous, saying it was me who had really inspired him to look towards the future, which was exceedingly kind of him. Our congratulations were cut short because the door leading to the kitchen then opened. The food was ready, as were the caterers.

We regained our seats, while the conversation remained centred upon Bill and Charlotte. A beautiful starter course appeared in front of us, and the first of many toasts was proposed by Harry. "To Bill and Charlotte." What a wonderful start to the evening. Fiona and Lorraine were sitting opposite me. As Bill talked about their plans, I gestured towards the girls with a kind of "when will this be you?" look. They knew what I meant and smiled at each other.

"I *do* like a nice wedding," I said to Bill, while looking at Fiona.

The conversation jumped around as it always did with that group. They knew quantitative easing and money supply were a constant backdrop to my life in Washington, and so they asked me about that. Where did Alan see this current financial crisis ending? I was unable to give them any answers because there were none. I said what Alan had said so often, that it was all one giant financial experiment. I did add that he felt the problems would come much later when the system would have to be unwound.

Then the conversation moved back to the others. Molly asked them if they had any regrets about leaving the Village. There was a universal 'no' to that question, so Molly asked them why they went there in the first place, when they were clearly younger than the average community resident. Audrey said she could speak for all of them. She explained how each for their own reason had given up on life, carrying a burden from the past which seemed too heavy to carry any further.

I asked them to tell me again about Stanley, knowing how important he was to their story. Bill said he thought Stanley had changed their lives. He didn't think they would have been there that day had it not been for him. Audrey explained that before Stanley came along, the last thing they wanted to do was to talk about their past. They went to the Village to escape it, not to relive the past. It seems that the remarkable Stanley somehow changed all that, offering them the opportunity to confront their past, and to deal with it together.

"And then *you* came along, Joanna," Harry said, "you weren't just a breath of fresh air; you were a hurricane. Look at us now, we really *are* different people."

Glasses were raised again, the toast was "Stanley". That was quickly followed by another proposal from Bill. This toast was "Joanna", and the glasses were raised again. I was taken aback, and humbled. There were some things I wanted to say, but I was not really sure what or how to say it. I was not sure where it came from, but I made a little speech.

"It's true I did feel you needed shaking out of that gilded cage you were in. That was presumptuous of me. I felt I could show you a different kind of life, so I set out to show you a glimpse of that life. That was also presumptuous of me; I had no right to do that. I haven't changed any of you - you were always the people I see here today. I hoped the life I showed you might change your outlook, but in fact the reverse has been the case. You have all changed *my* outlook and you've changed my life. I have so much more to learn from you, than you do from me. Your lives are full of real values, things which matter. The things that I pursued are superficial. I was the consummate hostess, the Queen of Washington. In fact, I know now, I was just an exhibit; I've always been on display.

Now that I am no longer an exhibit, what do I have left? You have all taught me such a valuable lesson. We all need meaning in our lives; without it, life is, well, meaningless. I would trade everything for what you have."

My little speech was met with a deafening silence. I was feeling a bit low, and I had bared my soul to them. I shouldn't have done that; this was their special night. I was hoping they would skip over it and move on, but I underestimated them. They were not prepared to let it go, almost squabbling over who would confront me first.

It was Bill who won the day. "That woman you just described, Joanna, that's not the woman we know. We only know the wonderful person who has inspired us and changed our lives for the better. Maybe you are no longer an exhibit, as you call it, but what you have left is the greater part of you that we see, the really beautiful part."

Harry interrupted. "Bill's right. I'm going to change your mirror, Joanna. You're simply not seeing what we see."

"You're wonderful, all of you. That's such a lovely thing to say," I said. "Don't let me spoil the evening, I'm just being silly."

Harry put some more logs on the fire, and our desserts appeared. I was pleased for the opportunity to change the subject. I looked around the table. Giles and Molly were in buoyant mood and kept whispering to each other. I wondered what was in their minds. Bill and Charlotte seemed to be floating somewhere above their dining chairs. Not only were they taking their first step into a new life, but they had also made it a giant step. I was so pleased for them.

Fiona and Lorraine held hands beneath the tablecloth. I imagine the burden of their concealed life had been a heavy one to carry. *Their* new life also began on that day. Audrey and Harry seemed to fit together like hand and glove. She was back in her ancestral home and had delivered on her father's wish to bring joy and laughter back to this wonderful old house.

But Charlie had been noticeably quiet; it seemed strange that Sylvia was not there. She must know how much he wanted to share that night with her.

The caterers had performed wonderfully; everything had been perfect. Harry made a little speech thanking them, and we stood up to give them a clap. They cleared away everything, leaving us only our coffee cups to deal with. Not only that, but they also provided all the ingredients for our Christmas Day lunch. When they left, we sat back with our coffee and chocolates.

Molly and Giles could contain themselves no longer. I knew they were up to something!

"We would like to tell you something," Molly said.

Being her mother my immediate thought was, 'Oh my God, my child is pregnant!'

Molly looked at my reaction. "No, Mom, it's not that."

Giles said, "I need you all to promise me that what we say here will go no further. That's really important."

Everybody nodded in agreement.

"We've done it!" Giles said. "Our AI system works; it is orders of magnitude faster than existing algorithms and it consumes far less energy. It *works!*"

We all knew how important this was. They were extremely excited, and so were we. Everybody rushed round the table to congratulate them. Giles could not stop talking. He was bombarded with questions. Of course, it was Bill who asked the sensible ones. No one else understood it, but we asked questions anyway. Bill wondered when it would be available to the wider world and Giles explained there was still more work to do. Molly confirmed it would need further development before being available to the wider world. Giles explained that other artificial intelligence systems being developed were all task-specific; all were algorithms trained for a specific application. Their new system would be much more adaptable, but they still needed to test it in a wide range of situations. He was in no doubt the finished system would have endless potential.

"Is this really going to change the world?" I asked.

"It is, Mom, it really is! This is like the first powered flight, or the invention of the internet; nothing is going to be the same."

We talked and celebrated into the night; it was immensely thought-provoking. Everyone there was taking their first steps into a new life, and it seemed that the wider world was taking a giant stride forward as well. The significance of that night weighed heavily upon everyone present.

Chapter Twenty-Five
JOURNEYS END

Christmas Day morning, and everyone gathered rather late. We had probably drunk a little too much wine, but I think it was the events of the previous evening that were even more intoxicating. Bill continued his conversation with Giles who was more animated than I could recall seeing him. Molly and I talked together, or more accurately, I listened. Fiona and Lorraine appeared to be unable to take it all in. A new identity, and a new home; it was a lot to absorb. Charlotte said she felt like Alice in Wonderland. Was this really happening? It was Christmas morning and it was like no other Christmas any of us had experienced.

It was late morning as we all sat in the comfy chairs in the dining room. Harry placed some additional logs on the open fire. They momentarily crackled, sending dancing flames searching for the chimney. Audrey produced a tray of tea and mince pies. Charlie smiled approvingly as Fiona arranged the bone china tea-set on the table. There was a white frost outside, but inside it was wonderfully warm. I could not imagine a more quintessentially English Christmas as I sat back in my armchair, allowing this magical moment to envelope me. Sadly, it was not to last.

Harry suddenly announced, "Sylvia's here, didn't anyone hear?"

We all jumped up to greet her. Charlie kissed her, Audrey grabbed her coat, Charlotte was pouring her a cup of tea. Despite the warmest of welcomes, it was immediately obvious that something was wrong. Sylvia was not her normal self.

"What's wrong?" Charlie asked.

Sylvia prevaricated for a moment, looking extremely nervous.

"I need to talk to you, Charlie. I suppose I might as well tell you all. You need to know."

"What is it Sylvia, what's happened?" I asked.

Audrey took charge in her usual reassuring way, directing us back into the dining room. She sat Sylvia down, and we sat around her. I realised something serious was going on. Charlie held her hand; she looked terrified.

"Take a deep breath, Sylvia, and just tell us what it is," Audrey said.

Sylvia looked around at each of us and took that deep breath.

"I'm sorry, Charlie, I can't do it."

"What do you mean, you can't do what?" asked Charlie.

"I can't move into Belmont with you, Charlie. I can't start that new life we talked about."

"What's happened, what's changed your mind?" Charlie asked.

"It wouldn't be right, Charlie. I've been such a fool! I adore you, Charlie Bartlett, I always have. We are a part of each other; you have been my life. My poor husband, Jack, he's been shut out all these years, but he never once gave up on me. When I told him about our plans here at Belmont, he looked so sad, and I saw something in his eyes that I have been to blind to seen before. He loves me, he always has, but fool that I am, I just didn't see it. We are so good together, Charlie you and I, but I don't see that look in your eyes and I don't think you see it in mine. We have only been seeing what we wanted to see, Charlie. It has taken me all this time to realise that needing each other is not the same as loving each other. We would have a contented life together, you and I, but I need *more*. Joanna has shown me that. I don't know why it's taken me so long to realise."

"I don't know what to say, Sylvia. This is so sudden!" Charlie said.

"What about your work with Charlie, and Molly and Giles?" I asked.

"I know you can't manage without me, Charlie, and I'm not sure I can manage without you. So if you will still have me, then nothing needs to change."

"Thank heavens!" Charlie said.

Audrey spotted the deficiency in Sylvia's proposal. She and Jack had a house near Bristol, and she had a flat in Cambridge. Charlie now lived in Oxford.

"You're one of us, Sylvia," Audrey said. "We want you with us, even if you can't live with Charlie. I haven't met your husband, Jack, but I'm sure he's adorable; we will all love him. When you've settled things, the two of you, think about converting one of the outbuildings here into a cottage."

Sylvia was overwhelmed by Audrey's offer. They put their arms around each other and we all stepped forward to hug her.

"Are you quite sure you have thought it all through?" Audrey asked.

"Yes, I'm quite sure. It hasn't been a last-minute decision. I am just so sorry, Charlie, that this has happened now, on Christmas Day. I simply could not see how to avoid it. This is all difficult enough without prolonging it for Jack. He's waiting in the car for me."

"Jack's outside now? Waiting for you?" asked Audrey.

"Yes, he doesn't know any of you other than Charlie. He said he would find it all a bit embarrassing."

"Well, you must bring him in, you know he's welcome."

"I know, I told him that, but we're going on to Cambridge, you see. We are going to stay in my flat, just the two of us for Christmas. So, you see, I think it's best that we just go."

I had to admire Sylvia's strength. What she had just done must have taken enormous courage. We could all see she was resolute about the matter. We had no option but to accede to her wishes, so we went outside to see her off and to introduce ourselves to Jack. There was a spark between the two of them; I could see it in Sylvia's eyes. This was obviously not a new love, but having been rekindled, it was burning with fresh intensity. Why there was no animosity from Jack towards Charlie, I could not imagine. He seemed to be such a nice man.

As we waved them goodbye, I had mixed emotions. I suspect we all did. I was devastated for Charlie and felt so sorry for Sylvia, until I saw that look between her and Jack. She had followed her heart, and I could not fault her for that. We walked back into the house, and our mood was the exact opposite of what it had been earlier. Harry put some more logs on the fire and Fiona offered to make some more tea, but this attempt to restore normality was doomed to failure. It had all happened so fast; I understood why Sylvia wanted to go, but her departure felt as if we were sitting in the wake of a tidal wave.

Charlie looked dejected and I felt dreadful. I had thrown them together, so it was all my fault for interfering. I stood in the kitchen with Audrey and told her how I felt, but she could not have disagreed with me more. She insisted it was for the best; Sylvia had to get Charlie out of her system. If I hadn't intervened, they would most likely have continued just as before. If I had achieved nothing else, then at least I had done that! She made me feel just a little less awful.

Everyone had to rally round to prepare our Christmas lunch, and so a sense of domestic normality pervaded what was otherwise a surreal situation. There was an enormous elephant in the room, and we all delicately stepped around it. I poured

Charlie a glass of his 38-year old whisky; that seemed to help. Christmas lunch was not a complete disaster; we narrowly escaped that accolade. We enjoyed some lovely wine, and the ambience of the wonderful dining room gradually ingratiated itself upon us once again. The general mood lifted slightly. I could see that Audrey had taken Charlie to one side to talk to him. Molly came over to me and spoke quietly to me.

"You need to talk to Charlie, Mom. I know it seems like a bad time, but you've both been dumped. You need to let him know."

"That's a terrible word, Moll! I've not been dumped; we drifted apart."

"Mom, you've both been dumped; you're both in the same position. This is Charlie we're talking about, the greatest love of your life, and he also happens to be my father. If there's any chance of you two getting together, you have to tell him."

"I don't want to force Charlie into a corner, Moll. I don't want him to feel sorry for me. I'm frightened to let myself even think about it, I love him so much. If it's not what Charlie wants, I would lose him all over again."

"I'll talk to Charlie."

"Promise you won't tell him about your Dad, Moll. I desperately don't want him to know."

"Ok, I won't."

Sometime later, Audrey took me to one side in the kitchen.

"I've spoken with Charlie. He doesn't know which way to turn."

"You didn't tell him, did you, Audrey?"

"No, I said I wouldn't, but *you* should tell him. You know he loves you; he's tried to deny it to himself because of Sylvia."

"Maybe it is too late for us, Audrey. It didn't work with Sylvia, perhaps it wouldn't work with me."

"You and Charlie were always intended to be together. That's why your marriage failed, isn't it? Because you could not let Charlie go, could you?"

I nodded, trying not to be tearful.

"I'm just frightened, Audrey. After all this time, I'm scared stiff of losing him again. What if it doesn't work out?"

"I'll talk to Charlie again."

The afternoon dragged interminably into the evening. Molly spoke to me about Charlie, and Audrey spoke to Charlie about me. All the while, everyone pretended things were perfectly normal. Audrey told me Charlie thought I would never leave Washington. Perhaps he was right, could I really walk away from my boys, my life? And what about Mrs Garcia? Oh, good heavens, I hadn't thought about Mrs Garcia! Would Charlie consider coming to Washington? He has Belmont; could he leave Molly, Audrey, Sylvia, and the others? I didn't think so. Audrey told Charlie I was not sure I could leave Washington, perhaps he was right. Molly told me Charlie said he didn't feel he could leave Belmont and the others; it simply wouldn't work out. He was resigned to his fate. I told Molly I felt the same. I was just too terrified to do anything. It seemed that we had reached an unspoken agreement.

Charlotte tried her best to lift our spirits.

"Perhaps it's time for our Christmas pudding. Does anyone have room for it now?"

There was a muted general agreement, and it was decided we should all return to the dining table. Charlie said he had a fine old bottle of vintage port. He suggested it would cheer him up to open it. Heroic efforts were made to restore the Christmas spirit, but to describe our Christmas evening as being a little flat, would have grossly exaggerated the fun we had. I felt just dreadful and kept apologising to everyone for being so preoccupied. They were all being so kind to me. I felt exactly as I felt that dreadful night in Charlie's car all those years ago when we said our final goodbye. Neither of us said anything, but we both knew it was over. Charlie sat staring into his glass of port, as if it were a crystal ball about to decide his future for him. I just sat staring into the distance, not really seeing anything. This dreadful paralysis would have continued into the night had it not been for Audrey.

"This simply cannot continue, not in Belmont!" Audrey pronounced. "This is supposed to be a happy occasion. It just *has* to be a happy occasion. I made my pledge to my father. Somehow you two have to resolve this ridiculous position you've created for yourselves."

Audrey in her authoritative way was not asking us; she was telling us. Her stern voice was enough to focus my attention.

"Do you remember, Joanna," Audrey continued, "you telephoned to tell me that Alan had left you. You were so low, I told you it was just a case of reshuffling the cards, throwing out the joker, and starting again. *This* is how those cards have fallen, Joanna. All you have to do is pick them up and start again."

"I asked you not to mention about Alan."

"Oh, don't be ridiculous, Joanna, of course I've told Charlie! Molly's told Charlie: we all know Alan has left you. It's nothing to be ashamed of."

"You two need to listen to your own words," said Bill. "You told me, Joanna, if I ever found the opportunity for love again, I should grab it with both hands. The same applies to you."

"You're the one, Charlie, who told me to forget about what other people might think."

Harry said. "You told me to forget about 'I should know better,' you told me 'there was nothing better'."

"It was only the other day, Joanna, when you told Lorraine and me that we had been ridiculous keeping our relationship a secret," Fiona said. "What do you think you and Charlie have been doing all these years?"

"Fiona's right, Mom. You and Charlie have lived a ridiculous lie, right from the first moment you met. You told me the biggest mistake of your life was when you didn't tell Charlie you loved him that first morning at Poppies. You both told us how much in love you were, but you don't tell each other."

"Can I say something?" Giles said. "You gave me the best advice I have ever had, Charlie. You said I didn't realise the gamble I was taking by risking losing Molly. You said I hadn't the faintest idea what a lifetime of heartache felt like. You described it as a pain that eats into your soul and never lets you go. You told me I would never feel another pain like it. It's my turn to tell you Charlie, if you turn your back on Joanna again, you'll never get over that pain."

"I can't bear it," Charlotte said, "please stop tormenting yourselves, both of you."

"It's true what everyone is saying, Mom. You are both right about all the obstacles standing between you. I have no idea how you could make it work; I only know that you *must*. Think back to what you told me, Charlie, about the 18th of June 1982 and the reason that I'm here. Your special moment was always when you kissed. You said you each inhabited the other, you were as one together. Those are *your* words, Charlie. You said the moment your lips met, there was no way back; there could only be one outcome. Neither of you has changed in the way you feel about each other. All you have to do is kiss each other; and there can only be one outcome."

"Molly's right isn't she, Charlie," I said, "nothing has ever changed for me."

"It's true," he replied, "nothing has changed for me."

"I'm still that same stupid woman who walked away from the only man she had ever loved. Will you give me another chance, Charlie?"

"You know the answer to that, JoJo."

I stood up, and suddenly I was standing in the Poppies Hotel wearing the Red Dress, about to walk into Charlie's arms. I stepped round the dining table and walked towards him. Those lost years just melted away with every step. Molly was right, there really could only be one outcome.

THE END

The Last Word

I do hope you have enjoyed the two "Autumn Daffodils" books as much as I have enjoyed writing them. If you have, then I would really appreciate a nice review.

peterturnham.author@gmail.com
www.peterturnhamauthor.com

Made in the USA
Las Vegas, NV
25 May 2022

49361214R00173